NIGHT CHILD

NIGHT CHILD

Alan Scholefield

CHAPMANS

Chapmans Publishers Ltd
141–143 Drury Lane
London WC2B 5TB

BRITISH LIBRARY CATALOGUING IN PUBLICATION DATA
Scholefield, Alan
Night Child
I. Title
823.914 [F]

ISBN 1–85592–078–6

First published by Chapmans 1992
Copyright © 1992 by Alan Scholefield

Photoset by Rowland Phototypesetting Ltd
Bury St Edmunds, Suffolk
Printed and bound in Great Britain by
Clays Ltd, St Ives plc

For Robin Ilbert

My very chains and I grew friends,
So much a long communion tends
To make us what we are:

Byron
'The Prisoner of Chillon'

My thanks for his help go to Simon Slater of Surrey Social Services.

Any mistakes are my own.

PROLOGUE

By the time the foxes came, Wylie was chilled to the bone. About midnight, a vixen and two cubs stepped warily from a thicket onto the path, heads jerking left and right, ears pricked, noses twitching.

In spite of himself, Wylie felt that old tightening of his stomach muscles, the slight crawling of his skin that had marked similar moments over the years.

He had to tell himself that he wasn't filming jaguars in Brazil, nor tigers in the Sundarbans of the Ganges Delta, nor elephants in the Masai Mara. He was in a tatty canvas hide on Hampstead Heath in London on a cold autumn night filming urban foxes.

He kept his eye to the image-intensifying night sight and watched them come towards the litter basket. In the viewfinder everything was grainy and coloured greeny brown. That was the trouble with using infrared film at night – you never got a decent look at what you were shooting.

The foxes vanished. One moment they were on the path, the next gone.

But at least he'd seen them. He had waited in the hide for three consecutive nights and had begun to think that the reports had been wrong, that there wasn't a fox for miles. But here they were, or at least here they had been until a few moments before.

In the distance he could hear the late traffic grinding up Heath Street towards Spaniards Road and all around him was the steady hum of a great city, already partly asleep. But in the cold darkness of the Heath, life was stirring: hedgehogs were hurrying along on their nightly business, so were mice and voles and stoats and weasels and feral cats and stray dogs – all trying to kill and eat each other. Below him, little more than a mile away, lions were grunting and roaring in Regent's Park Zoo and for a moment Wylie was back in his camp on the banks of the Kafue in Zambia and the lions weren't in cages but just outside the penumbra of his lantern.

He stared into the darkness until his eyes began to water. Shadows became solid objects, solid objects became shadows. Bushes and trees seemed to move. He knew well this trick of the night which he had named the Dunsinane effect.

He looked away, blinked a few times, looked back. It was one of the first things he had told Ellie when she was filming at night: never hold a view for more than a few seconds, because the mind begins to fill the darkness with images of its own.

Wylie was a big man in his mid-thirties and he was used to the tropics. Cold autumn nights felt wintry and he hunched down in his heavy sheepskin coat. It had been round the world with him more than once and was beginning to look, like its owner, slightly battered. He'd slept in it dozens of times, he'd used it as a pillow, as a blanket, he'd used it as a groundsheet for women who were not keen on damp grass, and once, in the Kalahari when he was filming Kung Bushmen, he'd even bartered it for food and returned a day later and bought it back again.

The foxes were back.

The two cubs followed the vixen onto the path. Ahead of them was the litter basket where they were said to feed. He had checked it earlier. It was full of chocolate wrappings and empty drink cans, styrofoam cups and polystyrene packing: not the best of diets. But he had brought with him a parcel of stewing beef and had placed it with the rubbish.

The camera, which was lined up on the basket, was a 16-mm Arriflex and it too bore the scratches and scars of a full life. Each one told a story: the dent from a fall in the Ruwenzori; the scratch from a car accident in Nairobi; and another from the accident in the southern African bush . . .

But he didn't want to think about that one.

He watched the foxes come to the litter basket and started the camera.

The vixen sniffed the air, separating the scents in her mind. Wylie wasn't worried. The scent of man was all over Hampstead Heath; it saturated the ground and the grass and even the leaves of the trees. Anyway the night was still. There was no wind to carry his scent.

The litter basket was on a short pole. The vixen went up on her hind legs and pulled at a plastic shopping bag. She drew it onto the ground in front of the cubs and poked her nose inside. Her head disappeared. Then she began to walk backwards and reappeared with the beef.

'Go on, eat it,' Wylie urged silently. 'It's bloody good.'

The vixen seemed to agree for she allowed the cubs to feed while she herself swallowed several pieces. She went back to the basket and began to pull out and investigate bits of plastic and paper. All this time Wylie's camera, wrapped in a couple of old jerseys to kill the noise of its whirring motor drive, was filming the scene.

The cubs were just like the wolf cubs he had filmed on Vancouver Island, he thought: playful, loving, yet each aware of social structure. What would happen when they grew to maturity? Would they stay on Hampstead Heath? Or would they search for other ranges in other wild parks and would the traffic kill them?

Suddenly they were gone again. Just a grainy blur, and the basket, now surrounded by torn paper, stood alone.

He checked his film magazine. He knew that the foxes hadn't finished their meal yet. Something had frightened them but they would probably be back. He decided to put in a new magazine while he had the chance.

He was rummaging in his holdall when he heard a noise near the litter basket. He thought the foxes must have returned and looked through the night sight. But they were not there. Instead he saw a shadow on the far side of the basket. A bush with overhanging fronds made identification impossible, but it seemed to Wylie that he was looking at an ape of some sort. It stood erect on its back legs. It wasn't square enough to be a chimpanzee, more like a gibbon or a young Chakma baboon.

The animal stood in the shadows for some moments while Wylie, his eye fixed to the night sight and hardly daring to breathe, went on rummaging in his holdall for the new magazine of film.

Who the hell would have a monkey in Hampstead, he wondered. Or had it escaped from the monkey house at the zoo? It had happened before, not once but several times to his knowledge.

On the other hand, it could be a pet monkey that had escaped from one of the houses in the Vale of Health nearby. People kept snakes and alligators and God knew what else in their houses these days, even potbellied Vietnamese pigs. So why not a primate?

More than a year's rubbish filled the holdall and he went on rummaging about with one hand trying to find a full film magazine while keeping the ape in view.

It would be interesting to see what the animal made of the litter basket. And would it eat the meat? Baboons were omnivorous but that wasn't true of all primates. If only he could get a better view of it. If only he could find the bloody magazine. What he really wanted, of course, was the foxes to return, then he'd have something really good: urban foxes and an urban primate sharing the leftovers of Big Macs and pizzas and hot dogs.

But only if he could find the magazine.

He came up with two, both of which were empty.

He froze. The primate moved and seemed to be about to come from the shadows to the litter basket. Wylie looked through the night sight and saw, sitting further along the path, the three foxes with their hot green eyes. His professionalism got the better of him, he abandoned the night sight and used both hands and a pencil torch to find the film.

It was inevitable that he made a noise, and by the time he found the magazine and clipped it into the camera, both the ape and the foxes had disappeared.

He watched the area until his eyes ached. Had it all been real or had it been a trick of the night? Had his imagination filled a strange experience with an even stranger fantasy?

He left the hide and searched the holly bushes near the litter basket, then he went further and further towards the Vale of Health and East Heath Road. But he found nothing, not a trace of the foxes nor the primate. Eventually he returned to the hide. There was no option but to wait and hope that they would return.

He stood by the camera as the hours passed, reacting to every slight noise. But only an old cat came to the litter basket and Wylie was still there when grey dawn arrived on a cold north-east wind.

The early commuter traffic was just beginning when he drove back to Lancaster Gate. He parked the Volkswagen camper and carried the heavy camera up to his rented apartment.

It was a featureless place, furnished in the greys and fawns of professional letting. He had been living in it since he had returned from Africa.

Usually, when he came in from filming he would hit himself with several Scotches and fall into bed. The whisky had become a crutch and he knew it and did not care very much. But this morning his mind was filled with images and ideas and his thoughts were racing as they used to do when he had first started as a documentary film maker with the BBC years earlier.

He made himself a large pot of coffee, sat down at his word processor, and made notes of what he had seen. Then he slept for a couple of hours. Later he went to the Westminster Reference Library and checked *The Times* index for recent stories about urban wildlife.

He found articles about foxes, hawks and badgers, all of which seemed to be getting along famously in urban situations. But nothing about urban primates.

He went back to the flat and poured himself a whisky but did not gulp it. Instead he drank it slowly and thoughtfully. Then he phoned the Natural History Museum, the BBC Natural History Unit in Bristol, and the London Zoo. There were no reports of escaped primates living on Hampstead Heath or anywhere else in Britain for that matter.

Had it been imagination?

No. It hadn't. He had to trust his years of experience. He had seen a monkey or a baboon, of that he was certain. If none of the natural history agencies knew of such an animal then it was an even better story. Perhaps it even lived on the Heath and only emerged at night to feed on rubbish. There were enough examples of that kind of behaviour: from leopards on the outskirts of African cities, to wolves in India, and black bears in North America – all living close to man.

And what he desperately needed was good footage, a good story. When he had first arrived back from Africa, he had been numb. All he could think about was what had happened to Ellie. Then one day he had done his sums and come to the conclusion that he had about nine or ten months of capital left before he would have to pawn something.

He had worked as a freelance for so long that little subconscious alarm bells had gone off in his mind. Nine or ten months was not good enough. He usually worked a year ahead. If he was financially secure for a year that was all he could ever ask for. But nine, even ten, months was scary. Still, he had only to make a few phone calls . . .

And that's when he had received his second shock. It wasn't at all a case of, 'Hello, Duncan, what would you like to do for us?'

Each TV natural history unit he phoned – and most were run by old chums who had used his material before – were hedgy. Didn't he know what had happened to TV during the last year? Didn't he know there'd been a drastic falling off in advertising revenue, that the studios were dripping with the blood of redundant staff? That all new projects were on hold?

Well, no, he didn't. He'd been in Africa.

Not that they wouldn't want his stuff. Hell, no. They were always pleased to have Duncan Wylie's stuff. He'd won two gold medals, after all. Except what they needed now was unusual, offbeat material to compete with the sport and movies on satellite and cable channels. He'd asked Jimmy Monkton of Nature TV what he meant by unusual and offbeat.

'Difficult to say, but you know it when you see it. Easier to tell you what it isn't: it isn't the inside of birds' nests or the life cycle of the gnat. Sharks, crocs, snakes, they're all good, especially if you can find someone who's been attacked by them. What you want to get is the attacked and the attacker.'

'Action stuff.'

'Sure. That's always a good seller. Charging elephants, fornicating rhinos. But offbeat, unusual.'

He now had a subject that was certainly unusual and certainly offbeat. It might just be the one to save him from going cap in hand to one of the production companies to ask for a job from someone he didn't know and who was five years younger than himself.

By six o'clock that evening he was back in Hampstead. He parked the camper in Flask Walk and took a stroll around the streets that faced the Heath. In the dusk he could look into the brightly lit rooms of the expensive homes. This was the richest part of the richest city in Britain.

He crisscrossed the area between Christ Church and the Heath and looked down onto the small huddle of houses called the Vale of Health in a fold of the Heath itself – a village, within a suburb, within a city.

It was incredible, he thought, that down there, in the dark of the Heath, there was an ape-like creature that lived in secrecy.

By full darkness he had set up his hide, focused the camera, and checked the magazine. He was ready.

Slowly London settled down. Lights began to go off. Traffic began to grow lighter. An old tramp wearing two overcoats and carrying several plastic bags startled him.

Earlier, Wylie had again placed food in the litter basket, but this time he had bought a more varied selection. He made ready to scare off the old man should he start to rummage about. But not even this tramp could be bothered to look for food in such an unsavoury place and, without a sideways glance, he went on his way, perhaps to some Salvation Army binge.

The hours passed. Wylie began to feel that he was on a loser; that the opportunity had come and gone and he had failed to take it. But around two o'clock in the morning the foxes came.

He switched on the camera. It was like a replay of the night before. The vixen went to the litter basket and dragged out the food. She and her cubs began to feed.

Her head suddenly went up. Then, in an instant, they vanished.

Wylie held his breath. He looked for the shadow by the over-hanging branches but the ape did not come from there. Instead, after a few moments, he was able to make out its shadow crouching behind a low bush to the left of the basket. If it had planned to make life difficult for him it couldn't have succeeded better. Approaching the litter basket from this direction, it was almost invisible from the hide. It came slowly and softly, like the foxes themselves; nervous, listening.

Through the night sight Wylie could only see a dark blur. Leaving the camera running he used his naked eyes to try and penetrate the dark. He could hear paper being pulled from the basket, but could not see what was happening. He realised he was sweating in spite of the cold.

The foxes were back and looked as though they were about to contest the feeding ground. The primate clearly did not wish to fight for the food and simply melted into the darkness.

Wylie was ready. He picked up a lightweight video camera and ran softly after the animal.

A path led off to the left. He could just make out a small moving shadow travelling into the Vale of Health.

The Vale is made up of a dozen or more houses. It is a strangely sinister place. The story goes that because of its isolation the Great Plague of London reached it last. There is only one road into it from Hampstead and few people walk it by night.

The houses were asleep as Wylie entered the area. He saw the shadow for one instant more, then it vanished.

He reached the place where it had disappeared. It was an overgrown beech hedge about eight feet high that surrounded one of the houses. At ground level there was a hole made by dogs or cats – or the ape itself – but too small for Wylie. He went along the hedge until he found a gate and let himself in.

The house was in darkness. There was a neatly trimmed lawn and flowerbeds. He looked carefully about him but could see no evidence of the animal. Perhaps there was a potting shed where it lived or perhaps it was only using the garden as a short cut.

He circled the house. The windows were tightly closed on the ground floor and were completely overgrown on the inside by potted plants run wild. It was like a house in a nightmare, a place from which the dreamer could not escape, where branches and trailing vines would grip and hold.

Perhaps the house was empty, he thought. The animal might have found its way into an empty house and was using it as a lair.

He stood by one of the downstairs windows and shone his torch through it. The rank plants made him feel he was looking at a jungle scene. He somehow expected to see the ape swing into sight on the trailing vines.

The torch had a powerful beam and it travelled about the room like Tinkerbell in *Peter Pan*, a circlet of golden light dancing on floor and wall and staircase. And then it danced on something else. A foot. A woman's leg. The leg was twisted unnaturally; so unnaturally that Wylie sensed he had come upon something very terrible indeed.

ONE

'One-and-two-and-three-and-kick! . . . One-and-two-and-three-and-kick!'

Madame Eva Raymonde lay back on the pillows and watched her daughter.

'One-and-two-and-three-and-kick!'

The heavy legs, brown from the sun lamp, jerked into the air from under her miniskirt in a parody of a chorus routine.

'I should have been a Tiller Girl,' Hilda said, breathing heavily as she danced. 'Or a Rockette. Radio City in New York. I could've danced there. One-and-two-and . . .'

'When?' her mother said. 'After you became prima ballerina at Covent Garden?'

'Laugh if you want to. Or one of the Bluebell Girls at the *Folies Bergère*. I would have loved that.'

The legs jerked into the air as she spoke, and her big breasts, unfettered by a bra, bounced up and down under her black T-shirt.

'Saint-Saëns wrote music for you,' her mother said. '"The Dance of the Elephants".'

This was an old joke. Too old to respond to.

Dusk was creeping into the big room, the best in the house. Against one wall was the four-poster occupied by Madame. An eighteenth-century escritoire stood opposite it almost invisible under a pile of old newspapers. Near the doorway was a Bauhaus chair and on the wall above it a Dufy. Boris had been an eclectic collector of both antique furniture and paintings and Madame often thought with satisfaction of the other pieces in the house, which were her insurance against possible hard times.

She looked now at the ficuses and spider plants that gave the room a jungly look.

'I hope you've been watering the other plants,' she said.

'Of course.'

Although she had not been downstairs for months the thought of the drawing-room, with its fine furniture set off by vines and indoor plants, gave her great pleasure. The plants had been her idea. Boris would never have allowed them. But the point was, if you had plants you had to water them and they became humidifiers and stopped the antiques from drying out and cracking.

When Boris had been alive her bedroom had been the music room. This was where he had practised and where Madame had accompanied him. The Steinway, her precious Steinway, was still in the corner of the room, open, music on the stand, waiting.

One day . . . Perhaps . . . one day . . .

'I could still do it,' Hilda said. 'Not the Rockettes maybe but –'

'Rockettes!'

'All right, maybe I'm not as good a dancer as you were a pianist –'

'There's no maybe about it! You know what they called me?'

'Yes . . . we all know what they called you!'

'"The new Myra Hess!" That's what they said in the papers.'

'Not papers plural. In only one paper, the *News Chronicle* and we all know what's happened to that!' She bent and put her head on her knees. 'Look, I'm still supple. You couldn't do that. Never in a million years.'

Madame looked at her in distaste. 'Don't stick your bottom out at me,' she said. 'I don't want to see it. It's a disgusting thing to do.'

'What's disgusting about a bottom?'

'For God's sake you're nearly middle-aged. You've got a bottom like a . . . like a . . .'

'Like a what?'

'Hippopotamus.'

'You're always saying things like that. Trying to hurt me.'

'Hurt? Don't be so silly. You're my daughter. Why should I hurt you? But you won't face up to things. I've got to make you face up. It's a mother's duty.'

'We each have our duty? Is that it?'

'That's it.'

'*My* duty is to look after you, to be your skivvy. And *your* duty is to mock me and undermine my confidence! Which you've always done. Whenever I've wanted to do something you've said, no Hilda, you could never do it.'

'Rubbish!'

'What about learning to drive! You said I could never manage a car.'

'Well, you couldn't, could you? The man said he was terrified to teach you!'

'That's because you undermined my confidence. You know it is! And the time I wanted to work in that office. You said I'd never understand the work and –'

'That Mr Whatshisname. He phoned me. He said he was sorry but he couldn't keep you.'

'If you hadn't said I couldn't do it I would've been all right! But you never want me to leave the house!'

'Nonsense. You got pains in your stomach. How many doctors didn't you go to? You even had a barium meal and X-rays and what did they find? Nothing. Nerves, they said. That's what it was.'

'And who gave me the nerves?'

'For God's sake, Hilda, grow up!'

They paused, gathering strength.

Hilda went to the window and looked out. 'Autumn again,' she said. 'And I'm still here. Spring . . . summer . . . autumn . . . winter . . . Year in and year out.'

Her mother said, 'Put the lights on.'

'Please.'

She shrugged. 'All right if it makes you happy – please.'

'I like to be acknowledged,' Hilda said. 'You take me for granted.'

She turned back to the window seeing her reflection in the glass from the lamp on the Steinway. A plain woman running to fat, with a round face and shoulder-length dark hair, stared back at her. 'You're beautiful,' she whispered.

'What?'

'Nothing.'

The old woman pushed herself up on her pillows. 'I don't like you whispering to yourself. You do that to spite me, to annoy me, just because I'm helpless.'

'Helpless!'

'Of course.'

'Dr Innes said there was nothing organically wrong with you.'

'I suppose rheumatoid arthritis is nothing! Anyway, what does he know?'

'He doesn't know anything *now*.' She laughed to herself. 'He's dead, remember?'

Hilda placed her arms in the position for ballroom dancing and began a waltz. After a moment she paused and said, 'You know what he told me?'

'Who?'

'Dr Innes. He said had I ever heard the expression "the tyranny of the meek"? He was talking about you! Except for the fact that you're not meek at all.'

Her mother smiled, showing her teeth. She took the denial of her meekness as a compliment. 'I don't have to tell you what he said about you.'

'No, you don't. You've told me a hundred times.'

'And you've said that about the meek a hundred times.'

'Why react then?'

'It's *your* game. All I'm doing is playing it with you. But if you're going to remind me of what he said about me then I'm going to remind you of what he said about you. "Sheltered environment". Those were his words.'

'It won't be forever.'

'What?'

'Nothing.'

This was her weapon and she knew how to use it.

'What did you say?'

'I said it won't be forever.'

'No, of course not. Nothing's forever. I'm not going to live forever.'

They were silent for a few moments. Madame Raymonde picked up a magazine then put it down. She was fretful. She patted her long untidy grey hair and then switched on her bedside light. It was bright and hurt her eyes so she put on a white cap with a green visor. She peered at Hilda from under its peak like some elderly and myopic tennis player.

'What are we going to have for supper?' she asked.

Supper was what brought them together. It was like an oasis in the daily desert. They always ate it while they watched the *Six O'Clock News*. Afterwards Madame would walk up and down the room a few times. She thought of it as her 'constitutional'.

'Pilchards,' Hilda said. 'Pilchards and baked beans.'

'Tins,' said Madame Raymonde with a sniff. 'Never anything fresh.'

'You like tins. You never want anything else. I bought some fish once. You wouldn't eat it.'

'It was off.'

'It was smoked.'

'I don't like smoked things. They put colouring into them. Sometimes they don't smoke them at all.'

'That isn't true.'

'I heard it on television.'

'Oh, then it *must* be true. Anyway, I'm going out. If you don't want pilchards, don't have them.'

The room went suddenly still.

'Out?'

'Out to dinner.'

'But —'

'To a restaurant. A proper one with tablecloths and napkins and three knives and three forks.'

Madame Raymonde's lower lip began to tremble.

'Now don't start, Mother.'

'You're always going out these days. And what about me?'

'You'll be all right.'

'Hilda —'

'I'm going out, Mother, so don't start crying. It's not going to do any good.'

'You bitch! You selfish bitch!'

'That's right, you have a good yell. Make you feel better.'

The old woman adjusted her visor, picked up the *Radio Times* and began to read.

'Pilchards and beans. Okay?'

Her mother ignored her.

'Mother! If you don't answer you'll get nothing.'

Madame could have been in another room.

'I'm not going to put up with this. If you don't want to talk then don't! But I'm going to get the food anyway and I'm going to put it here and if you don't like it, don't eat it. I don't care if you go silent on me. I don't care if you don't speak. It was you who started the silent treatment last time, remember, but you who gave in.'

Her mother turned a page.

'And let me tell you something. I'm going out with a man. And we like each other. I haven't told you that. But we do. More than like. And we talk about the future. I haven't told you about that either.'

Madame slowly licked her finger and used it to turn another page. But the magazine was trembling slightly. She put it down.

'You? And a man? That's funny!'

'Oh, so it isn't going to be the silent treatment. I was looking forward to that. Not having to listen to you. The last time it was a month, wasn't it? And remember it's you who is bedridden not me.'

'And you remember that it's me who signs the cheques, not you! And me who has the money. Not you.'

It was the usual stand-off.

'It isn't even *your* money,' Hilda said. 'You didn't earn it.'

'I looked after your father all those years. You can call it back pay.'

'And what about me all those years? Out of sight, out of mind.'

Madame looked at her angrily. 'How dare you? . . . Anyway it was never as bad as . . .' She jerked her head in the direction of the door. 'Nothing like. I should never have let you do that. I blame myself every day.'

Hilda looked at her with loathing. 'You should have thought of that when you were bringing me up. The only thing I ever wanted was to marry and have a child but you were always in the way. It was my *duty* to look after you. Duty! Duty! Duty! Well, I had a duty to myself.'

'God knows, I'm just as guilty!' her mother said. It was almost as though she were speaking to a third person in the room. 'But what could I do?'

'Oh, for goodness sake let's not go into it all over again. It's not your business anyway.'

'You're cruel.'

'You don't know what cruelty is! You stuck me away!'

'That wasn't my fault and you know it! It was yours. It was after . . . well, you know what it was after. But that doesn't justify what you're doing to the two of us now.'

'If you mention him again I'm going to do what I said I'd do right at the beginning. I'm going to leave both of you. Walk out. And you can stuff the money.'

'God will punish you.'

'Oh shut up, Mother. I'm going to get your pilchards.'

'Hilda! Darling Hilda! Please don't go out!'

But Hilda had left the room and Madame Raymonde heard her going down the stairs to the kitchen.

'You're rotten through and through,' she said.

She switched on the TV and turned up the volume, as she often did when she was angry with Hilda.

The announcer's voice said, 'This is the *Six O'Clock News* from the BBC.'

She knew Hilda would hate that.

TWO

It wasn't a restaurant and there were no tablecloths or place settings; it was a pub, down the hill from Hampstead where Chalk Farm becomes Camden Town.

'But the food's good,' Harry said. 'Wouldn't have brought you here otherwise.'

Hilda didn't mind. The tablecloth and the knives and forks were only symbols anyway; symbols of freedom, of independence from her mother, of being with Harry – and the new life they were planning together.

'It's better than most restaurants,' Harry said.

'What are Spanish restaurants like?' she asked.

Harry leaned back. 'Depends where you go,' he said. 'Most tourists only know paella.' He pronounced it properly, giving weight to the second 'l'. 'Hardly any go to Alfredo's in Madrid for the suckling pig. It's just paella or *filete con patatas fritas*. Cheap food for cheap people. Fish. That's what the Spanish do best. Baby eels. And chicken. *Pollo al ajo*. That's chicken with garlic. Delicious.'

She listened avidly. She was never able to get enough of this kind of talk. He was so worldly-wise, and she was so . . . so lucky!

He lit a cigarette with a gold-plated Zippo lighter. She loved the way he did that. He even had a cigarette case, something she hadn't seen for years. He would take out the cigarette, and tap it gently on the case – and then . . . flick, flick, and the Zippo would light and Harry would draw the flame to the tobacco.

She put her hand under the table, placed it on his thigh and began to stroke it.

'What would you like?' He shifted his leg away, then stood up to look at the blackboard menu. 'There's chilli con carne, enchiladas, lasagne, spaghetti bolognese –'

She was bewildered. 'What's enchiladas?'

'Mexican.'

'And chilli con carne?'

'Also Mexican. But a bit hot.'

She was helpless.

'Try the lasagne,' he said. 'Everybody likes that.'

But what if she didn't, she thought. It would be awful to leave it.

'I think I'll have the spaghetti.' She felt safer with that. Her father used to eat it in great quantities.

'And to drink?'

She smiled at him. 'My usual, please.'

'Your . . . ? Oh, yes, Bloody Mary.'

He had taught her about Bloody Marys, just as he had taught her about a lot of things. There had been life before Harry but she did not like to remember it.

'I'll have to teach you to drink wine,' he said. 'You'll have to drink wine in Spain.'

She watched him go up to the bar. He was dapper in a dark grey suit of good cloth and cut. He wore a moustache, the centre of his skull was quite bald – outdoors he usually wore one of those Beatles caps which she loved – and he was on the short side. But to her he walked tall; and wasn't baldness supposed to mean virility?

When he came back she said, 'Tell me about Spain, Harry.'

'What about Spain?'

'Tell me about the house.'

'All right. Well, they have these thick-walled houses out there –'

'And that's what we're going to have. Because it's cool in

27

summer and warm in winter. And ours will have white walls.'

'Absolutely. Very white walls.'

'And geraniums in pots.'

'And wrought-iron balconies.'

'And somewhere I can dance.' She sipped her Bloody Mary.

'Oh, absolutely. We'll have a patio.'

'Tiled. Yellow and red tiles. And I'll have one of those long dresses and I'll dance for you.'

'Terrific.'

'I'll dance the flamenco.'

'Have you ever danced a flamenco before?'

'No, but I'll learn. I'm a natural dancer. That's what I should have been if it hadn't been for Mother. I had several offers, you know. I could have danced at the *Folies Bergère*. Even at Radio City in New York. You've heard of the Rockettes?'

'Of course.'

'Well, I was –'

'Have you thought?'

'What about?'

'What you're going to do with her. Are you going to bring her?'

'God, no, Harry. She'd spoil everything.'

'What then?'

'Leave her.'

'In the house?'

'Why not?'

'You can't just leave her.'

'A housekeeper or a nurse, then. She's got the money.'

'A home would be better. I know one in Surrey. Very nice. Expensive, but very nice.'

She paused. 'What about the will?'

'Doesn't matter now, does it?'

'I suppose not.' She put her hand on his thigh again. 'Harry . . .'

The food came.

'My father used to be able to twist his spaghetti onto his fork,' she said. She tried to twist round several strands of pasta but

28

they fell off her fork halfway to her mouth and splashed sauce onto the table. He watched with distaste.

'Cut it up,' he said.

'I'd like to learn. We'll be eating spaghetti in Spain, won't we?'

'That's Italy. In Spain it's rice.'

'Oh.' She felt a little crushed. Sometimes he was cold to her. She suddenly blurted out, 'I've never been to a hotel with a man.'

'I should hope not.'

'It wouldn't make any difference. We're going to get married anyway.'

'It would make a difference to me,' he said. 'I'm not that sort of person.'

Again she felt the chill of his displeasure.

'Is it your wife? I mean, is the memory of –'

'My wife's dead! Life must go on. It's just that I'm not that sort of person. After we're married, yes, of course.'

His leg wasn't there so she took his hand. 'God, Harry, I can't tell you how much you mean to me. I mean, my life was . . . well, it wasn't much fun, you know.'

'I can imagine.' He squeezed her hand, disengaged his own and lit a cigarette. He kept both hands on the table and began to click the lid of the Zippo up and down.

'Harry, you really mean that?'

'What?'

'About your wife. I wondered if she was coming between us. You know what they say.'

'What who says?'

'Well, it's often on television. Plays. That sort of thing. Where the dead wife comes between her husband and another woman.'

'I've told you. The past is the past.'

'Except for us.'

'How do you mean?'

'Well, I mean our past.'

'You should live in the present.'

'I know but the present isn't much fun. So I live in our past – and our future.'

He looked at his watch.

'I went to the travel agency,' she said.

'What?' His voice was alarmed. 'Why?'

'To find out about the ferries. You said we were going to Santander by boat and then we'd drive down to Málaga. You said we'd take a car of our own. A Mercedes. I wanted to see what the ferries looked like and when they sailed.'

'I don't want you going to travel agencies.'

'But I –'

'I'm the one that does all that.'

'But I just thought –'

'What if your mother saw the brochures? What would she think? She could ruin the whole thing!'

He was angry now and she felt deflated. 'I'm sorry, Harry. I didn't think it –'

'That's your trouble. You don't think. Remember our pact. What did we agree?'

'That you would do the organising.'

'And?'

'That you would look after the money.'

'And?'

'I wouldn't say anything to anyone.'

'Right.'

'Harry.'

'What?'

'When will we go?'

'When I say so.'

'But –'

'For Christ's sake stop it! Let me organise it! When everything's ready and when I say go, we go.'

'It's just that – well, she might find out, that's all.'

'How? You say she's too weak to go downstairs. When was the last time?'

'Months ago.'

'Well, then. But I see what you mean. Anyway we've had it all, haven't we?'

'Everything. I mean everything that we can. You know . . .'

'What?'

'Sometimes I wonder whether –'

'Listen, you were going to get it all eventually. All you did was anticipate. Anyway, I couldn't have managed on my own, not on my savings and the early-retirement pension. I explained all that to you. So it's too late to –'

'I'm not worried about that, Harry. It's just that . . . I don't want anything to stop us. Have we got enough in the bank?'

'For what?'

'For Spain. Enough to buy the little bar. Enough to get started.'

He looked over her shoulder, his eyes half-closed against the smoke of his cigarette.

'Nothing's ever really enough, is it?' he said softly. 'Not really. And that's the problem.' He put on his Beatles cap. 'Come on, I'll take you back.'

Madame Raymonde woke with a start. The TV was still on. It was the *Nine O'Clock News* and she flicked it off. She'd seen all the horrors of the world at six, thank you very much. She turned to Hilda's chair but it was empty. Then she remembered about her going out. It was typical of her selfishness. She had always been selfish, even as a child.

What was she up to anyway with this veiled talk of her 'future'? Hilda didn't have a future. Certainly not by herself. That was made clear at the last interview with the psychiatrist. She either stayed in the house with her mother or else it had to be in an institution of some kind.

No, there was no future for Hilda without her mother, and not much future for Madame without Hilda, if it came to that. Interdependence was the word.

And Hilda was being secretive about this man. But then she always had been secretive. That was another of her little ways. There had been other men in the past but they hadn't lasted long. One word from her about Hilda and that was the end of any romance.

If any man was hoping to get rich through Hilda then he had better think again. It was Madame who held the purse strings. And even when she had gone – something she did not like to

31

contemplate – her money and the house and the furnishings were tied up in a trust that would look after Hilda wherever she was sent.

They were locked together like a pair of Siamese twins, she thought. Which was how it should be. After all they were mother and daughter. Togetherness.

She remembered she had not had her 'constitutional' that day – another black mark for Hilda. Perhaps she should have it now. She knew that unless she got out of bed and walked, she would stiffen up completely – and then she would get bedsores. And with Hilda in her present mood, who knew what would happen if she became totally dependent on her?

She rose, put on her dressing-gown and took up the stick that stood near her bed. Slowly she walked across the room to the piano. The music on the stand was Schubert's A-Major Sonata, the last piece she had been practising. She allowed her right hand to run over the keys. The piano badly needed tuning. One day she would have that attended to.

She walked back towards the door. This reminded her of the walks she used to go on with Boris. No matter how late at night he finished, he would want to walk. She had walked through most of the European capitals at three and four in the morning. Sometimes that was all she knew of them: a dark and freezing walk.

Was that something burning?

She sniffed the air and felt her heart begin to trip.

Hilda had once left on the iron in her room upstairs when she had gone out to do the food shopping and by the time her mother had made her slow and painful way along the landing it had burnt through the cover of the ironing board. But this didn't smell like burning cloth.

Or was it purely her imagination? Sometimes she smelled burning when there was no burning and she put this down to a night in Manhattan after Boris had sung Mahler's '*Lieder Eines Fahrenden Gesellen*' at Carnegie Hall. She remembered that night well because she had had to give him a steam inhalant for a slight cold before the recital.

They had been in bed in their suite on the thirty-first floor of the Montpellier when the fire alarms had gone off and the sprinklers had spurted from the ceilings. She and Boris had hurried along the corridors to the fire exits and she had seen several people knocked over or brushed aside in the rush. Twelve had died in the fire, most of them elderly. From that time on she realised how much the old feared the smell of burning. And now she was old herself.

There was a telephone by her bedside, but what would she say? That she smelled smoke? Or thought she smelled smoke? Or imagined she smelled smoke? And then she would have firemen trooping into her bedroom. They would see her in her nightclothes. A fireman might even hoist her onto his shoulder.

Then there was the water. In the Montpellier their suite had been untouched by flames but water from the sprinklers had ruined their clothes as well as a lithograph Boris had bought that day at Parke-Bernet. What if there was a small fire, like the one Hilda's iron had caused, and because of that her antiques and pictures were ruined? Best try and make certain before she called for help.

She made her way onto the landing. Here the smell was stronger and she knew it was not her imagination. Even the air around the landing light had a bluish tinge where smoke was collecting.

She guessed what had happened. Hilda in her selfish haste to go out and enjoy herself had left something on the stove. If that was so, all she had to do was switch it off, remove whatever it was, and the fire danger would cease.

But what if the fire had already taken hold?

She peered down the staircase in the direction of the kitchen but could see nothing. Surely, if there were flames they would be reflected on the wood panelling and the walls?

She decided to go down. But first there was something she had to do. She passed her daughter's room, a bathroom, a guest room, and came to a door on the far side of the landing.

She turned the key in the lock and opened the door. The smell was rank.

'I don't know if you can understand me,' she said to the gaping darkness of the open door. 'But there may be a fire in the house.' She knew she should do something more but was far too weak. 'I can't help you,' she said. 'You must help yourself.'

She turned and slowly made her way back to the top of the stairs. She was in pain now. The whole middle section of her body, thighs, bottom and stomach, had fattened and spread over the years she had spent in bed, so that although she had a narrow face and shoulders she had swelled out like a pear. Her flesh wobbled as she moved. Her muscles, or what was left of them, strained and contracted and strove to keep her upright.

Going down the stairs was like descending the north face of the Eiger. First she put the rubber end of her stick on the stair below, then lowered one foot, then the other. Each step was taken separately. Each was a triumph, a victory. There were fifteen stairs, all covered in dark red Axminster.

Halfway down she had to rest. Here the smell of burning was stronger and she was convinced that it came from the kitchen. Fear alternated with a more reasoned voice which said, 'Hilda made you pilchards with baked beans. She would only have needed to open tins, heat the contents and serve. It must be the pot itself which she's left on the stove.'

But even so, her fear was making her shake.

She reached the ground floor and nearly fell. Her head was swimming and she kept herself upright with her stick as a climber might use his ice axe. Slowly the giddiness left her and she went on down the passage to the kitchen. Here she could feel an unnatural heat and the smoke was thick enough to burn her eyes.

Just as she thought, Hilda had left the stove on. The ring was bright orange. On top of it was a stainless-steel pot which contained the leftovers of her supper. Smoke was pouring from it.

She switched off the stove, put the pot in the sink and turned on the water. With a whoosh of steam the emergency was at an end. Thank God she had not called the fire brigade.

Her muscles were crying for relief and she sat down on a kitchen chair. Her heart was pounding and her breath was short.

But she'd done it!

34

She looked around. At first glance everything seemed to be the same as when she had last been in the kitchen. But then, as she grew used to her surroundings, she missed things: Boris's collection of antique coffee grinders no longer occupied the top shelves of the Welsh dresser. And a small collection of Victorian kitchenware – copper pots, brass graters and ladles – was also missing.

And the plants!

What had happened to them?

They had stood in terracotta pots on the kitchen windowsills, spider plants and vines, decorative, pleasant to look at. Were these monstrosities the same plants? They had run wild, had covered the windows and half the wall, twining themselves towards the light on anything they could grasp. And then they had died. Instead of green, the stems and leaves were the quality of dun-coloured paper.

Neglect. Hilda's greatest sin. She neglected everything, including herself.

She'd really tell Hilda off this time. Then she paused. Better not be too severe. What if she went raving again as she had in the past? She might even leave. She might resort to violence. Madame wouldn't have put anything past her.

She had long ago found the *raison d'être* of their interdependence: that Hilda was still basically a child who must be dominated by strength of will and personality.

This she had done and it had worked. Hilda was still at home. Still her companion. But it was a fragile psychological edifice and could crumble at any time.

What made things dangerous now was the man. *Who was he?*

Madame had been confident for a long time that no man in his right mind would want Hilda. In her anxiety, she recalled that there were men about who were not in their right minds. Hadn't the government emptied the madhouses onto the streets?

Sitting there in her kitchen, which she had not seen for such a long time, she felt a sense not only of mortality but of panic.

There wasn't much she could do about Hilda except what she was doing. But she could do something about the plants. She'd

35

get Hilda to order more for the kitchen. And what about the other rooms?

She heaved herself up from the chair and made her way along the passage towards the drawing-room at the far end of the house. A half-moon was in the sky and silver traceries fell onto the drawing-room floor through the tangle of plants at the French windows.

She found herself looking at floorboards when she should have been looking at Persian rugs. She should have been standing in a room filled with furniture and paintings – but it was almost empty.

Was her mind playing tricks?

She groped for the switch and flooded the room with light.

'We don't have to go in just yet,' Hilda said.

Harry had parked in the lane near the house and the streetlight was some distance away. To Hilda it was like a scene in a movie: the night, the car, the soft music on the radio.

'What?'

'It's early. It's not ten o'clock yet.' She pressed herself against him. 'Let's talk about Spain. Let's talk about the bar. Will we serve food?'

'You've got to serve food in Spain if you have a bar. It's the law.'

'They call them . . . You told me once but I've forgotten.'

'You mean those little snacks? Tapas.'

'That's right. Tapas. We'll serve those, won't we?'

'Absolutely.' He got out of the car.

'Oh.'

She got out her side and they went along the hedge to the gate. She gripped his hand. 'Why don't you come in. My mother's upstairs and –'

'And she won't come down. You told me.'

He opened the gate.

'Harry, let's go to a hotel.'

'Listen, I –'

He felt her fingers grip his arm. 'The drawing-room light's on!'

'Well?'

'It's never on!'

'You must have left it on.'

'I never go there. Not at night. I don't like it. D'you think there are burglars?'

'Burglars don't go switching on lights.'

She ran up the path.

'The hall light's on too!'

He followed her at a trot.

She unlocked the front door and they burst in together.

'Mother? Mother?'

Hilda ran into the drawing-room. Madame Raymonde was leaning against the wall just inside the door. She had the telephone in her hands and was trying to dial but the stick in her right hand was making it difficult.

'What's happened?' Hilda said. 'What are you doing here? Have you had a fall?'

The old lady looked at them with hatred in her eyes. 'You bitch!'

'Me? Whatever have I done?'

'You've stolen everything!'

The three of them gazed briefly round the room. In the bright light the walls were marked by dust squares where the pictures had once hung.

'You rotten bitch!'

'Shall I take the phone?' Harry said, leaning towards Madame Raymonde.

'Leave it! I'm phoning the police!'

'I wouldn't,' Harry said.

Hilda said, 'All I've done is . . . anticipate. They were going to be mine one day, the paintings and the furniture . . . everything!'

'*Anticipate!*' Madame turned on Harry. 'You put her up to it! She'd never have thought of it for herself!'

'Put her up to what?' Harry caught hold of the phone and pulled. The old woman clung to it but her muscles were no match for his. She released the phone and he put it on the floor. 'What paintings?' he said. 'What furniture?'

Hilda registered the humour. 'Yes . . . what paintings?' She shrieked with laughter. 'What furniture?'

37

Madame pushed herself away from the wall and walked slowly into the hall.

'Mother!' Hilda tried to catch her arm. 'Mother, listen!'

'Don't touch me, you bitch!'

She waved her stick.

'Do you think I want to touch you?' Hilda's voice was rising and her eyes were becoming vacant. 'You filthy old woman! Filthy! Filthy! I'm going to leave you! Harry and I are going to get married and you can rot here!'

Madame Raymonde stopped and a bitter smile crossed her face. 'Married! You?' She turned to Harry. 'Take her and good riddance! Don't you realise what she is?'

There was a note of triumph in Madame's voice that enraged Hilda. She began to use her fists on her mother. The old woman raised her stick and tried to beat her off, but in her weakness the blows were ineffectual. Hilda began to scream with rage.

'That's enough!' Harry said, coming between them. 'For Christ's sake, you'll be heard across the Heath.' He caught the two women and forced them apart. Madame lost her balance and fell heavily against the staircase. Her head hit the bannisters with a sickening crack and her upper dentures flew out onto the carpet. She slid down so that she was lying half on the floor and half on the stairs. Blood began to trickle from her ear and her right foot jerked rapidly.

'Mother!' Hilda flung herself down next to her. 'For God's sake, are you all right?'

She raised her mother's head. The old eyes stared into hers.

'Mother!'

Harry went down on one knee.

Hilda said, 'What's happened to her?'

He felt her pulse and then leaned his head to her chest. His hands were shaking.

'Oh, God, Harry, what have you done?'

'Me! That's rich! It was *you* who started the rough stuff.'

'I didn't push her!'

'Nor did I! She tripped. Fell. It was an accident.'

'Look!'

'What?'

'Her foot's stopped jerking.'

He leaned forward and felt her pulse again.

'She's gone,' he said.

'Oh, my God.'

Both were crouching over the body and they stared at each other in silence for a moment. Then Hilda said, 'What are we going to do, Harry?'

He wiped sweat from his face. 'I don't know.'

'We could say it was an accident. That she fell.'

'Great. And what about the room? Don't you think they'll ask questions?'

'I'll tell them it was all mine. That I sold it.'

'You think they'll believe that?'

'Oh, Harry . . .'

He picked up a cushion and placed it over Madame's face so he would not have to look at the eyes.

'Are you sorry?' he said to Hilda. 'Really sorry? No more Mother to look after any more.'

The change in circumstances slowly gripped her. 'She's gone! Forever!'

'That's right. Forever.'

'I'm glad. Really glad.'

He looked at her in an odd way. 'You never can tell how things will end up,' he said. 'Remember how we started? In just a small way.'

'A painting.'

'That's right. One painting. But then that wasn't really enough, was it?'

'Not when we thought of Spain.'

'That's right. Spain . . . Pity about Spain.'

'But, Harry, we can still go, can't we? I mean . . .'

'Did you really think that was on?'

'What're you saying, Harry?'

'"Tell me about the house, Harry . . . And the bar, Harry . . . And the food, Harry . . ."'

She frowned, not understanding.

'Christ, you poor bloody fool.'

'Don't make jokes, Harry. Not about Spain.'

39

Suddenly she put her arms on his shoulders. 'Kiss me!'

He tried to step back but she held him, almost knocking off his cap.

Her mouth was hot and wet and he recoiled.

'You did it, Harry!' There was admiration in her voice. She began to unbutton her blouse. In a moment she had thrust her large, brown, sunlamped breasts at his face. 'Now!' she said. 'Here on the floor!'

'What about her?'

'She's dead, she can't see!'

'No, I mean *what about her*? I can't just leave things as they are!'

'Why not?'

'Oh, Jesus. Don't you understand? There's a witness!'

'What witness?'

A thought came into her head and she glanced up towards the landing.

'You,' Harry said, and caught her by the throat. 'I never wanted it this way. You must believe that! Never! But things have got out of hand!'

He squeezed harder.

'I'm not a wit . . .'

'And you're crazy! How the hell could I ever trust you?'

'Harry, I love you . . . I'd never . . .'

That was as far as she got.

THREE

It was nearly three o'clock on a cold autumn morning and in the Vale of Health the house blazed like a beacon. Three police cars and an ambulance were parked in the small road that led to the front gate. The occupiers of several other nearby houses, hearing the commotion, had switched on upstairs lights.

By the time Detective Inspector Ferry reached the house, two police cars had already answered Wylie's 999 call and a short time later the duty doctor arrived. Several of the uniformed men were holding handkerchiefs to their faces for the smell in the downstairs hall was bad.

A police photographer was taking detailed shots of the bodies.

'How long have they been dead?' Ferry said to the doctor who was overseeing the loading of the two corpses into body bags.

'Three, maybe four days.'

Detective Constable Holder, who was in his early twenties and who had never been in close contact with decomposing tissue, had to go into the garden.

Ferry questioned the doctor for a few minutes about the cause of death.

'The old woman was beaten with something or fell, and the younger was strangled. You'll know more accurately after the PM.'

The doctor left at the same time as the ambulance.

41

Ferry questioned the uniformed officers and was given the lay-out of the house.

'Anybody around?' he said. 'Neighbours? Anyone who saw anything?'

No one from the surrounding houses had been near the place.

'Too bloody upmarket to stick their noses in,' Ferry said, and went into the drawing-room.

He was a short man with a square face and gingerish hair that clung to his scalp in a mat. He walked on the balls of his feet like a boxer. He'd been born in the East End of London, in what had once been a community of dockworkers but was now the biggest apartment and office development in Europe – Dock-lands. He thought of it, bitterly, as Yuppieland.

He was casually dressed in field-green cords, trainers and a leather windcheater. He usually thrust his hands deep into the jacket pockets, hunching his shoulders and adding to the appear-ance of someone who was aggressive and impatient.

'Holder!' he called.

The young detective, tall and skinny, came to the front door.

'Get in here!'

The uniformed officers had already searched the house, but Ferry began his own search with Holder tagging along behind, notebook at the ready.

They went through the drawing-room and the kitchen, noting the burnt pot and dead plants, and then began a search of the upstairs rooms. One of the uniformed officers accompanied them.

'Any lights on when you got here?' Ferry asked.

'Nothing. Complete darkness. But the central heating was on full blast. The doc said that's what caused the bodies to decompose so quickly.'

'This must have been the old woman's room,' Ferry said. 'A piano? In a bedroom?'

'Maybe she liked music,' Holder said.

Ferry looked at his notebook. 'Madame Eva Raymonde. Sounds like a gypsy fortune-teller.'

One of the fingerprint team was dusting the bedside table for prints.

'Anything?' Ferry said.

The man shook his head. 'Wouldn't be surprised if it wasn't a professional job. I mean someone's wiped the downstairs pretty clean.'

'Of course it's professional,' Ferry said. 'You don't empty a bloody room full of furniture into the local taxi.'

They went into the bedroom next door. 'Looks like a little girl's room,' Ferry said.

The bed was pink satin and there was a teddy bear pyjama case on the pillow. The walls were a mass of photographs cut from glossy magazines: weightlifters, bodybuilders, film stars, lifeguards – all in a state of seminudity. The dressing-table was covered in bottles and creams. More pictures were stuck on the mirror.

'You wait till you see the other room,' the uniformed officer said.

They crossed the landing. 'This one?' Ferry said. 'What's the smell?'

'Drains.'

They went in.

'Jesus!'

Although the light was on, the room was gloomy. The bulb was weak and near the ceiling. In one corner was a cot-bed with a stained mattress. There was no other furniture, not even a carpet. But the floor was covered in sheets of white paper on which there were dozens of drawings. The walls of the room were dark with graffiti. The window was uncurtained but the lower panes were obscured by paint and wire netting.

'Looks like a secure cell in an asylum,' Ferry said. 'What's that over there?' He pointed to a door.

'Bathroom.'

Ferry opened the door and recoiled. The smell was worse.

There was a lavatory, and an old-fashioned free-standing bath on ball-and-claw feet against one wall. Every surface was decorated with graffiti. Even the bath. Here too the small window – of frosted glass – was guarded by wire netting.

'Switch on the light,' Ferry said.

'There's no bulb.'

The only illumination filtered in from the room next door.

43

Holder was beginning to go pale again. He bent towards the lavatory.

'Not here!' Ferry said.

But Holder kept his position. 'Sir . . .' he said, choking.

'Go outside!'

'Sir, I think there's something at the back of the bath.'

'What?'

Holder went down on his knees and peered into the darkness beneath the bath.

'Well?'

'It may be a dog, sir.'

'Put your hand under and feel.'

'Could get bitten, sir.'

'No dog in his right bloody mind is going to bite you, Holder.'

'Don't think it is a dog, sir.'

'It's not another body, is it?'

'Don't think so, sir.'

The uniformed officer passed a torch to Holder. By this time Ferry too was on his knees.

Holder switched on the torch.

'Oh my God!' Ferry said.

They were looking at a child. It had worked its way between the bath and the wall. The eyes stared blankly into the torch beam, then the child twisted away so that its face was not in the direct light.

'Jesus Christ,' Ferry said. He lay down on his stomach. 'It's all right. No one's going to hurt you.'

The child made no move.

'You think it understands?' Holder said.

'How the hell should I know? Give me the torch.' He let the beam travel down the child's body. It was dressed in torn jeans and a jersey. 'Can't tell if it's a boy or a girl.'

'Come on now,' Ferry said softly. 'You can trust me.'

He put his arm under the bath but couldn't reach the child.

'Can we move the bath?' he said to the uniformed officer as he straightened up. 'I can't make it from this side.'

'We'll fracture the pipes, sir. Water all over the place.'

Ferry went to the end of the bath. It was like shining a light

44

into a badger set or a fox's den, except that the child's eyes did not glow as animals' eyes do.

'Hello,' he said. 'What's your name? Here, Holder, take the torch.'

Ferry squirmed under as far as he could but the child withdrew its legs just out of his reach.

'Swop me,' Ferry said. 'You're a thin slab. You try.'

Holder's arms were long. 'I can touch a foot.'

'All right then, grab and pull.'

'I don't like to . . .'

'For Christ's sake, get a move on.'

'In case I hurt –'

Holder's fingers wrapped themselves round the naked foot of the child. He began to pull. Suddenly the child let out a kind of wail. It was a sound more animal than human. Ferry had never heard anything like it and it sent him cold.

Slowly Holder drew the child out and carried it into the light of the next room.

'God save us!' the uniformed officer said.

It was a boy. His hair was matted and his body was covered in dirt, his teeth were yellow and his clothes were torn. He made no move to resist as they placed him in the centre of the room.

'You'd think he'd be crying, sir,' Holder said.

'Poor little sod,' Ferry said.

The boy looked at them blankly.

Ferry went down on his haunches and faced the child. 'What's your name, old son?' There was no response. He turned to Holder. 'We're into something very nasty here. Get on to the station, tell 'em what we've found. Get a WPC organised. And they'll need to contact social services. I've seen something like this before. Only once, but I wish to Christ I hadn't.' He said to the boy, 'My name's Peter. You don't have to be afraid of me.'

The thickness of his voice would have surprised his friends and family who knew him as a macho bantam-cock.

He turned to the uniformed officer. 'How the hell can people do this sort of thing?'

*

45

London North police station is in the Finchley Road, a new three-storey building set back from the busy traffic with its own security gates and parking area. Duncan Wylie sat on a bench in the waiting-room. From his position he could see the computer area. The screens and the rattle of the printers reminded him of a bank. Uniformed officers and plain-clothes CID personnel moved through the rooms, drinking coffee and smoking and laughing.

Wylie was wound up and exhausted and his anger was near the surface. It didn't help that people were getting on with their work and seemed to be ignoring him.

He went up to the desk sergeant who was working on papers in front of him.

'How long do I have to stay?' he said.

There was a note of anger in his tone which the sergeant noted and disapproved of.

'What was your name again, sir?'

'Wylie. Duncan Wylie. You know damn well what my name is. Someone said I had to wait and make a statement. Well, I've been waiting for bloody hours.'

The sergeant, a sandy-haired man in his forties who had spent the past ten years dealing with irate citizens in the front office, put down his ballpoint pen and shuffled the papers.

'What was it in connection with?'

'Oh, for God's sake. I was the one who phoned, remember? About the body.'

'Oh yes, that's right, sir. The gentleman who saw the, what was it, sir . . . ? An orang-utan? A gorilla?'

A passing police officer chuckled and Wylie realised they were going to have their fun.

'On Hampstead Heath, wasn't it?' the sergeant said. 'Not actually your rainforest, is it, sir?'

Wylie went back to the bench. Screw you, he thought. He'd barely sat down when the big glass doors leading to the car park slid silently open and a group of policemen came in. He saw a tall, thin plain-clothes detective, followed by a shorter man carrying something large wrapped in a blanket.

'You got a WPC organised?' Ferry said to the desk sergeant.

46

'WPC Commins. She's waiting. But, Peter . . . she's only a probationer.'

'Why the hell couldn't you –'

'Because of the flu. That's why. But she's okay.'

A small knot of policemen, some in uniform, some in plain-clothes, watched with interest as Ferry carried his bundle through into the offices beyond. As he entered the doorway the blanket fell back and Wylie saw what he was carrying.

He rose. A strange and troubling idea was entering his head. He went up to the desk but before he could open his mouth the sergeant said, with sudden bitterness, as though Wylie was somehow to blame, 'More like a child, wouldn't you say, sir?'

'You mean that –'

'That's right, sir. Not really an ape or a monkey at all, was it?'

'Listen I –' Wylie broke off and tried to follow the child through the doorway. The sergeant was down in a flash barring his way.

'I'm sorry, sir, but you can't go in there. Inspector Ferry will want to talk to you in a little while.'

'But –'

'Would you like a coffee, sir? There's a machine in the corridor.'

Wylie knew when he was beaten.

Woman Police Constable Janet Commins was young and insecure. Like Ferry, she had only been at London North for a few weeks. She was tall and dark with a high colour and was still going through a period when she was embarrassed and apprehensive about the canteen cowboys who were constantly rubbing up against her breasts and bottom – and then apolo-gising.

So now she was nervous as she watched Ferry and Holder bring the bundle to her. She'd been warned that a child had been found and she had telephoned the night duty officer of the North London Child Protection Team. She wished the social worker would arrive.

'There you are, old son,' Ferry said. He put the child down gently on a chair in one of the interview rooms.

For the first time they were able to look at him in a good light. He was thin and white, like some night creature that rarely saw the sun. His face was pinched and his dark brown eyes blinked in the hard neon strip. His hair was long and hung almost to his shoulders, his fingernails were also long, some of them had broken, all were dirty. He wore baggy jeans, a size too big for him and an old dark blue jersey with holes in it. His feet were bare. Ferry thought that both pieces of clothing could have been bought at Oxfam shops or from street markets. The boy looked like a kid in an old black and white Dickens film Ferry had seen on TV but whose name he couldn't remember.

'Well?' Ferry said.

Janet Commins said, 'Sir, I've called the Child Protection Team and a social worker is coming over.'

'Good.' He turned to the boy. 'Hear that? Someone's coming to see you. But first let's get you cleaned up and find out who you are.'

The boy stared at him unblinking.

'He's been like that since we found him,' Holder said. 'Never uttered a word.'

'No, but he's going to, aren't you, old son? You're going to tell us your name and what happened and everything.' He turned to Janet Commins. 'You got a basin of water or something?'

'A basin?' She was more nervous than before. She had never seen a child so . . . she searched her mind for a word but the only one that came was 'animal-like'.

And she was self-conscious in front of Ferry. She had heard about him. He'd come on a wave of rumour. How he'd been one of the top thief-takers in the East End. A hard man.

'Yes, a basin. Round thing. Holds water.'

She flushed. 'I know what a ba –'

'Oh, Christ, look let's take him into the bathroom. It'll have to be yours, okay?'

They took him into the women's room.

'You want me to . . . ?' Janet began.

'Of course. Haven't you got any brothers and sisters?'

48

'I'm the youngest.'

'Oh all right. I'll do it.' He pulled down a towel from one of the shelves, dipped it in warm water and began to wash the boy's face and hands. 'See if you can find a toy or something.'

The water in the washbasin went suddenly dark.

'How old do you think he is?' Holder asked.

'Dunno. Could be six. Seven perhaps. But we'll find out, won't we, old son? Bound to be papers in the house. Birth certificate, that sort of thing. We're only just at the beginning.'

A constable knocked and put his head round the door. 'Sir, the social worker is here.'

'Tell her to wait.'

Ferry finished cleaning up the visible parts of the boy and then said, 'That'll have to do for the moment. You'll have a proper bath when you get wherever it is you're going. But first of all we're going to have a little talk.'

He took the boy's hand and the child walked with him into the interview room. Janet Commins was holding a teddy bear.

'I found this,' she said.

'Well, give it to him.'

'Would you like it?' she said.

The boy stared blankly at her. She pushed the bear towards him but he shrank back.

'You don't think he's deaf, do you?' Holder said.

'Why should he be deaf?'

'Just wondered, sir. He's not reacting to your questions.'

'He will. Won't you?'

Ferry put him up on the table. 'Now we've got to get some information from you. You understand that, don't you?' He took the boy's hands in his own. 'What's your name, son? Won't you tell us? We're friends, real friends. We're going to look after you. Nothing bad's going to happen any more. So you can feel safe. And you can tell us your name and how old you are and all about what's been going on.'

There was a knock on the door and the same constable as before said, 'Sorry to interrupt, sir, but she's insisting we hand him over.'

'Insisting, is she?'

Ferry went out to the waiting-room. Duncan Wylie was about to rise to his feet, then sat back. The woman who had recently arrived was making even more of a scene than he had. He decided to keep his mouth shut.

She was in her late twenties or early thirties, Wylie thought, and wore enormous spectacles. They exaggerated her eyes which were china blue. She was thin-faced and intense-looking and her face was devoid of make-up. Her clothes were flowing and loose and Wylie guessed she would be a vegetarian or a vegan and that she would spend many Saturdays marching for the rights of minorities.

Now she advanced on Ferry. 'My name is Ruth Challis. I'm from North London social services. One of your people phoned about a child.'

'That's right,' Ferry said. 'I'm talking to him now.'

She made a little display of looking at her watch. 'It's twenty-five past four.' It was plain she thought this was no time to be talking to a child. 'I'll take him now.'

Ferry said, 'I haven't finished yet.'

'He's no longer your responsibility. He's mine. I'm in contact with foster carers. They're expecting us.'

'Sure. When I've finished.'

'No. Now.'

'Don't try too hard, Miss Challis.'

'Ms.'

'Okay. Ms. I want a few more minutes wi –'

'I'm sorry, Inspector, but I must get him settled for the night! He must be exhausted and frightened.'

'We're all exhausted. And yes, I suppose he must be frightened. After all, his mum and his grandmother were murdered a few days ago.'

Ferry's gingerish colour had seeped down from his head to his cheeks.

'All the more reason why I must –'

'Jesus Christ! With people like you it's no wonder social services are in trouble.'

She looked at him coldly. 'Would you fetch him, please. And his toys.'

'What toys?'

'Didn't you bring them? I should have thought –'

'Don't you understand? There *were* no toys. Nothing. Zero. He was locked away.'

For the first time she seemed unsure of herself. 'Is that what he said?'

'No it isn't. It's what we found. He hasn't said a single bloody word.' He turned. 'Holder! Bring out our friend.'

Holder emerged with the boy, the blanket and the teddy bear. Holder was carrying it. He passed it to Ruth Challis.

She bent down and took the child's hand. 'What's your name?' she said.

The boy looked at her blankly.

'I hadn't thought to ask,' Ferry said.

She ignored the sarcasm. 'I deal with all sorts of cases, Inspector. I'll deal with this one too.'

'Hang on. You'd better give me the address of the carers. He doesn't become yours and yours alone, you know.'

'Mr and Mrs Brind, 31 Newton Road.'

'I know the street.'

'Fine. Can we go now?'

'Yeah.' He went down on his haunches in front of the child, started to say something, patted him on the cheek instead. It was like patting cold marble. He looked over the boy's shoulder at the social worker. 'You better take good care of him.'

FOUR

Images.

Duncan Wylie's life was made up of images. Mostly they were images of animals and birds and fish, his bread and butter, so to speak, and of course there were images of people, mostly Ellie. Ellie washing her blistered feet in the Findhorn in Scotland after walking all night hunting for a wild cat's lair; Ellie in the Kalahari filming bat-eared foxes from the roof of the Land Rover; Ellie in the forest . . .

It was soon after seven in the morning and he was lying on his rumpled bed in the forgettable flat in Lancaster Gate, and the images of the previous night were crowding into his brain.

The boy.

First the fuzzy thing he had thought was a monkey; then the strange, etiolated creature he had seen at the police station, with its long hair and blank eyes.

After the boy had been taken to the foster carers, Wylie had gone into one of the interview rooms with Ferry and made a written statement. The whole episode had been abrasive. Simple questions had been stonewalled.

'If you won't tell me what's going on why the hell should I help you?' Wylie had said after an hour of sparring.

'Because I'll bloody well make you! Apart from anything else it's your statutory duty to help. You're a witness after the fact.'

'Just because I saw the woman and phoned?'

'Maybe and maybe not.'

'What's that supposed to mean?'

'It means that perhaps you're just someone who blundered into something – or perhaps not. You may have killed her for all we know.'

'That's really marvellous. I kill her, push the child out into the night, then take a camera onto the Heath, hang about, then phone the police.'

'There were two of them. Two women.'

'Two?' He felt a jolt. He thought then that Ferry might open up a bit, give him a few more details, but the hope was vain. He returned to the boy.

'What do you want to know?' Ferry asked.

'Well, who he is, where he was found, what he's told you.'

'You must be crazy asking questions like that and expecting answers!'

'If it wasn't for me you wouldn't even know about the murder . . . murders. I suppose they *were* murders?'

'What else?'

'Suicides? How the hell am I supposed to work it out if you won't give me any details?'

'I don't give a damn if you work it out or not. All I want from you is information.'

Wylie decided to be more pacific. 'I'm interested. That's only natural, isn't it?'

'Look, we don't know a bloody thing yet. The investigation is under way. Two women have been murdered. A mother and her daughter. We know their names. We know that the old lady was a concert pianist at one time. We found her grandson in the house – alive. We don't know who killed them or why or when. Okay?'

'What about the boy?'

'What *about* the boy?'

'Well, you know, anything at all.'

Ferry looked at him closely. 'What the hell's all this in aid of? Oh, Christ, I get it. You want to exploit this.'

'Exploit it? How?'

53

'Don't give me that crap. You make your living as a documentary film maker. You want to exploit the child. Make money out of him.'

'Rubbish!'

'You were filming wildlife and suddenly more than wildlife comes into your viewfinder. It's only human nature you'd want to sell it.'

Then Wylie told the first lie.

'The only trouble with that theory is I didn't get anything in the can.'

Ferry laughed derisively. 'You're telling me a professional photographer like yourself missed an opportunity like that?'

'I ran out of film. I was looking for a full magazine.'

'I don't believe you.'

'Okay, you can get the camera and check.'

And they had.

But the magazine containing shots of the child was hidden in the camper. The magazine the police removed from the camera was the one with the *previous* night's work on the foxes. Wylie had made the switch almost instinctively once he'd phoned. Something in his brain had said, *Don't let anyone have the film*. And that was even before he had made up his mind what he was going to do.

And what he was going to do was make his own film. Without Ferry knowing. Jimmy Monkton of Nature TV had wanted something offbeat. Well, this was offbeat. It was so offbeat and so dramatic he might be able to name his own price. He could see the title now: *Mowgli in London . . . Mowgli of the Streets . . .*

Something like that.

Because it was all there. Substitute the foxes for Mowgli's wolf pack, substitute Hampstead Heath for the Seeonee Hills, substitute the two women for the terrorised villagers, the murderer for Shere Khan the tiger . . . and you had it all. Kipling 1990s style. You couldn't miss!

But it would have to be carefully done. He already had a hazy notion of how he would work: he would parallel Ferry's investigation. And if that didn't work then he'd operate in his wake.

Even though Ferry had been tight with facts, Wylie already had three pieces of information: the women's names, the fact

54

that one had been a concert pianist, and – he reached for a piece of paper and looked at what he had jotted down at London North – the address of the boy.

On the other side of London, Detective Superintendent Begg was lying in his bed, eyes open, staring at the ceiling, wondering if he should get up or whether he could close his eyes and summon up a last half-hour of sleep. He had been awake since five. He was sleeping badly these days and he thought he might go along to the police surgeon and ask for pills.

Beside him, he could hear the regular breathing of Amanda. No, not Amanda, Mandy. But he thought of her as Amanda and would like to use the name. It was a good name and there were too many Mandys.

He stretched out his hand softly and stroked the skin of her arm. This was the time of day when he was most easily aroused, but he didn't like to wake her. She was only really at peace when he was there although she would have denied that; not hotly for she never did anything hotly, but with a cold and indifferent contempt.

Why her, he wondered. There were dozens of women he met in the course of his work who would have made reasonable bed companions. So why Amanda?

Because when you became unhinged about someone, that was it, there was no one else.

The phone rang. He switched it off before it could wake her and took it through to the sitting-room. Grey morning light was coming in from the river, flat and leached of colour, and the room had lost the cosy warmth of the night before.

'Yes?' Begg said.

Ferry identified himself and Begg let him speak uninterrupted for some moments until he reached a point where he could no longer believe what he was hearing.

'A what?' he said.

'He thought it was a monkey or an ape or something similar. Called it a primate. But it wasn't.'

'Are you having me on?' The tone was irritated.

'No, guv'nor. That's the truth.'

'But it wasn't a monkey. Nor a fighting bull, nor a yeti; nothing like that?'

'It was a child. Little boy of six or seven.'

'In the house with two dead women?'

'Yeah.'

'Hang on. Let's get this straight. This photographer was making a film on the Heath, was he? And the child came to take food from a litter bin?'

'The boy was hungry. Must have been. The women had been dead for three or four days according to the doc, but we'll know better after the PM.'

'What about food in the house? I mean, why would he be foraging in litter baskets?'

'Everything in the house was in tins. That's what they lived on. Tins. Baked beans. Tuna. Stews. That sort of thing.'

'Are you telling me a seven-year-old kid can't open a tin? Jesus, they open child-proof bottle tops faster than adults. Anyway, this is all conjecture. I mean the kid could have broken into the house about the time the photographer followed him. Maybe this man Wylie frightened him and the kid ran into the house. Maybe he came from somewhere else entirely.'

'Not this kid.'

'Go on.'

'We found his . . . his room. If you can call it that. I once worked on a case in Hoxton. Little girl who was locked away in a cellar.'

'But you say he wasn't locked away. That he'd been seen on the Heath and followed into the house.'

'That's what bothers me. The room was a kind of den, you know what I mean? Like he'd been imprisoned there but then someone had unlocked the door.'

'No other way out? Window? Nothing like that?'

'Nothing like that. There was wire over the windows. I mean, the place had been made into a cell. When I first saw it I thought of the seclusion rooms in a mental hospital. And he'd been cooped up there all right. The smell was enough to stop a train. Drawings all over the walls and everywhere.'

'Well, if he lived there he may have seen something.' There

was a pause. 'Has he said anything? I mean has he told you what he saw? Or anything about it?'

'No, guv'nor. Not a thing. He hasn't uttered a word since we found him.'

'Is he dumb?'

'Don't know. Holder thought he might be deaf. If he is, then he could be dumb as well. Could be mentally handicapped. Maybe that's why he was hidden away.'

'Christ! All right. You go and get some sleep. I've got that rape in Swiss Cottage on my plate and the robbery over in West Hampstead. But I'll have a look at the papers on this as soon as I get in.'

'Okay, guv'nor.'

'By the way, where is the child?'

'Foster carers. Social services organised them.'

'You got the address?'

'Yeah. I got it.'

'Leave it for me.'

Begg put down the phone and stared at the wall. A messy one, he thought. A real mess. He went into the kitchen and made himself a cup of coffee and carried it out onto the balcony. High up on the eighteenth floor the morning was cold, with a wind that puckered the surface of the Thames below, but the air was clear and he could see across to the south bank. Sometimes he would stand on the balcony and stare at Rotherhithe through binoculars, trying to recognise streets or buildings he had known in his youth. But it was hopeless.

Both banks were unrecognisable now. Where once had been the West India Docks, the Surrey Commercial Dock, the Greenland Dock, the Quebec Dock, the Nelson Dock, the Royal Victorian Victualling Yard – names that to Begg were like a drumroll from Britain's imperial and mercantile past – now stood blocks of expensive and largely unwanted apartments.

But behind them, hidden from view by the new river people, all was much the same: the council flats, the rubbish dumps, the empty gas holders, the mean streets, the estates where drugs were pushed and where the old and the frail were too frightened to go out in the midday sun.

A river bus commuting from Greenwich to Charing Cross came buzzing up Limehouse Reach throwing a bow wave. He thought that the phrase 'the wrong side of the tracks' could usefully be reworked to 'the wrong side of the river'.

Well, he was not on the wrong side of the river any longer. Who'd have thought when he was a kid in Rotherhithe that the opposite bank of the Thames, the north bank, would become fashionable among the yuppies. The word yuppie hadn't even been invented then.

He'd taken Mandy to Rotherhithe not so long ago to show her where he had grown up. She wasn't impressed, but then nothing impressed her.

He'd been impressed – unhappily impressed – by the number of blacks who had fetched up there. It had always been a place for migrants: Chinese, Goanese, Turks – men who'd worked the ships. His mother had washed dishes in a Turkish restaurant and they had lived on the leftovers she brought home. For a while he'd even taken pitta filled with cold kebabs or houmous as his school lunch.

He lit the first cigarette of the day. He felt nervous and charged up and told himself it wouldn't be long now before he left Dock-lands forever. He'd never thought of early retirement before he met Amanda, now he could think of nothing else.

And now this. A bloody messy one. And Ferry. That made everything worse. He didn't like Ferry; he'd seen his sort before; grown up with various permutations of Ferry; chips the size of paving slabs on their shoulders; inverted snobs; envy merchants.

He'd just got London North to his liking, his team anyway – Begg's boys. He'd managed to get them out of their bomber jackets and their denims into decent suits. He'd managed to get them to have their hair cut and to shave off their Zapata mous-taches. London North was as up-market as a policeman could get and he wanted it reflected in his team. And now this wide boy, this Jack-the-lad, this ginger-headed git, had arrived with a reputation for getting the job done.

He'd gone out of his way to help Ferry make the adjustments to his style. But there had been that business of the black tie, for instance. Only an ignorant bastard would have done that. The point was he didn't fit into a place like London North.

He'd have to watch Ferry very very carefully. Especially over this one.

He began to shiver with cold and went back inside. Amanda was still asleep. She was naked, on her back. He let his eyes move up from the gold chain round her ankle, to the long thighs, the dark bush of hair, the firm high breasts. Twenty-eight years old. The flesh still firm. He had been planning to wake her with a coffee and take it from there, but Ferry's call had changed that. Better get in and try and sort out things.

He began to dress. He did so with a care that was almost fastidious. The same taste marked the furnishing of the flat. Modern, but good stuff. He kissed Mandy's sleeping head and went out into the morning. The apartment block was built at the edge of the water. He ran down the walkway to the floating dock. A river bus came racing upstream.

He bought a set of papers and took his seat among the business men. Nothing yet about the double murder. Too late for the final editions. But they'd get to it.

The water was grey-brown. A police launch passed them going downstream. The men looked cold.

Newton Road in North London had been built in the late twenties. The houses were double-storied with bay windows, each on its separate plot, each with a small front garden and a larger one at the back. They had been originally for bank clerks and shop assistants but over the years the street had gone up-market and the houses were valuable.

It had been a legacy that had enabled Ralph and Margaret Brind to buy number 31 in the 1960s.

They were school teachers, or at least Ralph was. He was deputy head of a middle-sized comprehensive. Margaret had recently lost her job. If they could, they would have sold the house, but in the present recession the street was a forest of For Sale boards.

When their family had been younger they had sometimes

fostered children for the social services. But their own kids had grown up and left home. The Brinds were in their late forties, both were apprehensive at what had arrived on their doorstep early that morning.

Now, as Wylie lay on his bed planning, as Ferry drove home through the morning traffic, and as Detective Superintendent Begg left the river bus at Charing Cross Pier and made for the tube, Ralph and Margaret Brind were standing in their kitchen, still in their nightclothes, sipping mugs of coffee and looking at each other and wondering if they had been wise.

'We need the money,' Ralph said. 'That's the logic of it.'

'I know but . . . I don't like thinking of it only in those terms,' Margaret said. She was a small, bespectacled woman going grey. Her husband was large and running to fat and talked frequently of taking up squash again.

'What's that supposed to mean? Logic is logic. Money is money.'

She thought back to the arrival of Ms Challis with the boy. She hadn't cared for her. She liked and respected the older social workers, women who had had their own families and who knew what life was about, but found the young ones with their buzz words and trendy jargon arrogant and hard to take.

But she soon dismissed Ms Challis from her thoughts; it was the boy who dominated. His face reminded her of a photograph she had once seen of a starving child. Not that his body looked starved – when she had bathed him she had seen there was flesh on his ribs – no, it was just that his face with its large eye sockets gave the *impression* of hunger and disease.

'I wonder what his name is,' she said.

'He'll tell us as soon as he's ready. I've seen kids like this before. For some reason they stop talking, then just start up again.'

'The reason's plain enough, Ralph.'

'Of course. Sorry. It'll be our job to help him get over it. Anyway, I've got to get to school. What time are you taking him for the admission medical?'

'Ms Challis said someone from social services would call about four.'

60

'I'll try to be back.'

After she had seen Ralph off, Margaret Brind made herself another cup of coffee. Had they done something foolish? Did they really want a young person in the house again? Especially a complicated case? She and Ralph had promised themselves that once the kids left home they would sell the house, invest the money and do all the things they had wanted to do and couldn't – like going on a walking holiday in the Black Forest, visiting America, buying a cottage in France. But they hadn't been able to sell the house in the recession.

Weren't they adding to their responsibilities, restricting themselves even further?

And how long would they have to keep the boy?

No one could tell them.

She had put him in Cliff's old room and she thought she would just peep in and check that he was all right.

The curtains were closed against the daylight but she could see instantly that the bed was empty.

Oh God, she thought, he can't have got out!

But the bottom of the window was closed and locked.

She looked under the bed where Cliff had often hidden from her when he was a little boy. But he wasn't there. She heard a faint noise, a kind of scratching. She looked in the corner next to the wardrobe. The boy was sitting on the floor in the little space between the wardrobe and the wall. He watched her with his huge brown eyes. Then his head began to rock from side to side making a scratching noise against the wallpaper.

'Are you all right?' Margaret bent down in front of him.

He looked through her and did not seem to see her.

'Won't you tell me your name? Then we'll have something to call you by.'

The eyes stared. The face remained expressionless. The head moved from side to side.

FIVE

'Call me a perfectionist if you like. I mean, I want to get things right. It's not just dialect. Any fool can do dialect. No, it's intonation and timbre and pitch. Voice is personality . . . that's what I've always said. Take Kennedy and those harsh New England vowels and consonants . . . the voice *was* Kennedy . . . When I was in *King of Hearts* I . . .'

Hannah Wilton found her attention straying. Not that Mitchell Bourke would notice. Once he got on to his interpretation of roles he might talk without stopping for a whole session.

Her consulting rooms were done in soothing pastels. She had long since abandoned a couch. Instead the patient occupied the recliner and could sit up or lounge or even lie back – just as he or she wanted. Hannah herself sat in a large brown leather chair with a notebook and pencil and sometimes a small hand-held recorder which she would switch on if she wanted something particular.

There was nothing particular about Bourke. He came to see her once a week and she thought there wasn't much wrong with him that the lead in a good TV series wouldn't cure. Like most actors' lives, his was a series of lurches from one emotional or financial crisis to the next. He'd been in a number of soaps in the seventies and early eighties. Now he was having what he liked to call his midlife crisis. But the problem was it had coincided with a lack of work and the fact that his most recent wife – a woman half his age – had walked out on him.

'Why do you think you're a perfectionist?' she said.

'Because I'm old-fashioned. I believe in giving value for money. If I take on a part I give it everything I've got and I wish that applied to some of the others I've worked with.'

He was lying back on the recliner studying himself in the mirror above her. Sometimes, just for the hell of it, she moved the chair before he came so she could see him readjust it. As he spoke he watched himself; his own best audience.

He probably wasn't so much disturbed as lonely, she thought. Three marriages, each wife younger than the last; a screen idol in his twenties with boyish good looks and wavy black hair.

Well, the looks had gone now, the skin was mottled, the hair thin. He needed someone to talk to and paid Hannah to listen.

The session came to an end. 'Can the patient ask the doctor out to dinner?'

He smiled the smile that twenty years ago had been in every women's magazine.

'I'm afraid not,' she said. 'A rule of the house.'

This was a kind of charade they went through, not every time, but often enough recently to make her embarrassed. What she should say was, 'Look, Mitchell, I don't want you to come any more. And I don't ever want to go out with you.' But how could she? It would be too destructive. Perhaps she was all he had right now.

He smiled at her as though he had not asked the question and had not been refused. It was weird, she thought. Perhaps there *was* something wrong after all.

'Same time next week?'

'Mitchell . . . I'm . . . look, isn't this costing you the earth?'

'It's only money,' he said. 'Anyway it's doing me good.'

She saw him to the door.

He turned and said, 'You know you can't go on like this for ever.'

'Like what?'

'Well, how long is it since Dick and . . .'

'Eighteen months,' she said quickly.

'Life's for –'

She just couldn't bear to hear him finish the sentence and said, 'Goodbye, Mitchell. See you next week.'

She crossed quickly to the window just in time to see him on the steps. He paused, put on his cap, and looked back at the apartment building. Then he got into a large shiny car and drove away.

She locked and barred her door. The action of locking up reminded her suddenly and painfully of a winter she and Richard had spent in France in a remote farmhouse in the Massif des Maures near Hyères. She had been pregnant then with Tom and they had rented the house so that Richard could work on his book *Eyewitness and Memory*.

The Provençal nights were frosty and clear and every evening he would finish work at dusk and then he would light the fire in the living-room and go round the house closing the shutters. She would always remember those three things: the chilly grey light of dusk, the smell of the pine logs as the resin in them began to burn, and the clack-clack of the shutters closing. Then the house would become their world until the following morning.

She hastily tried to wipe out these thoughts for they were coming at the most dangerous time of the day. Instead she went to her bedroom and changed into a blouse and a pair of old jeans. As she did so she glanced at herself in the long cheval glass, which they had bought in a small junk shop in Inverness and lovingly restored. She saw a woman in her early thirties, medium height, brown hair cut short, wide-spaced brown eyes, and a broad face with high cheekbones.

She was putting on a bit of weight, she thought, which was probably a good thing for she had become too thin – not something she could ever have contemplated a couple of years earlier. Her skin was improving too. It, with her eyes, had always been her best points.

Enough of this self-regard, she thought, and made a face at herself in the mirror. It was nearly six o'clock. She usually had a glass of wine while she watched the BBC news. Even though she frequently did not feel like it she cooked every night. It would be too easy, she thought, to skip meals and graze.

She decided she would have pasta with a pesto sauce. Later she would return to the language tapes. She was learning German. On alternate evenings she studied the history of art. At weekends she drove out of London and went to look at archaeological digs. She told herself she was living a full and interesting life.

She had just poured herself a glass of chardonnay when the doorbell rang.

'Sophie!'

'I thought I'd come without phoning . . . then you couldn't make excuses.'

'Don't be silly. I love to see you. You know that.'

Her mother-in-law hugged her, then held her at arms' length. 'You're still too thin,' she said.

Dr Sophie Maxted was a large woman, amply proportioned, who wore long, flowing clothes and, this evening, a soft yellow wrap around her throat. She was in her sixties but had a skin almost as smooth as butter. She had always been a good-looking woman and was still handsome. She threw the wrap onto a chair in the hall and went into the drawing-room.

One side of the corner apartment overlooked the Finchley Road. It was the larger part of a remodelled mansion flat built before the first war. The rooms were beautifully proportioned, with moulded ceilings giving an air of past elegance.

The evening rush hour was at its peak and the fourth-floor window looked out onto a solid line of traffic. 'I couldn't live with this!' Sophie said.

'I don't mind it. At night I like to watch the red taillights go up the hill. It's like an Edward Hopper.'

She turned off the news.

'I was just having a glass of wine.'

'I'd love one. Was that Mitchell Bourke I saw going down the street? Are you still seeing him?'

'I think I've got him until some juicy part comes up. That's what he needs. He was telling me how good he was at voices. Asked me out to dinner.'

'You said no, of course.'

'Why "of course"?'

'I just can't imagine you saying yes, that's all.'

65

'You wouldn't expect me to go out with a patient would you?'

'You can hardly call Mitchell Bourke a typical patient. Anyway, didn't you tell me he knew Richard from the tennis club?'

'He *says* he knew him. Refers to him as "Dick".'

'No one ever called Richard "Dick".'

'At first I thought he was just lonely. Now I wonder if he has a mild paranoid state.'

'The trouble with people like us is that we can see signs of this and that in almost anyone if we want to. In ourselves too, for that matter.'

Sophie sat down in one of the big Thai bamboo chairs that gave the room a feeling of the East.

'Have I ruined your evening?'

'Of course not.'

'What was it tonight?'

Hannah smiled. 'German, if you must know.'

'What about your art course? Are you still doing that?'

'"Mantegna and the Road to Venice". Every other evening.'

'And your diary?'

'I'm afraid it's become nothing more than, "Got up. Made a cup of tea. Sat down." A kind of Peter Cook joke.'

'I get worried about you.'

'I know you do. You mustn't. I'll worry about me.'

'It's eighteen months, darling.'

'I know exactly how long it is.'

Sophie fumbled in her bag, took out a packet of cigarettes and lit one.

Hannah watched her in astonishment. 'Goodness,' she said. 'I haven't seen you do that for a long time.'

'I'm sick of giving things up. Anyway there comes a moment when you don't care any longer.'

'God, how bloody selfish of me! Tell me!'

'It's malignant.'

'Oh, Sophie!'

'I thought it probably was. And now they want to cut bits out of me and . . . it's all too horrible to contemplate. So I said no.'

'You mean . . . ?'

66

'At some point you have to take charge of your own body. Of your own future.'

'But —'

'I've been to the best. It's unanimous. That's that.'

'But, darling, they can do marvellous things these days.'

'Look, I've had a wonderful life. I did what I wanted to do and I think I've helped people. Not many perhaps, but some. I had a husband I loved. A son I loved. A grandson I loved. And a daughter-in-law I love very much. Why should I compromise on quality now?'

Hannah fought back tears.

'Don't do that,' Sophie said. 'You're not helping.'

'Darling, you can't just do nothing.'

'I'm not going to do nothing. I'm going to do what animals do when they get ill. I'm going on a starvation regimen. Then we'll see.'

Hannah felt suddenly irritated. 'You know you make me very cross. Here you are a medical expert yet you won't let your own profession care for you.'

'Crazy isn't it? But that's the way it crumbles. Anyway, I haven't come to talk about that.'

'I'm going to have another glass of wine. What about you?'

Sophie held out her glass. 'I thought you only had one an evening.'

'Two. But to hell with that tonight.'

Sophie watched her as she poured the yellow-green wine into the glass. 'Don't leave it too long.'

'What?'

'You know what I mean. I wanted to see you married again. I wanted another grandson. Now . . . well, maybe it's getting a bit late for me, but not for you.' She paused. 'Well?'

'Well what?'

'I'm waiting for you to say something.'

'Darling, we've had this out before. I'm not going to be drawn.'

'Mourning is one thing but you're engaged in a kind of emotional suttee. Don't forget Richard was mine too.'

'He was my husband!' Hannah said fiercely. 'And Tom was my son!'

'Yes, of course. And I'm not going to try and –'

'Well, that's a relief,' Hannah said, smiling frostily.

Sophie held up her hand. 'Not another word.'

'Good. Now let's get back to you and what you're going to do.'

'No, let's not get back to me. Let's get to the reason I came here tonight.'

'Oh, I thought it was to inject proper feelings into your daughter-in-law.'

'I suppose I deserved that. No. That just happened to come up. It's always in my mind.' She sipped the wine then said, 'Something's arisen which I won't have time to deal with.'

'Work?'

'I wouldn't normally give it up. But I don't like starting something and . . . well, perhaps not seeing it through. I had a call from Sidney Rosenberg at North London General. You remember him?'

'Of course. Pediatrics. He referred a couple of patients to me a few years ago.'

'Well, Sidney had just examined a child. A boy of about six or seven, no one's certain how old he is. Anyway, this little boy has been locked away for a long period, months perhaps years, by his mother or his grandmother or both.'

Hannah tightened her lips.

'No one knows exactly how long he was shut away or why, because both the women are dead. A double murder. It all happened in a house in the Vale of Health. A photographer apparently discovered the murder.'

'I read about it. But there was no mention of a child.'

'That was a decision by the social services and the police.'

'And?'

'The Social Service Child Protection Team have placed the boy with carers. The child then had his admission examination at the local GP's, who quite rightly thought he should be seen by a pediatrician.'

'But why did Sidney refer him to you?' Hannah said, puzzled. 'Why didn't he keep him in the system?'

'Two reasons. Apparently the flu epidemic has laid low several of the child psychiatrists at North London General – and I can tell you that at the best of times there's a shortage. Now it's critical.'

Sophie paused again.

'And secondly?' Hannah prompted.

'And secondly . . . Sidney thinks the boy may be autistic.'

Hannah felt as though she had taken a blow in the stomach. For a moment she was breathless. Then she said, 'And you want *me* to take him?'

'I want *you* to take him.'

Hannah rose from the rug and went to the window. She folded her arms and hugged her chest, staring out but not seeing the cars.

'I don't know how you could even *think* of such a thing!'

'I thought about it pretty carefully. It's obvious. I want to but can't. You don't want to but can.'

'No.'

Sophie lit another cigarette and held out her glass. She said defensively, 'When you get to my age you can do pretty much as you like. Anyway this is my final fling before the fruit juice.'

Hannah filled her glass and then her own. She swallowed half in a single mouthful.

'I thought you'd say no,' Sophie said, smiling to ease the tension.

'You thought right.'

'In fact I bet myself on the way here that you'd react like this.'

'I'm glad I didn't disappoint you.'

'It's only natural. But there are one or two things you might consider.'

'Sophie, I really don't want to discuss this!'

'But I want to. And if Richard were still alive he'd want me to and he'd want you to as well.'

'That's unfair!'

'Fairness? Is that what you expect? Then what about the boy? What can he expect?'

'You can't make me feel guilty about the boy. I feel guilty enough already!'

'That's self-indulgence. I'm sorry if that hurts but it's true. The same with this mourning business. You're like some medieval flagellant except that the blood you draw is mental.'

'I'm not going to argue,' Hannah said.

'Why not? You used to argue about everything. That's why we loved you so much. You were always discovering the other side to questions. That's what made you such a good psychiatrist.'

'Physician heal thyself. That's what this is all about, isn't it? You're not really thinking about the boy you're thinking about me.'

Sophie's large handsome face changed. 'If you weren't my daughter-in-law and if you weren't someone I love very much, I'd . . . well . . . never mind. Just think of this: there's a child in desperate need. Eventually he will get help. Eventually the system will get to him. By that time he might be unsalvageable. You could help now.'

Slowly Hannah shook her head. 'No, you're just saying that. I know you too well. You're so much like Richard. You're saying to yourself: Hannah is in trouble. Hannah is unfinished business. I may die before she pulls herself out of it. Ergo what can I do?'

Sophie looked at her for a long moment and then said, 'I wish I *was* as brave as that. I really wish I was. I'm frightened. Of course I am. But think how frightened that child must be. And if you can't think of the child then think of this: are you going to spend the rest of your life listening to people like Mitchell Bourke?'

Again Hannah slowly shook her head. 'Ask me anything but that, darling.'

After Sophie left, Hannah was unable to settle. She ranged around the apartment, a glass of wine in her hand. She abandoned the idea of food – just thinking about it made her feel ill.

Her mind was a mass of conflicting thoughts: Sophie's illness, the child, herself, not in any order but tumbling over each other. Emotionally she felt disturbed and upset but mainly she felt a sense of grievance, of injustice.

She had only just begun to get over Richard and Tom. The first weeks and months had been terrible, too terrible ever to discuss with anyone, especially Sophie who was suffering herself. At that time she had seriously considered suicide. Beneath the apartment block was the residents' parking area and she had thought of gassing herself in her car.

She had bought a length of hosepipe and a connector and it would have been a simple matter – except that the garage never seemed empty for long. People were always coming and going. You couldn't continuously run a car's engine down there without the possibility of someone blundering into your final act.

So she had driven into the countryside. There had been a dig near Winchester in Hampshire and she had left it after a few minutes and found herself in narrow country lanes. There were certainly gaps in the hedgerows where she could park but the countryside, too, seemed filled with activity: there were farmers, and hikers, and horse riders and bicycle riders and lovers and dog walkers – any one of whom would have stuck his or her nose against the car window and seen what was going on.

Anyway the whole thing became too much, the impetus retreated and she knew she would have to live through her grief.

Now, of course, she realised that subconsciously she had never wanted to kill herself at all. She checked her own feelings in Bowlby's book *Attachment and Loss* and rediscovered that she was vulnerable, suddenly, to many forms of stress-related disease. As a bereaved widow and mother she was now seven times more likely to have a heart attack. Ironically, in view of what she had been planning for herself, this worried her. It was one thing to toy with suicide, another to discover how much at risk she was doing nothing at all.

And so she had 'pulled herself together', in her father's phrase. She had faced the loss, sold the apartment, bought a new one, started up her practice again and in so doing had also restarted her life. Work, that old standby, had come to her aid. She worked at one thing or another from seven in the morning to midnight.

She had begun to feel the first glimmerings of a change in her own situation recently. Each dawn did not seem quite as dark as the last. She actively began to look forward to her weekends in the country, she became genuinely interested in the problems of her patients – some of which were as bad as her own and some worse. To discover someone worse than oneself was always – how could she put it? – cheering?

Prowling about her apartment as the hours sped by, she felt the sense of injustice grow. Damn Sophie! Damn her for breaking the protective layer.

She found herself in her consulting room. The shelves of books gave it an air of purpose. On the bottom shelf, under the bound journals to which Richard had subscribed, was a collection of large leather-backed writing books of the kind she imagined von Humboldt or Livingstone might have used to write their travel journals. These were the diaries that Sophie had mentioned.

Her father had given her the first when she started at university and since then she had written them up, not religiously day by day, but when she had something interesting to report about her life or her family or the world. The last half-dozen were different. On the leather spines she had written in ink: *Tom 1*, *Tom 2*, *Tom 3* . . . all the way to six years old.

These were all she had of him: she had given away his toys and clothing, just as she had given away Richard's clothes and sporting gear. She had not looked at these since the tragedy but she had never wanted to part with them even though she was afraid of them. They were like bombs on her shelves which could explode at any time.

Now, perhaps because of the unusual quantity of wine she had drunk, perhaps because of Sophie's bravery, or perhaps because the time had come, whatever the reason, she sat down at her desk, switched on the green-shaded Tiffany lamp, and pulled out the book titled *Tom 1*.

Hannah began to have doubts about Tom in the early stages of his life. The first incident she recorded was six weeks after he was born when she went for the regular post-natal checkup. The room had been full of other mothers and babies. Tom had begun to cry hysterically. This set off many of the babies but they soon stopped after being comforted by their mothers. Tom went on screaming despite Hannah's best efforts and finally one of the nurses had to take them to a separate room. She was overworked and snappish and when she discovered that Hannah had been unable to breast feed she hinted that this was the cause of Tom's outburst. It was the first time Hannah had been made to feel guilty, but not the last.

It was also the first of many such scenes and she dreaded taking Tom to what later became a procession of checkups and investigations.

She began to notice abnormalities. Were all babies terrified of unshaded light bulbs? And then there was the rocking motion he made in his pram. As everyone knew, that was a classic manifestation of a lack of love, of rejection. But she *loved* Tom. Sometimes it seemed to her she loved him too much. She had never rejected him. Never. And she was constantly hugging and touching him — so the tactile bond was there. Richard loved him too, always picking him up and playing with him.

Richard took after his mother. He was large and good-looking and sophisticated and friendly. The perfect father.

So why was Tom rocking?

They discussed this aspect of his behaviour. Both were puzzled. Hannah gave him more and more attention. But this did not seem to help.

And he was crying more. And screaming. As soon as he woke — sometimes at five in the morning — he would start. Hannah tried everything she could think of, but nothing seemed to work. Then, as suddenly as he had started, he would stop. Richard moved to another room. Lack of sleep was affecting his work. Hannah had abandoned hers.

She began to feel isolated and that, in turn, aggravated her increasing sense of guilt. It was an echo of the nurse at the post-natal clinic: somehow Hannah was to blame. She told herself that this was the kind of guilt for which she treated some of her patients. Its roots were plain. It was *not* her fault. And yet . . .

There were also long periods of silence when Tom would play obsessively with a spoon. Often she would watch him. The concentration on the little face was fierce and she began to feel that if she simply left him he would go on playing with the spoon forever. At first she worried about the periods of silence, just as

73

she had worried about the hysterical outbursts. But weariness won. She got used to the silences and eventually welcomed them as blessed relief.

His obsession with spoons never left him. He would take them and hide them whenever he could. Once, a few years later, she found fourteen hidden in his room.

Before he was two, Tom began to drift away from her. 'Drift away' was the only phrase she could find to describe his growing lack of interest in her. He did not look her in the eyes. He did not react when she came into the room or left it. It was as though she was becoming an irrelevance in his self-absorbed life – and it wounded her.

Those first years were ones of bewilderment both for Hannah and for Richard. But Richard had his work. Hannah, who had always had a great deal of confidence, now found herself filled with doubt and indecision. Whenever she spoke to Richard about Tom he said some children developed in their own ways. Tom was too young for them to form a judgement.

By two and a half Tom had not spoken. He made sounds but did not seem to give them any meaning. Eventually Richard said, 'He's not like other babies. He's different. I think we should see someone.'

'Different' was the word they had both begun to use. Other words were too brutal. But they were soon to be spoken out loud by the specialists to whom they took Tom. They were given a variety of diagnoses: mental retardation, thyroid deficiency, aphasia, high-tone deafness, even juvenile schizophrenia.

One of the strange by-products of these consultations was that while both Hannah and Richard worked in the field of mental health they were, in the presence of the specialists, just as fearful and unsure of themselves as any lay parent.

And then one day the word autism was mentioned. Hannah was shattered. Like most psychiatrists she had come across cases in journals but had never been face to face with one. The word itself had an apocalyptic ring: it indicated zombie-like behaviour; madness.

She sought out the literature, she read the anecdotal accounts by other mothers with autistic children. She discovered that autism defied definition for there were many forms and many degrees. Severe autism was permanently mentally crippling but lesser forms meant that children could grow into adulthood, take part in the community, hold down sheltered jobs, especially those with a mathematical base.

Later, when she met other mothers at a self-help group she discovered a common denominator: the children lacked empathy, they did not know what it was to give or receive love.

It was here too that she watched in astonishment an autistic child read a story to a dyslexic child. The one could read but could not understand; the other could understand but could not read.

And it was then, for the first time, she realised the complexity of the problem which Tom was facing.

But that was in the future. For the time being the discovery of books and self-help groups gave her the comfort that she was not alone. She learned to live with it. And so did Richard.

SIX

Peter Ferry's break-up with his wife, Alison, had coincided with the death of his mother. His father, Albert, had been shattered. He and Gracie had been married for forty years and in all that time had not been parted for more than a few days.

Peter would never forget the sight of his father at the cemetery in Bethnal Green. He had always been a big man, a dockworker, a lumper, strong and full of energy. At the graveside he seemed hardly able to lift the trowel to sprinkle soil on the coffin lid.

He had come to live with Peter in a small terraced house in Holloway. It seemed the sensible thing to do at the time. It was planned as a temporary measure, until things sorted themselves out, but it didn't take a genius to see that things were not going to sort themselves out very easily.

The old man had spent the first few days lying on his bed weeping. He stopped shaving and his beard had sprouted white. Peter had never seen his father cry before, had always thought of him as a 'hard' man. He had to remind himself that this was the man who had worked in the Pool of London and who prided himself on the fact that his muscles and his back had shifted thousands of tons of cargo.

After a few weeks Peter had wanted to get rid of him. His presence was making a bad scene worse. But how?

One evening Peter came back to find the house a mess, the beds unmade, the dishes unwashed, and his father sitting in front of the TV, a bottle of whisky at hand. It was the third day in a row that this had happened.

He had lost his temper. 'We can't go on like this, Dad! I know Mum's dead and all, and I miss her too, but for Christ's sake you've got to pull out of it. I mean, I come home and I've got to make the beds and wash the dishes and tidy up. It's not on!'

It shook his father. He had never been spoken to like that before. It was a first for both of them. But it did the trick. Albert Ferry began his role as house mother – although he would not have known the phrase. He'd go down to the post office to collect his cheque if it was pensions day and he'd do the shopping and he'd phone the police station to find out if Peter was working late and when he was likely to be home, and he'd prepare a meal.

At first they were only fish-and-chip suppers he bought at the shop around the corner, but later he began to make tentative efforts at cooking. Sometimes Peter wished he'd go to the Indian takeaway or the doner kebab house, but the old man didn't like foreign food. So they had egg and chips or sausage and chips or bacon and chips or steak and chips – four or five times a week. Albert Ferry fancied himself at cooking chips.

A strange new relationship built up. Albert became like Gracie the way he fussed and worried about the hours his son kept. 'No wonder you and Alison broke up,' he grumbled, as Peter came home late yet again. 'I'm bleedin' cooking at eleven at night.'

But that was only part of the problem. Alison was an attractive, dark-haired young woman, who came from the North of England. Ferry had met her on a package holiday in Majorca and they had been married two months later. But Alison was from an extended family. She had four brothers and two sisters, all of whom were married and had kids. Her mother and father were also still alive. She had grown up in a street of terraced houses where everyone knew each other. There had never been a time in Alison's life when she was alone.

In London she knew no one except Ferry. Her days were spent by herself and so were many of her nights because of his duty rotas. Certainly her mother-in-law lived nearby but Alison had early made a decision that she did not really like London cockneys – except Peter, of course. She found them too fly and didn't understand their humour. They in their turn didn't understand her accent. The marriage lasted two years and then Alison departed for the broad vowels of her native heath. Ferry's masculinity took a severe beating.

After his mother died and his father came to live with him, he and Albert settled down to an Odd Couple relationship and as the months passed it began to look more and more permanent. Sometimes Peter worried about this – but the longer his father lived with him the more difficult it was to broach the subject of where he would eventually go. So he let things slide, waiting for something to happen.

Albert became fascinated by his son's cases. He would stay up late just to hear the latest in a running murder investigation. It gave him a feeling of importance being in the know. When Peter was transferred from the East End to London North, Albert said, 'Don't suppose they murder each other up there. Too many tea parties. Too bloody lah-di-dah.' The murder of the two women changed that.

He knew the Vale of Health, for the Hampstead fair was held nearby in August every year. He and Gracie had taken Peter there as a child. Peter could still remember seeing the Pearly King and Queen. Then they had walked in the Vale of Health to look at the houses of the wealthy.

When Peter first told his father the elements of the case the old man's reaction was to sympathise with the child, 'Poor little bleeder.'

Now, as Peter returned from work Albert placed his meal in front of him and waited for the next instalment.

'Chips . . . chips . . . chips . . .' Peter said. 'Don't you know how much cholesterol there is in fried chips?'

'Potatoes are good for you.'

'Yeah, but not as chips.'

'Take my advice, son, don't worry so much about your health. It's the worryin' that kills you.'

'I mightn't live long enough to worry. Anyway, what about you and smoking?'

'I roll me own. They can't do no harm.'

'Who're you kidding?'

'Never mind about that. What about the investigation?'

Peter ate his chips one by one dipping them in tomato ketchup. He liked to tease his father, make him wait for it.

'Well?'

'Well, there was some strange news today. By the way, did you cook these chips in lard or what?'

'Lard, of course. How else d'you – ?'

'You should use polyunsaturated oil. Not lard.'

'Your mother cooked chips in lard all her life. If you don't want them don't eat them. What about this strange news?'

'The post mortem results came through. The woman never had a baby.'

'What's that mean?'

'Just what I say. She never gave birth. You can tell. I mean they, the pathologists, can tell whether a woman's given birth or not.'

'I still don't –'

'Come on, Dad. The old woman couldn't have had the boy, 'cause she's too old. Okay? *She'd* given birth, of course. To the younger woman. But not to the boy.'

'Hilda.'

'That's right, Hilda.'

'Well, use the names then. I can remember the names. Madame Raymonde – Christ, who could forget it? – and Hilda.'

'That's her. Hilda. Well, she never had a child.'

'So?'

'So whose child was it?'

Albert knew his son was pulling his strings and didn't like it. But what could he do? He said, 'Well?'

'That's exactly what we'd like to know. Whose child it is. I've got fifteen detectives trying to find out just that. We've spoken to all the neighbours. The two women lived in that house for sixteen years but they hardly spoke to anyone. It's the kind of place where people keep to themselves. They had a gardener once a week but he never went into the house. No one saw the kid. The window glass of his room was painted over at the bottom. Couldn't have seen anything if you tried.'

'What about the furniture? You can't take furniture away without someone seeing.'

'That's right. One or two of the neighbours did see a van. But you can park up a little lane and you're hidden by the bloody hedges. But okay, you see a van . . . so what? It needn't have been big stuff. Pictures, small tables, rugs . . . you can get that sort of stuff in the boot of a car.'

'Can't you trace it? If it was valuable wouldn't there be records?'

'None in the house. And we've been to the banks, of course. The account was at Barclay's in the High Street in Madame Raymonde's name. They also had her will. But nothing that could identify separate pieces of furniture. Half the people who own stuff like that can't afford to insure it. And if there were no records or photos of individual pieces they could be sold anywhere. London, Edinburgh, Bath, Gloucester, Winchester . . . you name it. Every decent-sized country town has got its antique market and its auction rooms. The stuff may even have been taken abroad and no questions asked. There's a new report out, Dad, art theft is the third major crime after drugs and arms smuggling.'

'So what do you think about the boy?'

'Family. That's the first thing to check. He's probably the son of a sister or a brother. His side of the family may be dead. So they were looking after him.'

'What a way to look after him!'

'We're checking family connections.'

'Finish your chips.'

'Can't eat any more.'

'Have some tea then?'

Albert poured out a cup. It was a terracotta colour.

'When did you make that?' Peter said. 'Yesterday?'

Albert poured himself a cup and rolled a cigarette. The slightly sweetish, sickly smell of a roll-up permeated the room.

'You're like Begg,' Peter said. 'You smoke too much.'

'How're you getting on with him?'

'So-so. I don't think he likes me much. He's a snob. You can tell that by the way he talks. And half the rest of 'em have been to college. BA this and BA that.'

'Studying books never made a good copper.'

'You can say that again.'

'They want to get out on the streets. Meet the people. When you was little we always had coppers in the street. We welcomed them.'

'Welcomed them! You lot were always beating them up.'

'Well . . . not always.'

'They had to walk in twos.'

'You know what I mean, son.'

'Begg wants to see the boy. Keeps on poking his nose into the case.'

'That's reasonable, isn't it? I mean, it's his case too. He's the boss.'

'Some bloody boss!'

'Peter, you got to co-operate. Even though you mightn't like him.'

'I'm not licking anyone's arse!'

'I'm not saying that. But you want to get on. I know you do. You've been ambitious since you was little. You'll never get on if you're obstructive. Or if you have a chip on your shoulder.'

'What's that supposed to mean?'

'Ever since you went to London North you've been different. Touchy, if you know what I mean. Listen, all police stations are the same. Just because this one's in a posh neighbourhood doesn't mean the coppers are posh. Same coppers everywhere.'

'Yeah, I know . . .'

'It's not the black tie business that's bothering you still, is it?'

'No, 'course it isn't.'

'Because it's not worth it. You can't know everything. We all have blind spots.'

The black tie business had been the worst humiliation Ferry had suffered since joining the police. He'd only been at London North a few weeks when he'd been invited to a retirement smoker for one of the DIs. Begg had given the invitation verbally and had said, 'Black tie.'

For some reason he did not understand – and he had thought and thought about it – he had simply missed this phrase. So far as he could tell, he'd never heard it spoken nor seen it written

81

down. He'd gone out and bought a black string tie and had worn it with his light grey suit. Everyone else was in a dinner jacket with a black bow tie.

'You gotta forget all about that, son.'

'Okay, Mum.'

Albert laughed with relief. 'Anyway what about the boy? What's happened to him?'

'Still with those foster carers.'

'Has he spoken yet?'

'Not a word.'

'When you was little you used to draw things sometimes. You'd get cross and wouldn't talk but you'd draw things.'

'They've tried that. The point is he doesn't seem to know what a pencil's for.'

'You know, son, he might have seen something. Might be shocked.'

'If he did it's all locked up in his head.'

'You've got to unlock it.'

'I know. Social services are talking about letting a psychiatrist see him.'

'Oh, Christ. One of those. You finished?' His son nodded and pushed the plate away. 'It's a waste me making a decent meal if you don't eat it.'

Peter felt overfull. 'Listen, Dad, lay off the spuds for a while, will you?'

Duncan Wylie had always used his camper as an office wherever he was. It was fitted with a telephone, a small TV set, writing table, typewriter, specially made cupboards for his movie and still cameras. It was parked now in Newton Road less than fifty yards from the Brinds' front gate on the opposite side of the road. He had set up the Arriflex so that he could cover the front door, the gate, and part of the pavement. The big telephoto was hidden by a small satellite dish aerial. In a sports bag on the front seat was his lightweight video camera. He had cut a hole in one end of the bag for the lens. This gave him the flexibility that the Arriflex denied.

From the camper he had a good view of the Brinds' house. There was no activity that he could see so all he could do was wait. As he waited he read the papers and a heading on page three of the *Chronicle* caught his eye: *Child Discovered In Hampstead Double Murder*. The story read:

A child was found in the Vale of Health house where the double murder of former concert pianist Eva Raymonde and her daughter, Hilda, occurred.

Although Scotland Yard would not deny or confirm his presence, it is understood that a six-year-old boy was found alive in another part of the house. He is thought to be the son of Hilda Raymonde and the grandson of Madame Eva Raymonde.

Police are working on the theory that the child might have witnessed the murder and have placed him in foster care at a secret address where they can question him.

Wylie's first reaction was one of anxiety that someone else had got onto his story – he thought of it as 'his' – then he began to realise that anything about the boy could only enhance interest in what he would eventually have to show. And no one – *no one* – had the night shots he had taken on the Heath.

And they, so far as he was concerned, *made* the story. He was still excited by its potential. If, and it was a big if, he could get enough footage to make a documentary – enough of the unfolding murder investigation, enough of the background, enough people, lives, detail – then he had a world beater.

Well, he'd made a start. He'd sat down and worked out the kinds of people who would know something about the two women. Then he'd gone back to *The Times* index in the Westminster Reference Library and looked up Madame Eva Raymonde. He had been surprised at how little there was, a few references to recitals in the fifties at the Wigmore Hall and that was about it. Not much of a concert pianist it seemed. One of the recitals had been reviewed, not very well, on a page containing an advertisement for a Schumann recital she was giving the following week – this was in 1959 – and underneath her name was the phrase 'Management: Inter Arts'.

He'd looked them up in the telephone book and had been astonished and pleased to find they were still listed. Wylie never really believed in durability.

'Inter Arts,' the voice said on the telephone. 'How may I help you?'

'I'm trying to find out some details about a client of yours.'

'One moment please. I'll put you through to Miss Black.'

'Miss Black's office.'

Wylie repeated his sentence.

'We don't discuss our clients.' The voice was both hostile and wary.

'Well, this is really an ex-client.'

'It doesn't make any diff –'

'I mean very ex indeed. Dead, in fact. My name's Wylie. I'm making a television documentary about her life.'

'Who is she?' The voice had changed. There was now less hostility, more interest. He assumed that the word television had done what it usually did.

'Madame Raymonde.' He waited for a reaction. None came. The name couldn't have made an impression on Miss Black. Maybe she didn't read the tabloids. Maybe she only read the arts pages in the up-market papers. 'She . . . uh . . . died recently.'

'I don't think she's one of ours, Mr Wylie.'

'She was in the 1950s.'

'Oh. Well. That was a little before my time.'

Wylie turned his tone into a smile. 'I was sure of that. Do you have anyone who might have worked with her? Someone who was young at the time. Just starting, perhaps.'

'Hang on a second.' He heard pages being riffled. 'Look, this is just a long shot but Miss Morgan – that's Miss Gwyneth Morgan – retired a couple of years ago. She'd been with the firm since the year dot. She might know.' She gave him an address. 'It's in the wilds of Wales somewhere.'

He thanked her and rang off.

SEVEN

'Sophie?' Hannah said into the phone. 'How are you?'

'I suppose you could say as well as could be expected.'

'What does that mean?' Hannah took up her fountain pen and began to doodle on her pad.

'I'm fine. Starvation is good for the character. It's just that it's not much fun at the beginning. Headaches and –'

'That's not what I meant at all and you know it! Where are you? Are you in your bedroom?'

'If you must know, I'm in a chair in the living-room wrapped in a blanket, trying to finish *The Times* crossword. And you mustn't go on like this. I'm not some fragile plant.'

'Are you in pain?'

'No.'

'Are you sure?'

'Of course I'm sure!'

'I don't trust you.'

'Never mind me. What about you? Have you seen him yet? It was today, wasn't it?'

'I'm waiting for him now. And I wish I wasn't. I feel . . . I don't know how I feel . . . tense, wound up like a clock spring . . . scared.'

'You don't need to be scared. You'll see how easy it is after the first few minutes.'

'That's what I keep telling myself. I feel it's like my first consultation. And you're to blame!'

Sophie gave a faint chuckle. 'Do you good. Make you face up to yourself. Anyway, I knew you would.'

'Did you indeed?'

'I knew once I'd left you'd brood and when you finished brooding you'd say yes.'

'I went back to the diaries. I haven't looked at them. Haven't been able to go near them since . . . well, since it happened . . .'

'Say it.'

'What?'

'What happened.'

There was silence. 'Don't push me too fast. I sometimes think that if I fall I won't get up again. And I don't have your courage.'

'You don't know what you have until you try.'

'Look, let's not talk about me. I phoned to find out how you were.'

She was lying and thought that Sophie probably knew it. She had phoned because panic had caught her in the throat.

'Have you had a report?' Sophie said.

'I didn't wait for one. I thought if I was going to do it I'd better do it before I changed my mind. So I phoned Sidney Rosenberg and we had a talk. There's no sign of sexual abuse, thank God. And he's apparently in pretty good health. Underweight but otherwise all right.'

'Has he spoken yet?'

'No. I talked to the carer, a Mrs Brind. Does the name mean anything to you?'

'Don't think so.'

'I wondered if you'd ever had a referral while she was the foster carer. She sounds rather nice. But she's frazzled, poor thing. She's never had a case like this. He won't sleep in his bed. Won't eat properly. He'll only eat tinned food, baked beans, that sort of thing. Nothing fresh. She says he just holds the fresh food in his mouth as though unsure of what to do with it. Doesn't chew. Then spits it out.'

'Did Tom do that?'

'He spat out anything he didn't like. But then so do most

babies. He just kept it up longer. I don't think it's evidence of anything really. And he's terrified of water. Doesn't like being bathed.'

'Probably because he never has been. Was he very dirty when they found him?'

'Ingrained apparently, but Mrs Brind has managed to clean him up.'

'And not a word.'

'Not even a sound, she says.'

There was an imperious ring at Hannah's door. 'I've got to go. Talk to you later.'

There were three of them and Hannah had not expected this. The third was Ms Challis, the social worker.

They came in like a family: mother, daughter and grandson. Hannah went down on her haunches in front of the boy. 'Hello,' she said. 'I'm Hannah.'

The boy looked past her, over her shoulder.

Ms Challis stared at Hannah through her large round glasses and said, 'This is most irregular. We had expected to see Dr Maxted at the clinic.'

'Yes, I know. But she's . . . she's not very well and I thought it might be better to see him here rather than at the hospital. It's more informal. Less pressure . . .'

'I hope it's not going to become –'

'I think Dr Wilton's right,' Margaret Brind said, running her hand nervously through her grey hair. 'The more informal the better.'

'I think I'd better be the judge of that,' Ms Challis said.

Hannah smiled at her and said, 'No, I think *I* had best be the judge of that unless you'd rather we didn't start at all. Then you can make your own arrangements.'

'Well, I –'

'If I'm going to be in charge of his case then that means what it says.'

A faint flickering of anger was running through Hannah's muscles. It gave a prickling feeling to her skin. She had not felt it for a long time and it suddenly felt good, as though one of her senses was returning to her.

'Come on,' she said to the boy, 'let's go into my room and see what I've got for you to look at. No . . .' she held up her hand as Ms Challis moved to follow. 'I want to see him alone, if you don't mind.'

She took the boy's hand – it was like taking the hand of a zombie – and led him into her consulting room.

23rd November

This is not really a diary, *Hannah wrote*. More of a journal to expand the case notes. Perhaps one day it may be published.

It was evening and she was writing at her desk in the golden glow of the Tiffany lamp.

The idea came to me once he had left and I went out and bought a large writing book NOT the same as the books which contained my earlier journals. Once I had the idea it seemed that I was giving expression to something that had lain in my mind for a long time.

The basic reason for doing it – I tell myself – is that since autism is unresponsive to treatment or investigation by most forms of analysis including Gestalt, all the evidence we have on it is anecdotal, largely by mothers who have brought up autistic children. So someone trained in psychotherapy *must* take the trouble to add to that evidence.

I'm sure Sophie would agree. But it's got to be 'popular'. No long words or difficult ones like Gestalt. In other words no psychobabble. It's not for academics. It's for ordinary people faced with this frightening behaviour pattern.

The boy. He has no name. I find this disturbing. All the human beings I have ever come across have had names. The name is the person, the person the name. If I just call him Boy he sounds like someone out of one of those old Tarzan flicks with Johnny Weissmuller.

The first thing I did was to examine him physically. I know

88

that Sidney Rosenberg did all this but I wanted to look at him for myself.

He stood as though catatonic and let me examine him. He is very thin, ribs showing. His thinness makes his head seem larger than it should be and he has a high-domed forehead and deep-set brown eyes. I thought of Munch's painting, *The Scream*.

And that reminds me: Mrs Brind said that she had not seen the boy cry. Nor, apparently have the police nor Ms Challis. Tom never cried either when he was this age.

Sidney had mentioned marks on the back of his hands and I looked at them carefully. Tom had them too. It came from anger and frustration. If I stopped him doing something he would suddenly begin to bite the backs of his hands in impotent rage.

The boy's hands carry scars on the fingers, little white lines, almost as though they had been drawn. Tom's were more like little ridges.

That is the first similarity; not quite the same but near. Nothing is ever *precisely* the same. One must proceed empirically.

I notice that the boy never meets my eyes. His view is always somewhere over my shoulder.

Tom did this. He never looked me in the eyes either, until I began to try and make him. I started a process of getting down on the floor with him for twenty minutes or so each day and bringing my eyes to his level. It took some time but eventually he began to look directly into my face. But I was never certain whether he was actually *seeing* me.

The boy makes me uneasy. His line of sight is just off me, but unlike with Tom, I have the feeling that he is *deliberately* not looking at me.

But that may only be my feeling. The fact is that he isn't looking at me and Tom didn't either.

I had bought a selection of toys, but he was not interested. He sat in the easy chair by the window staring over my shoulder. I showed him a packet of crayons and gave him a piece of paper. He didn't so much reject them as ignore them. I drew on the paper with one of the orange crayons. He paid no attention.

During our session I kept up a flow of conversation about anything I could think of: this is a ball, this is a car, would you like to play with them? No reaction.

Tom didn't listen to me either, but there was a subtle difference: with Tom you knew his mind was busily conducting its own impenetrable affairs; the boy seems consciously to be holding his mind in repose.

I have a feeling that the similarities, or at least the immediate and obvious ones, between Tom and the boy, are like mirror images; the same but not quite the same.

I remind myself that nothing is ever the same between two human minds.

At the same time as Hannah was writing her journal, Duncan Wylie was in a cutting-room at Wilderness Films in the West End of London. He had had a long working relationship with Arnie Marks, who owned the facilities house, and used the place like an office and club when he was in London. Usually he worked in the daytime when an editing machine was free, and there would be much toing and froing between editors and film makers as they looked at the rough cuts of each other's work.

But not this time.

What he had was too important. He worked alone.

He ran the film through the monitor for the umpteenth time. There was the path on Hampstead Heath, there the litter basket. Into shot came the foxes, their eyes hot green, almost fluorescent in the browny green of the image intensifier.

He watched them smell the meat and come towards the litter basket. There! They were gone. Just the trees now and the bushes. He stopped the film, then let it roll on very slowly. He was looking to see if he had missed something. But, no, he couldn't see the boy in those shots.

He ran the film on. Then there was the break when he had stopped filming, then he started again and this time the foxes came to the litter basket. First the vixen went up on her hind legs and pulled out the plastic shopping bag.

He could almost hear his mind urging, 'Go on, eat it. It's bloody good.'

She and her cubs began to feed.

Gone again! Just a grainy blur. And now, from the left-hand side of the basket, came the figure, softly, nervous, listening, much clearer on film than at the time.

Then the delving into the basket.

He moved the film forward manually frame by frame. Now that he knew what the figure was he could see plainly that it wasn't ape-like. Much more upright. Thinner. But if you didn't know . . .

The boy had something in his hands and was opening it.

He wound on.

The boy vanished.

At that point Wylie had stopped the camera, picked up the camcorder and run after the 'primate'.

That was really all he had of the night shots.

It wasn't much, but, Christ, it was enough! Especially when you knew the link with what he had seen in the house. You could cut that section – and the earlier piece of the night before – into a documentary three or four times.

He let the film rewind, put it in his bag and went home. He poured himself a solid whisky and put a cassette into his video recorder. This contained the material he had transferred to VHS. Then he sat down in front of his TV set.

Almost immediately he was looking at the outside of London North police station. There were some establishing shots of cars entering through the security gates, Black Marias arriving and leaving, and uniformed policemen and members of the public going up the steps to the entrance.

They all seemed totally unaware that he was standing with his sports bag containing the camcorder at a bus stop across the street. You'd think they'd notice that he never took a bus but it was a case of watching the watchers. A lot of police time is taken up by surveillance work; they never seem to consider the possibility that they, too, might be targets.

He ran the video forward until he reached the place he wanted. Two men came out of the police station and walked down the steps. They stopped on the last step as though posing for Wylie. One was of medium height in a suit and tie, the other was in brown cords and a denim jacket. That was Ferry. Wylie didn't know who the first man was but the way he spoke indicated that he too was a policeman; the way he dressed that he was a senior officer.

Didn't matter. Ferry was the one Wylie wanted.

The two men talked for about three minutes, then the man in the suit went one way and Ferry went back up the steps into the station.

There wasn't much mileage in that but at least it established the police presence. He might be able to use a few seconds of it and cut it into a section he had of the house in the Vale of Health. It would show where the boy had been taken that night.

The film ran on. This is what he wanted. This was new.

Newton Road. Trees losing the last of their leaves. Cars parked. Rows of neat semis. Come in close on one house. Garden path. Small piece of lawn spotted by leaves. Lace curtains. Now . . . the door opens. Woman in doorway. Yes, this is Mrs Brind. Now the other woman. Ms Challis, the social worker.

They pause as though waiting for someone. Mrs Brind makes to go back into the house. Ms Challis moves her hand to stop her. They wait. Ms Challis is saying something into the dark doorway. Argument between Ms Challis and Mrs Brind. Then suddenly Mrs Brind pushes past. Good for you, Wylie thought. Just possible to see Mrs Brind on her haunches talking to the dark interior. Marvellous stuff because you know, yet you don't quite know, what's in there. Could be anything, but you think it's going to be the boy and you're damn right.

Because here he comes. Wouldn't come out by himself. The viewer knows that. No need for commentary at this point. The perfect screenplay. Things are happening on the screen that don't need words. This is what movie-making is all about.

Slowly he comes out of the house. He's holding Mrs Brind's hand. Ms Challis still arguing, Mrs Brind shaking her head. It wouldn't surprise him, Wylie thought, if that bitch Challis was making things hard for both of them. Trying to make the boy act like a real boy instead of . . . well, instead of what he was.

Now, apprehensive, one step at a time. Into the chilly air. Like an animal who's been kept in a zoo suddenly allowed his freedom and not knowing what the hell to do with it. He had to remind himself that this was the same boy he had caught in the image intensifier raiding the litter basket. Now he was dressed up in warm clothing and an anorak and Wylie had to make the effort to recall an 'apelike creature'.

Zoom in and he was close on the boy's face. Big dark eye sockets. Big head.

Come on, come on!

And here they came. Down the path. Mrs Brind holding the boy's hand tightly. The boy pulling back slightly as they reached the car. Mrs Brind talking. Probably cajoling. Challis impatient. Mrs Brind getting in first. The boy finally joining her. Ms Challis slamming the door. Vroom, vroom . . . and off we go!

And CUT TO:

Exterior. Day. Block of flats in North London.

And here they are again. The three of them.

Jesus, he'd been lucky to get a parking place. He'd shot this from the side window of the camper. You couldn't see them getting out of the car but that wasn't important. There! Going up the concrete step to the big double doors of security glass. Challis pressing the bell. Clear as anything. Top right-hand bell. Challis leaning forward towards the entry phone. The doors opening.

And CUT TO:

Exterior. Day. Close up of doorbells.

Maybe use it, maybe not, but it's there if needed.

Yes, there was the name. Bright and new and eminently filmable: Dr Hannah Wilton.

He had sat on for an hour and had then been rewarded. The three women and the boy had come out of the building. He watched Dr Wilton. She was attentive but seemed slightly apart. Professional. She watched them get into the car and raised her hand, then she turned and walked back up the stairs. She had not made much impression on him except for her legs. He thought they were rather nice.

He'd check her out before doing anything else about her. He

jotted down her name and the number of the apartment. He wondered how good she was at her job; wondered if she'd be co-operative.

EIGHT

It is nearly a week since I saw the boy for the first time, *Hannah wrote.*

It was late afternoon but she had no other patients.

I have now seen him three times. Thank God Ms Challis is too busy to attend each time. Mrs Brind is an admirable woman. She is trying to get him to wash his hands himself. She is using behaviour modification, although she wouldn't call it that. Everything underlined by reward. He hasn't done it on command yet. It will be interesting to see if he does.

The second and third sessions were much like the first: getting to know each other. I tried to follow what I had done the first time. Showing him the toys. Talking to him. I want to get him used to human speech as much as possible. He may well have heard very little being shut away in that house.

I'm not sure if I am getting any more of his confidence, in fact today I seemed to go backwards. On the first occasion I brought my eyes to his level he did not seem disturbed. He didn't look at me but at least he remained as he was.

Today he reacted differently. I saw fear in his eyes. Something must have happened to make him frightened. But what? Earlier I wanted to test one of the characteristics some autistic children share. They are spinners. They like to spin things. Tom would sit for hours spinning a record on the turntable or the wheels of toy cars. He never played with a car normally. Never pushed it along the carpet. He always held it upside down and spun the wheels.

I gave him a toy car. He held it for a moment and then dropped it. So I took him into the sitting-room and showed him the turntable of the stereo. I switched it on and he watched it go round and round for a few moments, then his eyes became unfocused and I knew he was not interested.

I'm afraid that this is just part of the trial and error that will have to continue for a long while and I

The doorbell rang and Hannah went to the entry phone.

'Detective Inspector Ferry,' the voice said.

She let him in. He showed her his warrant card and introduced himself.

'Can we talk?' he said. 'I mean, have you got someone with you?'

'No, I'm free. Come into my office.'

'Nice,' he said, looking round the room.

'Thank you.'

'Is this where they sit?'

'Who?'

'The people who need . . . well, who come to you.'

'That's right.'

He sat gingerly on the edge of the black leather recliner.

'Sorry I didn't phone first but we're stretched. You know why I'm here?'

'The boy. Mrs Brind has mentioned you. Ms Challis said you might come.'

'Yeah. The social worker.'

The way he said it made Hannah feel she had something in common with him. She thought he looked like a cop out of *Hill Street Blues*. He was wearing an open-neck shirt, denim jacket, cords and tennis shoes that had once been white. His East End accent was marked.

'There are a couple of things we should talk about,' he said. 'The first is that the boy wasn't the son of the woman called Hilda. The pathologist said she'd never had a child.'

Her face registered surprise. 'But they said in the newspaper . . . Whose is he then?'

'That's the point. We don't know. We're assuming that he's the son of another member of the family. Mother dead. Or mother and father killed in an accident. So Madame Raymonde and her daughter, being nearest relatives, take on the child. But —'

'But what?'

'We haven't been able to trace any family at all. Not in this country, anyway. We've given it to Interpol. They may come up with something but it could take months.'

'If he wasn't a relative he might be the offspring of friends. He could be adopted. He might be a missing person.'

'We thought of that.'

'Of course. I'm sorry.'

'No, no. I didn't mean it that way. It's our job, see.' He smiled for the first time. She thought he looked bright and decided she liked him.

'I've got a room full of people working on those lines. We're going through records, we're going through newspaper files of missing kids. Trouble is, how far back do we go: two years? Three? Where do we stop?'

'Yes, I see.'

'So another of the things I've come to see you about is his picture. I wanted you to know. In a case like this we release pictures to the media and then wait to see if anyone gets in touch with us.'

'You're going to photograph him?'

'We spoke to social services. They've no objection. But I wanted to tell you.'

'And if I object?'

'Would you?'

'I don't like the idea. It could be disturbing.'

'You don't think a double murder is disturbing?'

She flushed slightly. 'Of course, but —'

'Look, it'll take five minutes. Our photographer is used to this

97

sort of thing. The kid will hardly know. And, well, I don't like saying this but –'

'But it doesn't matter if I object or not?'

He avoided a direct answer. 'I didn't want you to pick up a paper or switch on the news and see his face all over the place.'

He was trying his best and she was grateful. 'That was a kind thought. What are the odds?'

'Kids disappear every day. Some get snatched and go into paedophile rings. Some go into prostitution. Occasionally we find bodies.'

'But there isn't a register of missing persons, is there?'

'No, there isn't. Amazing, isn't it? They're setting one up but it won't come into use for a year or more. So we have to dig in the files. But the point is, when a kid goes missing someone usually sees something. Maybe they don't even know they've seen it. Then the picture jogs their memory.'

'And what then?'

'What do you mean?'

'Well, it all sounds so easy. You put his picture in the papers and someone comes forward and says, yes that's my little boy. I mean, anyone could do that. And how will you know? And for that matter, how would the person who really belongs to the boy know? As you say, he might have been in the house for years. He'd have grown inches. His physical appearance would have changed.'

'We thought of that.'

'You seem to have thought of everything.'

She had not changed her tone but he looked up at her and the nice smile was gone and she was seeing a face filled with sudden anger.

'Don't patronise me,' he said.

'I didn't mean to. I'm sorry. It's just that I'm . . . well, I've formed a link with the child. It's tenuous but it's still a link, and I don't want it broken or damaged. Please go on. How would you prove it?'

Ferry readjusted himself. 'In cases like this we use DNA and blood grouping. It doesn't prove that someone is definitely a relative but it can prove that someone isn't. And if the circumstantial evidence goes along with that then we make an assumption. We play the odds.'

'And they say you can't prove a negative. Would you like some tea?'

'No, thanks.'

'A drink?'

He shook his head. 'So you don't mind?'

'About the pictures? Not if you think they're essential. It's your job to know.'

She thought he might be about to leave but he leaned back in the chair for the first time and said, 'I'd like to ask you about the boy.'

'Go ahead.'

'The social worker says he's . . . well, that he's mentally retarded. I dunno the phrase she used. Made it sound like he was off his trolley.'

'Is that how you think of people who are disturbed? That they're off their trolleys?' She saw his expression change again and smiled to soften her question.

'I was on another case once,' he said. 'Little girl. She'd been locked away in a cellar. When we found her she was like an animal. Parents eventually said they'd locked her up because she was mongoloid.'

'We call that Down's syndrome these days.'

'Oh, yeah, sorry. What I mean is that it was *because* of the Down's syndrome they locked her up. They were ashamed, see.'

'And you think this child may have been shut away for the same reason.'

'Could be if he was . . . what you called it . . . disturbed.'

'I don't know. No one knows.'

'But you're going to find out.'

'I'm going to try to find out.'

'It's important, doctor.'

'Of course it's important! We don't want any child –'

'No. Not that. Look at it from my point of view. I've got a murder to solve. Double murder. No one can tell us anything. We've got nothing to work on. No one saw anything. Except – and this is just a possibility – except the boy.'

99

She paused, puzzled. 'But I thought you said he'd been locked away.'

He looked down at his hands for a moment. 'Yeah, well. The thing about that is that the door to the room was unlocked. He might have seen something.'

'Then he *wasn't* locked away!'

'We found him under an old bath, as far away from us as he could get. He'd been locked away all right except —'

'That the door wasn't locked!'

'I can't explain that. But I've seen someone who was locked away. They're similar.'

'And I've seen someone who was autistic and he was also similar.'

'Autistic. That was the word Ms Challis used.'

'It's possible. I don't know yet.'

'But what does it mean?'

'It means —' She stopped and leaned back in her desk chair. 'I wish I knew with certainty.' She tried to formulate sentences that weren't psychobabble but found herself floundering. 'I suppose the simplest explanation is that autistic children have great problems in understanding what they see and what they hear in spite of having normal eyes and ears. And that leads to . . . Look, try to imagine someone close to you, a boy, who lives in his own world . . . who doesn't share yours. You may love him but he doesn't love you because he doesn't know what it is to love. It isn't possible for us to imagine his world but he can eventually be made — if his autism isn't too severe — to fit into ours.' She paused. 'I'm explaining this badly. Do you know what a prefrontal leucotomy is?'

'They take away part of the brain, don't they?'

'Only in extreme cases and it's hardly done at all now. But the removal of that part removes part of your humanity. You are no longer a person in control of yourself emotionally because the part they remove controls responsibility and moral judgement. Well, autism is a bit like that. Part of you isn't so much missing as different from what we consider normal. It produces a different world, a different set of interests. I was going to say values but I'm not sure it produces *any* values. So we have a problem.'

'What's that?'

'If the boy is autistic and even if he did see the murder he might not know what he was looking at, might not have the primitive instinctual feeling that what he was seeing was brutal and bad and horrible. You see what I'm getting at?'

'That he could look at a murder and not know it was a murder.'

'Precisely. He might not store it. It might be unimportant and transitory.'

'But wouldn't that apply to all very young children?'

'I don't think so. We have certain built-in social reactions. It would depend on how long a child was locked away. What he'd seen, what he'd experienced.'

'So, even if it's there in his head – the picture I mean – we may never get it out because he doesn't know it's there.'

'Something like that.'

They looked at each other in silence.

Then he said, 'Can you do anything about it?'

'I'm trying. But first of all I've got to find out if he is autistic. He may be suffering a post-traumatic syndrome.'

'Have you had any experience with this . . . autism?'

She nodded. 'I treated a case once. Using that as the basis I'm trying to find comparisons.'

'And?'

'Nothing definite. It's early days yet. But it's important to know. Because if it is autism then you'll have to find another witness. The boy won't do.'

He rose and she rose with him. 'What about your theories? About the murder and the murderer?' she asked.

'At this stage that's a hard one.'

'I read somewhere that you always try to create a profile of a wanted killer.'

'Yeah. Sounds marvellous, doesn't it? But it isn't all that easy. We're looking for a man because strangling is a male crime. Someone who knew about valuable paintings, furniture. The trouble is the two ladies were hermits, if that's the right word. No one saw any comings or goings. We don't even know if there was one man or more than one. We don't know how big the pieces were that were stolen. Two men? Three men? Who knows?'

She came to the door with him. 'Inspector, would you do something for me?'

'I'll try.'

'Let me see the house. It may help.'

He thought for a moment and then nodded. 'That'll be okay. I'll ring you. Take you myself.'

The wilds of Wales was right, Wylie thought, as he drove the camper through the high moorland that skirts the Radnor Forest. He had left London in darkness and it was now mid-morning of a misty, cold day, with light snow on the tops.

A sign said 'Radnor Wells 1 mile', and he took a small side road that led down to a valley hidden from the moors. The surrounding countryside was brown and grazed almost to the roots by sheep, but the little town nestling in the valley was surrounded by tall conifers. There were rows of neat stone-built terraced houses, half of which had For Sale notices on them. The most obvious thing to a stranger was the silence: there was hardly a soul or a car to be seen.

He drove slowly through the town. Its centre was dominated by two huge hotels, both in a state of sad decay, with rusty wrought-iron lacework and peeling window frames. Here indeed was a rarity, he thought: a British ghost town. He decided to shoot background material on his way out.

He asked directions for the Radnor Wells Hotel and finally found Miss Gwyneth Morgan on the opposite side of the valley about half a mile from the centre of the town.

He had imagined she was living in retirement in the hotel, one of a group of faded gentlefolk with their own napkin rings and marmalade pots. But when he reached it he discovered that she was the owner, that this was her home.

'My great-grandfather built it before the turn of the century,' she said, after Wylie had introduced himself. 'My father lived here until he died some years ago. Now look at it. A gnarled old ruin. Just like me.'

She had chosen her words aptly. She must, he thought, have been in her seventies. She was tall and thin with iron-grey hair and had the gnarled quality of a hawthorn tree growing against the wind. She was plain, with a large jaw and large hands but she seemed friendly enough.

'Come along in,' she said. 'Let's have some coffee.'

The Radnor Wells Hotel was in an even greater state of decline than the ones in the town.

'Eighty rooms,' Miss Morgan said. 'And seventy-five of them unusable. I live in the rest. Imagine what this place was like before the first war. People used to come from all over the West Country to take the waters.'

She had made her own suite of rooms cosy but he was conscious all the while of the other part of the hotel, the greater part, looming above and around them.

Her drawing-room was from another era. It still bore the sign 'Residents' Lounge' on the door and was filled with mahogany furniture, antimacassars, and even an aspidistra on a small inlaid table in the bow window. In a magazine holder there were copies of *Country Life* and the *Tatler* which looked twenty or thirty years old. He had a strange feeling that ladies in long Edwardian dresses and gentlemen in blazers would soon be coming in for their morning coffee after taking the waters.

There was one anachronism: the walls were covered by record sleeves. There were hundreds of them and they gave a kind of glow to the room; brightened it up.

'My boys and girls,' she said, seeing him glance at them. 'That's how I always thought of them. I loved them all, even when they were naughty, and no one can be more trying than a singer or a soloist when they want to be. Egos the size of the Ritz.'

He saw names he had not heard of for years; Victor de Sabata and the Orchestra of the Augusteo, Rome; Noel Mewton-Wood, Eileen Joyce, Dinu Lipatti, and names of singers and orchestras he had never heard of. He was looking at a musical past.

'We live in hope that one day people will come back. But why should they? There's nothing here. Even the water tastes filthy. Come along. I'll show you.'

He followed her into the echoing corridors. She opened a door and he caught a smell of sulphur. 'The Pump Room,' she said.

All that was left of it was a series of corroded pipes, a pump handle in the middle and three or four china mugs on thin steel chains.

'You pumped up the water and drank it from one of those mugs. Grandfather put the chains on them. People were pinching them as souvenirs.'

She went on throwing open doors and looking into musty rooms where ceilings had fallen onto beds and damp was peeling away the old chintzy wallpapers.

'Would you allow me to film in here?' he said.

'Let's go back and talk about it.'

They returned to her living quarters and she sat in one of the Morris chairs and covered her knees with an afghan.

'You said you were interested in Eve Raymond.'

'I've got it down as Eva Raymonde,' he said.

'She changed her name. In those days a British name was thought hopeless for a musical career. It had to be something Continental. Anyway poor Eve . . . what a terrible thing. And Hilda too!'

'I was the one who found them,' Wylie said.

'How awful.'

'Did you know there was a child in the house?'

'No, I didn't. I didn't know Hilda had been ma – Well, of course, one doesn't need to be married these days.'

'I've been asked to do a documentary about the murder,' Wylie lied. 'And since you knew Madame Raymonde . . .'

'I'm perfectly willing to help,' she said, touching her grey hair. 'But I think we should talk about it first. I mean, there are some things that might be better left out.'

'I always have a session first anyway. Madame Raymonde was one of your clients, wasn't she?'

'Oh, yes, I've known Eve . . . well, that's past tense now. We weren't the first agency she used. Her mother took her to Simpson and Lowther when she was a child. She was a prodigy of a sort. Most prodigies never hold their promise. We see the most amazing juvenile fiddlers and pianists but by the time they reach their late teens they've lost whatever they had, or haven't matured to match their talent. Technique . . . technique – I got so tired of the word. He has a "big technique" they used to say. And I used to reply, Yes, but does he have a soul?

'Eve was a bit like that. She could rattle off a Mozart piano sonata by the time she was nine, but by the time she was nineteen she hadn't improved much. In those days Britain had an empire and soloists of Eve's calibre were still able to make a living. Nowadays they'd be travelling the school and library circuit. In the fifties and early sixties Eve played in places like Uganda and Tanganyika, Northern and Southern Rhodesia.'

'Did she make a good living?'

'Heavens no. Just managed to pay our percentage and her travel. Nothing over whatsoever. And it was a killing life. You made all your own arrangements and travelled to the most fright-ful places by train and bus and ship.'

'You know the theory is that she and her daughter were mur-dered because of valuable antiques and paintings.'

'I read that. But they were Boris's, not hers.'

'I don't know about Boris.'

'The Russian baritone. Boris Milikov. He defected to the West. He'd left his wife in Russia and met Eve over here. He couldn't get a divorce so he couldn't marry Eve but they set up house together.'

'In Hampstead?'

'First in Chelsea.'

'Is he the father of Hilda?'

'She was born soon after he and Eve set up house. That was the end of Eve's career. It wasn't much anyway and she was relieved to stop. But Boris would have ended it anyway. He said he was the artist, she just a tinkler. She went all over the world with him so it didn't end her travelling. It must have been a terrible life. She had to see to his food, wash his socks, send out his laundry, check it when it came back, do all the hotel bookings, see that he had a bed-board because of his back. Later on she had to learn how to massage his back and his neck. Oh, all sorts of things. She was his slave really. And he treated her like dirt.'

'What about Hilda?'

'Poor Hilda.'

'Why poor Hilda?'

'She was just a complication. Her father didn't want her. Nor did her mother. They were travelling all the time. Couldn't look after her. She went to boarding school when she was about eight – and stayed there. I mean through the holidays as well.

'I felt sorry for her and had her to stay in my London flat one Christmas. It wasn't a success. She was about fourteen or fifteen at the time. Mad about men. Anything in trousers. She brought a tramp to the flat once. Said he was her boyfriend. You can see why. I mean she'd been ignored right from the beginning. Since she was a baby. Is this the kind of thing you want?'

'Absolutely,' Wylie said. 'Perfect.'

'I'm not sure it should go into a documentary.'

'Let's talk about it.'

'Well, sometimes when Eve and Boris were in London and staying at the house in Hampstead she used . . . she used to lock Hilda away. I don't mean sending her up to her bedroom when she was naughty. I mean days, even weeks, of being by herself. Hilda loved her father. Wanted to be with him when he was home. Eve didn't like that. She wanted Boris to herself. She was like a kind of doormat. He would use her most dreadfully and she would come back for more. Anyway, she used to pack Hilda off to her room and lock it.

'I remember once when she was about eighteen or twenty she went on one of her "runaways", as they were called. She was eventually found after about a week with a man near the Tottenham Court Road tube station. They were sleeping rough together, sharing a sleeping-bag. Her hair was matted and her clothes torn, her body covered by dirt.

'Eve kept her in her room for a long time after that. I suppose it was better than sending her to an institution. Do you think we should talk about that?'

'Yes, I do,' Wylie said. 'I think it's very important.'

NINE

On the fifth visit Hannah sensed that there had been a change in the boy, but she did not know what it was. It was something about the way he came into the consulting rooms with Mrs Brind. More confidently? She stared at him intently. He was so like Tom. She hadn't really noticed this before. He was dressed in grey cords and a blue shirt and a green and white anorak. Tom had had a green anorak. It was the eyes that so reminded her, dark and luminous and . . . blank.

'I like the anorak,' she said to the boy.

'We bought it this morning. Didn't we?' Mrs Brind said.

'It suits you.'

They spoke to each other through the boy, including him in almost everything they said, even looking at him when they spoke. Neither had planned it that way, it had simply happened. Hannah had once had a case of a married couple who hated each other and who only spoke to each other through their dog. This was different. She and Mrs Brind got on well.

So far as Hannah was concerned, the woman was unfussy, practical and seemed genuinely to like the boy. And she was in awe of Hannah: she was the doctor, the expert. Hannah found this flattering.

The visits had taken on a routine. First Hannah would spend some time with both of them while Mrs Brind reported any changes in behaviour, then Mrs Brind would go out into the waiting-room while Hannah had him to herself.

Usually there was a series of negatives to report but today Mrs Brind said, 'There is one thing: I've told you that he's passive most of the time, well, yesterday he did something positive.'

'In what way?'

'I usually leave a glass of water for him in his room. Yesterday he was with me in the kitchen and I forgot to offer him water. The glass must have been empty because he went up to the sink and put his hand on the tap.'

'Go on.'

'I wasn't sure what he meant. I touched the tap but he didn't seem to react. Then I touched the sink and various other things but his hand went back to the tap. He was trying to tell me something, you see. He wanted water. So I gave him a glassful and he drank it.'

Hannah smiled at the boy. 'Well, aren't you clever?' She turned to the small, grey-haired woman. 'That *is* good, Mrs Brind.'

Mrs Brind flushed with pleasure.

Then Hannah said, 'Does he like running about or bouncing up and down?'

'Not really.'

'And the rocking?'

'He still does it. Perhaps not quite as much. You see, I touch him whenever I can and hug him. They say that the tactile thing is very necessary.'

'Who's they?'

'I must have read it. Isn't it true?'

'Oh, yes, very true.'

Hannah had his case notes in front of her and looked down at one entry. 'Mrs Brind, do you think he understands anything you say?'

'I honestly don't know. I've told you I've been trying to get him to go to the bathroom by himself. But that hasn't worked even though I say it over and over again. "Would you like to go to the bathroom?" Or just "bathroom". Then I take him by the hand and lead him and say it again.'

'It's early days yet,' Hannah said. The phrase echoed in her head. It was what Richard used to say about Tom.

'What about light and dark?'

'He doesn't like the dark. Hates it.'

'He may have been kept in a lighted room. I'll try to find out.'

'Oh, and one other thing: he doesn't seem to feel the cold as much as we do. If I put on his jersey he keeps it on. If I don't he doesn't seem to mind. Or at least he doesn't show he minds.'

That evening Hannah went to see her mother-in-law. She had not visited her for a week – Sophie had told her she wanted to be by herself for a few days – and was shocked at how thin she had become. The handsome face with its shiny plump skin had fallen into decay like an abandoned building. But the eyes were bright and she professed to be cheerful.

'But no more grapefruit juice when this is over. Not another drop.'

Sophie had travelled a great deal in Africa and her house was a mass of beadwork and carvings from the Okavango and the Kunene. She was sitting up in bed with a soft Shetland shawl about her shoulders. Her grey hair was loose. In the bedside light her gaunt face seemed to look out from a Goya portrait.

To Hannah's insistent questioning she finally said, 'Never mind me. I'm bored to tears with me. Tell me about the boy.'

'I'm beginning to see a pattern. Little things. So reminiscent of Tom. The boy doesn't seem to mind heat or cold. Tom didn't either.'

'Let me play devil's advocate,' Sophie said. 'In Japan they're carrying out an experiment right now keeping young children quite naked in classrooms while they're being taught. No heating on. The children are flourishing, apparently.'

'Okay.'

Then Hannah mentioned the water and the tap. 'Tom used to do that. It was uncanny hearing her say it.'

Sophie shrugged. 'Maybe.'

'There is one thing. I can't explain it but it's happened several times. When I have him alone I've been trying to get him to

109

understand numbers. I've got a little group of marbles and we sit on the floor and I count. Each time I take a marble away I put it in a separate pile and say, one, then two, then three, and so on. And he seems interested. I mean he looks at the marbles and then at me and then at the marbles. But each time I've got to six I've noticed a sudden change in him. It's as though . . . Well, it's difficult to put into words. But imagine a horse jumping perfectly over the first five barriers and then something causes it to baulk at the sixth — always at the sixth.'

Sophie frowned. Then sipped the grapefruit juice. 'This is changing the subject slightly. Have you thought of aphasia?'

'But that's the loss of all verbal skills due to brain damage. There's no evidence that his brain is damaged in that way. No, I don't think so.' Then she said, 'He seems so lost, poor little chap.'

Sophie looked at her closely.

'Well,' Hannah said, 'how am I doing?'

'The boy seems —'

'No, darling, not the boy. Me. You see we're a kind of double act. He comes to me, I come to you. Physician heal thyself, remember? Your idea. And it does seem to be working! It really does!'

'As your psychiatrist — if I were your psychiatrist — I'd have to say you were looking better, and —'

'I'm sleeping better.'

'I think that's excellent. Except . . .'

'Except what?'

'Oh, nothing. Forget it. I'm just so pleased you're coming out of it.'

She was smiling at Hannah but her eyes were troubled.

It was late when Ferry reached his house. He found his father dozing in front of the TV. The news was just coming on but the sound had been turned down. Newspapers were scattered round his father's feet and Ferry picked them up and plumped the cushions on the sofa. As he did so he caught a memory of his mother. He could see himself as a small boy when they lived in

Hawkins Street. His father would sit in front of the TV and fall asleep soon after he had his dinner – that's if he wasn't going down to the boozer. And his mother would put her finger to her lips and she would tidy up round him. He could see her now. Tidying. He smiled grimly to himself. It wasn't going to happen to him.

'That you, son?'

He went into the kitchen and opened the oven. His father, yawning, followed.

'What's that?'

Ferry put a Pyrex dish on the table. In it was a dark, dry substance, with turned-up edges.

'That's *pommes Anna*,' his father said. 'At least it was at six o'clock.'

'What the hell's pomanna?'

'You said you didn't want no more chips. This is French. Potatoes and onions done in the oven.'

'Looks more like something out of a kiln.'

'It looked good at six. I had some. Not all French food's rotten.'

Ferry scraped the hardened mass into the bin.

'You never phoned,' his father said accusingly. 'You want your meal when you come in the door but you never think I have to prepare it.'

'I got caught up.'

'You're always getting caught up.'

'Where the hell did you get a recipe for *pommes* whatever?'

His father held up a small brown book. 'Fifteen pence at the Women's Institute street market. A bargain that is. What kept you? That Vale of Health business or was you out boozing?'

'Boozing? Do me a favour! I had to go and see Begg. Not in his office, of course. Had to travel bloody miles in the rush hour.'

'But don't you see him at the station?'

'Twice a day. Sometimes three times. He says the top brass are coming down on him about the murder. I mean, we got nothing . . . *nothing*! So he takes it out on me, the bastard.'

'Don't let that chip grow any bigger, son.'

Ferry ignored him. 'You should have seen him. Like some bloody big shot.'

'How d'you mean?'

'He was at this health club in the West End. Very posh. Very trendy. Unisex. All girls and blokes lifting weights and rowing and riding those exercise bikes. Receptionist looked at me as though I was dirt.'

And so had Begg. Ferry had sensed that. Could see it in his eyes as he'd come across the floor, stepping round the bodies. Begg was lying on a table in a cubicle waiting for a massage, watching Ferry come towards him.

It was Begg's look that made him acutely aware of what he was wearing. In his dirty trainers and his old leather jacket he knew he was out of place. Begg's eyes took it all in and the word that formed in the air between them was – yob!

He told himself it didn't make much difference. Begg had thought like that since he had arrived at London North. He'd never hidden his feelings.

'This is a different patch from what you're used to,' he'd said when Ferry had first arrived. 'Hampstead's about as up-market as you can get. Lots of money, lots of influence, lots of everything. Just you remember that you're not rousting out some dosser down by the river. And for Christ's sake buy yourself a suit.'

Now, Begg turned slowly over onto his side, a towel covering his middle, and looked up at Ferry. 'You went to see the psychiatrist. What's the news?'

'She thinks maybe the boy's got . . .' Ferry consulted his notebook. 'Got a thing called autism.'

'What the hell's that?'

'I asked her. It's not easy to explain, guv'nor.'

'Try.'

'Well, seems like the kid's got something missing in his head. Doesn't see things the way we see things, doesn't understand our world. Lives in a world of his own.'

'And?'

'So if he's got this autism then it doesn't matter what he saw, even if he saw both murders. He wouldn't know what he saw. Wouldn't be able to tell us anything at all.'

'Wait a minute. Are you telling me that even if we have a witness we haven't got one? Even if he saw it he wouldn't know he saw it?'

'That's about the size of it.'

'Jesus. So what's she up to then?'

'Trying to find out if he has this autism. There're other things he might have instead. Like shock. If he's not autistic then he *may* be able to help us. But could be a long business. I mean, he can't even talk yet.'

'And if he is whatever it is?'

'I dunno, guv'nor. I honestly don't know. I've never come across anything like this before. And I've been thinking.'

'Thinking?'

He made it sound as though it was some arcane form of self-indulgence.

'We may be barking up the wrong tree. The boy might have been in the room all the time. Doesn't mean to say that because the door was unlocked he came out. What about if someone unlocked the door without him knowing? To bring in his food or something. We found burnt remains in the kitchen. Or one of the women was going in to see him when whoever it was comes in the front door? That way the boy mightn't even know the door was unlocked. I mean, he'd been in the room for months and months, maybe years. I bet he wasn't trying the door every day, maybe not even every week. Being a kid he'd probably have been too scared to come out even if he could've.'

Begg shrugged. 'What about the kid's picture?'

'Going in tomorrow's papers.'

'Anything from the house-to-house inquiries?'

'Not a thing.'

'What's the name of this problem again?'

'Autism.'

'I want a written definition of it on my desk first thing.'

'Right, guv'nor.'

'And what about Wylie?'

'I think he's clean. We've checked him. He's who he says he is. Used to be with the BBC. Won a couple of awards.'

'Awards don't mean a thing.'

'Guv'nor, there's no way he would've hung around taking pictures after killing the two women.'

'He's all we've got.'

'Anyway, he's just got back from Africa.'

'What the hell's that got to do with it?'

'Nothing. Except . . . well, you get a feeling about people.'

'Oh yes, you're the bloody murder expert, aren't you? Do me a favour.'

'Sure, guv'nor.'

'Don't argue all the time. It makes me tired.'

Albert Ferry, in his son's kitchen, said, 'You think the picture will work?'

'Christ knows.'

'What are you doing?'

'What's it look like? Making a sandwich.'

'That's not the way. Here, give me the knife.'

'I can make my own.'

'That's not how your mother made a sandwich. I know, I ate them for forty years.'

TEN

The elephant was invisible.

Wylie knew the animal was only a matter of yards away but the growth of the Tsitsikama Forest was so thick he could not see it.

'Just sit tight,' he said to Ellie, who was resting the camera in the open window. 'He'll let us know where he is. He'll move. He'll flick an ear.'

The bush was silent. There was no birdsong. No shrilling of Christmas beetles. Not even the sound of a breeze. Only the slight ticking of the car clock.

'Anyway,' Wylie said, 'he won't attack a vehicle. They never do.'

As he spoke the big bull burst from the grey-green wall of bush and was on top of them. Wylie could see his huge tusks — the left one broken — and then the vehicle was tossed over on its side and the doors burst open and all he could see was the great browny yellow tusk coming at him. He was trying to get away. His limbs were weak and slow. It was like swimming in heavy oil.

Then came the screaming.

He woke with a terrible fright, drenched in sweat. The scream was the ringing of the telephone. He was in his own room. On his own bed. In London. In reality, of course, it was Ellie who had screamed and Ellie who was dead.

'Yes?' he said.

'Mr Wylie? Inspector Ferry.'

'What is it?'

'I wanted to check if you were in town.'

'Where the hell would I be? You told me not to leave without telling you first.'

'That's good, Mr Wylie. My guv'nor's a bit worried about you. I'd like to talk to you again.'

'Okay. Call me.' He put the phone down on Ferry and lay back on the bed.

The nightmare faded but did not disappear. It settled into the back of his mind, shadowy, but always there.

He made the effort and switched his thoughts to the problem in hand. If Ferry was going to start looking into things more thoroughly; if he was going to go over everything again; if he should want him for hours on end – then he, Wylie, would have to act more quickly. He swung himself from the bed and went into the bathroom to take a shower.

At London North, Ferry was holding the receiver to his ear. The sudden cut-off left him irritated. Maybe he hadn't shown Wylie who was boss. That was something he'd do before long. And maybe Begg was right. Maybe Wylie could have done it. Normal people didn't photograph animals at night.

He dialled Hannah. 'You wanted to go through the house,' he said. 'I could take you today.'

'I'm seeing the boy at three and I haven't any other patients. Would mid-morning suit you?'

He picked her up at eleven and they drove to the Vale of Health. It was a bright, cold, Saturday morning. Scores of people were walking on the Heath.

'It seems improbable that two people could be murdered here,' Hannah said.

'There's nothing improbable about murder. We see it every week. Sometimes you think everyone is killing everyone else. But really it's not all that many. To me the surprising thing is there aren't more.'

'That's a very depressing thing to say.'

'I dunno. Seems like I'm looking on the bright side.' He indicated the strollers. 'Look at them.' She looked at the prosperous couples, some with dogs and kids. 'Where I was born we had no parks or heaths. Just the streets. They dunno when they're lucky. Yet they still kill each other.'

'Where was that? Where you were born?'

'Near the Isle of Dogs. What they call Canary Wharf now. My father was a docker on the Thames. Worked there all his life until the ships stopped coming. I'll take him back there one of these days. Show him what's happened to it.'

The Vale of Health looked beguilingly like an English village in the winter sunshine. Police tapes fluttered in a slight breeze, and metal barriers cut the lane off from the public, but a few people were standing at the road end looking at the house. Most were elderly.

'Pensioners,' Ferry said. 'Gives them something to do.'

They went through the gate. The grass had grown and the flowerbeds were unkempt. The windows were still covered on the inside by dead plants. Even on this bright day the place had a gothic, scary feel to it.

Ferry acknowledged the salute of the constable on duty, then unlocked the front door and let them in. The sounds of London disappeared. The house was silent. Motes of dust drifted in the sunrays that fell through the half-blocked windows. It was freezing cold.

There was a faint odour and Hannah thought it must have something to do with death and tried not to register it, but as they moved further into the house she changed her mind and decided it was a faint smell of burning.

'This is where they were found,' Ferry said, pointing to the foot of the staircase. Two shapes were outlined in chalk. She felt a sudden revulsion at what had happened and what she was doing. It was like walking into a crypt.

She followed Ferry into the drawing-room. Dead plants were everywhere. She could see the dusty rectangles on the walls where

117

pictures had hung. Apart from a heavy sofa, two heavy arm-chairs, and a magnificent bow-fronted rosewood display cabinet that stood eight feet tall, the room was empty.

'What they were after was in this room,' Ferry said. 'The antiques. The pictures. Trouble is there are no records – or none that we've found. We don't even know what's missing.'

'You said "they". Do you think there are more than one?'

'Could be.'

'Two men could carry that display cabinet.'

'Maybe.'

'But not one.'

'Unless they knew it wasn't valuable or too well-known.'

They went upstairs. 'This was the old woman's room,' Ferry said.

The bed was still rumpled, just as it had been left. Hannah moved to the piano.

'It's a lovely room,' she said. 'What's going to happen to the house?'

'We're still searching for relatives.'

The bedroom window had a view of the garden and the lane. The knot of onlookers was still at the metal barrier. A figure stood to one side looking up at the house. There was something about the shape and the cap that was familiar.

They looked into the *en suite* bathroom: bathsalts stood on the edge of the bath, a cupboard contained medicines. Towels still hung on the rails.

'They both used this bathroom,' Ferry said, then led her into the second bedroom. The male pin-ups still covered the walls.

On a dressing-table was a pile of Dutch and Danish magazines. They concentrated on the male genitalia and what could be done with them. Hannah flicked over a few pages. 'Goodness,' she said. 'How very painful.'

They moved along the upstairs landing and he said, 'This is where he lived.'

The smell of musty drains was strong. She examined everything minutely, including the graffiti. Suddenly she was gripped by a flood of compassion for the boy. She could visualise him here week after week, month after month – a little boy tortured

118

mentally and physically, his only outlet the perpetual drawing, the one thing he was allowed to do.

'They're just jumbles,' Ferry said.

He was right. They didn't seem to have any meaning. They looked like series after series of lines, yet each series seemed to be apart from its neighbour. As though it was meant to be a separate drawing.

'I've given him dozens of crayons and pencils. He won't draw.'

'He didn't at the station either.'

'Unless . . .' She paused as a grotesque thought entered her mind.

'Unless what?'

'Unless there was another child.'

'What do you mean?'

'Maybe there was someone else *before* the boy. I mean, look, I'm only speculating . . .'

'Go on.' He had turned and was staring at her.

'Well, all I'm saying is that the boy might not have been the first. What if there had been an earlier child? An earlier captive?'

'And it died.'

'Yes.'

'And was got rid of. Oh, Christ! Here! In the garden!'

'Yes.'

'Or somewhere in the house! Jesus, I hadn't . . . Is it possible?'

'The person who did this to the boy would be capable of just about anything, wouldn't you say?'

They spent another fifteen minutes in the house and then Ferry locked it up again. The little knot of people was still standing at the bottom of the lane. The figure Hannah had seen from the window had begun to walk away and she caught him up.

'Hello, Mitchell. What are you doing here?'

'Just looking,' he said. The once handsome face was half-hidden by the peak of his cap.

'That's a bit ghoulish, isn't it?' She smiled.

'I used to live close by.'

'Did you know them? You never told me.'

'Well, I –'

'Did you know them, sir?' Ferry had followed Hannah.

She introduced them to each other and Ferry repeated the question.

'Oh, no, not really . . . I mean . . . No one knew them. They kept to themselves. I used to see the younger one shopping in the High Street. But that's about all.'

He seemed embarrassed by the questioning.

'I'd like to talk to you, sir,' Ferry said.

'What on earth about?'

'The two ladies.'

'But I've said –'

'I know that, sir, but we're trying to find out as much as we can about them. Can you give me a phone number where I can contact you? And an address?'

Reluctantly Bourke complied. 'But I've got nothing to add, you know.'

'That's fine, sir.'

In the car Ferry questioned her about him. She explained he was her patient and said, 'What you're asking for is privileged information.'

Ferry scowled at her.

'What's wrong with him?'

'Nothing that an adoring young woman wouldn't cure.'

She told him who he was and a bit about him. 'He's a seventies face. You might have seen him in some of the soaps. And he's had parts in the eighties too. You don't think Mitchell did it, do you?'

Ferry's face remained closed. 'You'd be surprised at the people who kill,' he said. 'Most seem unlikely.'

He dropped Hannah at the flat. It was lunchtime but the thought of eating did not appeal to her. She was glad to have seen the house and the room, it gave her a partial picture of the boy's background. But it also brought an immediacy that changed her relationship with him. She could see him all too plainly in her mind's eye; she could feel his suffering.

She went into her consulting room, pulled out her journal and wrote *Saturday* and drew a line underneath it. It would help, she thought, to describe what she had done and seen.

The house is like a tomb, *she wrote*. His room is like nothing I've ever seen before. The drawings don't make sense. Could there have been another child? It's a terrible thought but Ferry says they'll search the house and garden.

She wrote on, expanding the visit, until she began to think of Tom, seeing Tom instead of the boy. Losing herself in memory.

Because it was Saturday, the day Mrs Brind did her shopping, Hannah had arranged to fetch the boy and deliver him back.

The police guard, which had been placed on the house for the first few days, had now been withdrawn and Mrs Brind was at home alone.

'It's such a lovely day, Ralph's taken him to the park,' she said.

They drove the few hundred yards and walked towards the children's playground. In the sunshine it looked like a view into Hannah's own childhood: swings, roundabouts, seesaws. Except for one major difference: around the play area was a picket fence with the notice *Adults Including Parents May Not Enter The Play Area*. That was what distinguished her childhood from those of the dozens of little children all milling about there. In her childhood she had felt no threat from adults. Now not even parents were trusted.

She looked for the boy but could not see him. Ralph Brind appeared carrying two ice-cream cones.

'Where is he?' she said.

He scanned the area, frowned. 'He was here a moment ago!'

She ran into the play area, pushing and pulling at the children, turning little boys round so she could look into their faces. Some burst into tears. There were shouts from parents standing outside the fence, but Hannah took no notice.

He wasn't there.

She ran out again.

On this bright Saturday afternoon the park was full of families with children. She ran from one to the other, with Ralph and Margaret Brind lumbering behind. She sped on past a small pond where boys were sailing toy boats, and where tiny children were feeding the ducks. She raced past dank hedges of rhododendrons, past a concrete space for skate-boarding, until she came out on a grassy area where young men were kicking footballs.

At the far end Hannah saw a man and – 'There he is!'

They ran faster. The man had a video camera and was taking shots of the boy. The child stood rigid. The man moved him into another position and picked up the camera. Hannah began to shout. The man saw them and turned the camera on them.

'How dare you!' Hannah shouted.

Wylie smiled reassuringly. 'Don't worry. He's okay.'

'I'm going to call the police!'

'What for? What'll you tell them? That I took shots of him in the park? Listen, I know who you are. You're the psychiatrist, Dr Wilton. But you don't know who I am. My name's Duncan Wylie. I was the one who found him. If it wasn't for me he might be dead by now.'

Hannah hardly registered what he was saying. She went forward to the boy but found Mrs Brind there ahead of her. Mrs Brind threw herself onto her knees and put her arms around the child. And then slowly, like puppet arms being moved on strings, his own arms rose from his sides and curved around her neck.

Something inside Hannah, something she had not even known was there, seemed to cry out. She looked up and saw that Wylie was staring at her.

ELEVEN

Two days later Hannah saw the boy for another session. During that time she had done a great deal of thinking about herself and about her reactions to what had happened – without coming to any conclusion.

She relived the moment she had searched the play area, relived the panic, a panic which had turned to anger when she confronted Wylie.

Even now, thinking about it, she felt rage. He had been so – she could not immediately think of a word . . . uncaring? – that she had been on the verge of causing a major scene.

Her voice had turned into a shriek that had caused the footballers to stop playing. When they began to run over to see what was going on Ralph Brind had scooped up the boy and they had gone back to the car.

Another picture formed in her mind: the boy with his arms round Mrs Brind. This was the 'behavioural difference' she had subconsciously recognised a few days earlier. It was the way they had held hands. At the start it had looked unnatural as though he was being forced to do something against his will. But when they had come into her consulting rooms the week before it had looked quite natural; like a little boy and his mother.

Earlier that day she had tried to explain all this to Sophie.

'I suppose it's only natural,' she had said. 'It's transference; part of the healing process.'

'I'm not sure who you're talking about,' Sophie had replied. 'Yourself or the boy?'

'Myself, obviously.'

'The healing process is also important to him.'

Hannah heard a certain crispness in Sophie's tone.

'Of course it is!'

Then Sophie said, 'Rule One –'

'I know, I know. Never become involved with the patient.' And then she said sharply, 'You should have thought of that before you started playing God.'

Was she becoming involved?

She was interested in his case, fascinated – but involved? True, she looked forward to his visits but that was purely professional. The real benefit accrued in a different way: she was brooding less about Tom and Richard. She no longer thought of the sleeping pills in the drawer by her bed as her security against the problem of living; she no longer even needed them for sleep.

'Hello, how are you today?'

'He's fine,' Mrs Brind said, bringing him into the room.

The boy stood by her side, his hand in hers. Hannah looked closely. Perhaps she had imagined things. He looked as uninvolved as he had ever been. The scene with Mrs Brind in the park could have been pure reaction.

'And how have you been after your fright?'

'I'm not sure if it's affected him or not. It's difficult to tell.'

'Well, we're going to try something new today.'

As Mrs Brind went to sit in the waiting-room, Hannah took the boy's hand. 'Come over to the sofa. I'll draw the curtains.'

She looked out onto the dark winter streets. Near a lamppost she saw the figure of a man. He was too far away for her to make out his features. Mitchell? But in his heavy coat and cap she could not be sure. He seemed to be looking up at the apartment block.

'I'm becoming paranoid,' she said to the boy. 'Just because someone's looking up at the block it doesn't mean to say he's looking at *my* apartment. Probably a policeman. Watching over us. Or you anyway.'

She wasn't entirely convinced but it made her feel better.

She had a large drawing book in her hands. On the desk were half a dozen pencils of different colours. She seated herself next to the boy on the sofa, took one of the pencils and offered it to him.

As usual he did not react. But she persisted.

'Look, this is what I saw on the walls where you lived.' She drew a series of squiggles and loops.

The boy remained static, uninvolved. She remembered how Tom had reacted to pencils. He had chewed them down to the lead. Then he had ripped up the pages of the drawing book. What he had *not* done was to sit quietly and be uninvolved.

'I wonder if you did the drawings? The policeman that found you, Mr Ferry, is going to try to find out if there was anyone else there before you – or maybe even with you. Was there? Was there another child? A brother or a sister? A friend?'

Just then there was a soft knock at the door. Mrs Brind put her head round. 'Someone's buzzed your street phone. Would you like me to answer it?'

'Please.'

'I wonder who that is,' Hannah said to the boy. 'Do you think it's the man near the streetlight?'

Mrs Brind came back. 'It's that man from the park, Mr Wylie.'

'I don't want to see him.'

'I told him you were busy.'

There was a long buzz on the entry phone.

'Right. I'll go.'

Hannah picked up the receiver. 'Yes?'

'It's Duncan Wylie. I'd like to talk to you.'

'I don't want to talk to you. Please go away.'

She put down the receiver. Instantly there was another long, nerve-jangling buzz.

'If you don't let me in I'm going to stay here and buzz until you do.'

She paused, angry and uncertain. Then she said, 'Five minutes, that's all I can give you.'

She asked Mrs Brind to take the boy into the sitting-room. 'I'll talk to Mr Wylie in my office.'

She switched on the TV and left them, the boy sitting in a chair, Mrs Brind standing near the window.

Wylie was bigger than she had remembered. He was wearing khaki trousers, an olive-green shirt, desert boots and his elderly sheepskin coat. He looked, she thought, like an explorer.

She stood behind her desk and left him standing in the middle of the floor. It didn't work. He took off his sheepskin coat, dropped it on the sofa and stretched out in the patients' chair.

'Is this where they bare their souls?'

'What do you want to see me about? I should have thought you'd done enough damage already without –'

He held up his hand. 'Hang on a second, doctor. It is doctor, isn't it?'

'Yes, it is.'

'There are so many of you now: counsellors, psychotherapists, industrial psychologists, child psychologists, psychiatrists . . . I get confused.'

'Mr Wylie, I have a patient and –'

'I know. It's the boy. I followed him.'

'Have you been watching us?'

'It's my job, remember. I'm a photographer. I've come to apologise for Saturday. I had no right to scare everyone like that. I realise that now. I'm sorry.'

He did not look like someone who was very sorry, Hannah thought.

He smiled at her. 'I can't do more than say I'm sorry, can I?'

'I should have thought that was the least you could do! I mean, why did you do it in the first place?'

'Because if I'd asked, no one would have agreed.'

'Don't you understand the harm you may have done? Don't you realise how delicate the boy is mentally? I mean –'

She did not finish the sentence. From the sitting-room there came a loud crashing noise as though a bomb had gone off. Above it she heard a shriek.

They ran for the door.

The sight that greeted them made Hannah's blood run cold.

The first thing she saw was that Mrs Brind had hold of the boy round his middle. He was struggling and trying to hit her with a copper vase. At the same time he was making a high-pitched noise. On the floor in front of him was the TV set. It lay on its back, the glass screen shattered, smoke rising in thin trails from the broken innards.

Mrs Brind could hardly contain the boy's struggles and seemed in imminent danger of falling over. Wylie scooped him up. 'I've got him now.' He held him above the floor until his struggles grew less manic. 'It's okay, it's okay . . .'

Mrs Brind's face was chalky. 'I don't know what happened,' she said. 'I was standing here and he was sitting just as you left him. I gave him the drawing book and a pencil. But he was watching the TV screen. He does that sometimes. Without seeming to take anything in. And then suddenly he leapt to his feet and picked up the vase and before I could do anything at all he rushed at the TV set and began to attack it!'

Wylie set the boy down on his feet.

'He's all right now.'

Hannah knelt in front of the child and tried to take him in her arms. It was like enveloping a cadaver. She took one of his hands. 'What was all that about?' She led him to a sofa, sat him down and put her arm round his shoulder.

'It was like a dam bursting!' Mrs Brind said.

She joined them on the sofa and took the boy's hand.

Wylie said, 'I've often felt like kicking in a TV set.'

Hannah smiled. The tension among the adults was broken but she could feel the boy trembling.

'I wonder if I shouldn't take him home,' Mrs Brind said.

'I think that might be a good idea. Ring me if anything happens, it doesn't matter what time.'

She saw them out and came back into the sitting-room. Wylie, whom she had almost forgotten, had lifted the TV set and said, 'Where would you like me to put it?'

'In the kitchen, I suppose.'

He carried it through. 'Look, I'd better be on my way. I'll see you some other time.'

She did not want to be alone. 'Since you're here, won't you

have a drink?' It wasn't graciously put and she saw a slight cynical smile cross his lips.

She gave them both Scotch on the rocks. Flowers from the vase were scattered about the floor and she picked them up and mopped up the water.

'Has it happened before?' he said.

'Absolutely not. Quite the opposite. I'm still trying to deal with it in my mind. It's something new and I don't know why it happened unless . . . unless it was your presence – I mean after what happened to him on Saturday.'

'But he didn't see me. He was already here with Mrs Brind.'

'Sorry, I'm confused. Maybe it was the pencil and the drawing book. Maybe when she gave it to him it triggered off something.' She pushed back her hair which had fallen across her eyes. 'That's the trouble, you never *really* know why things happen.'

'Same with animals,' Wylie said.

'No, it's not the same at all.'

Her voice put him in his place. She had lost control of the situation, now she had regained it.

'Well, if you've finished . . .' She put down her drink preparatory to seeing him to the door.

'Thank you, I'd love another.'

He stretched out in a low bamboo chair. 'Nice,' he said, looking round at the room. 'Cambodian?'

'Thai.'

'Ever been there?'

'No. I've never been to the Far East.'

'I did a series on elephant training in Burma. Fascinating. They use them in the teak forests.'

She stood, waiting for him to go.

He said, 'Why don't you get yourself another drink and sit down. We've got a lot to talk about, at least I have.'

'I don't think –'

'For God's sake, it may just help you with your patient.'

She poured herself a small whisky and sat on the edge of a chair.

He said, 'Let's start with me and then you have your say and we'll see if there's any common ground.'

'You said you found him.'

He told her briefly what he had seen and how it had happened.

'So it was you who found the bodies?'

'Body. I didn't see the other one. The police still aren't positive that I didn't do the ladies in myself.'

He waited for her to smile at such an unthinkable proposition but instead she was measuring him. Could he have been the man under the streetlight?

He said defensively, 'I can assure you I didn't but since you don't know me my assurances aren't worth much.'

She did not reply.

'Don't the police think the boy may have been a witness?'

'Yes.'

'So what's he doing here?'

She looked into her glass. 'I'm not sure if –'

'If there's something wrong with the boy I want to know. He's mine. I found him.'

'He's not anyone's, Mr Wylie!'

'I didn't mean that literally. Is he disturbed? If not, why is he seeing a psychiatrist?'

'Why are you so concerned?'

'I'm out photographing wildlife and this starving kid walks into my lens. Why shouldn't I be interested in the poor little chap?'

'All right. I'll tell you briefly.'

When she had finished he said, 'What's autism?'

Again she spoke for a short time. His face registered disbelief. 'For God's sake,' he said, 'why make it more complicated than it is?'

She flushed. 'Have you a better explanation?'

'Well . . . look, when I saw him I thought, my God this is Mowgli. A wolf boy. The foxes are the wolves. A wild child like that kid in France. I mean, it was just so amazing . . .'

'You're a romantic, Mr Wylie. I'm afraid this is no Mowgli.'

'But why autism? Why not shock? Why not anything? It's like someone coming to a doctor with a winter cough and he starts by saying it might be lung cancer. Don't you try a cough mixture first?'

129

'And your cough mixture for the boy would be . . . that I should read Kipling?'

'Don't patronise me.'

'I thought you were patronising me.'

They stared at each other.

He sipped his drink and said, 'That wasn't a good start, was it?'

'Mr Wylie, I'm not really interested in starts or middles or ends. This has nothing to do with you.'

'Oh, yes it has. You see, I'm making a documentary about him. That's why I filmed him in the park. Weren't you even curious?'

'Of course I was! Curious doesn't begin to describe my feelings. I thought you might be the murderer.'

'Me the murderer! Why would I – ? Yes. My God, I see.' He paused. 'I have a confession to make. You know, I'd almost forgotten there was a murder. I mean, I've been concentrating on the boy. On you. On the Brinds. On Miss Morgan.'

'Who's Miss Morgan?'

He told her about his visit to Wales.

Hannah's interest quickened. 'And she said that Madame Raymonde used to lock her daughter away?'

'For long periods, I gathered. Weeks. Why?'

'There's a correlation. At least in child abuse there is. It's often the child who has been abused who abuses his or her own children!'

She paused and then said, 'Going back to what you were saying about the crime, it's strange but it happened to me too. Like yours, my interest has been centred solely on the boy. Everything else was remote. I'd almost forgotten there was a murder and a murderer.'

'I bet the killer hasn't.'

She felt a sudden chill.

He went on, 'Or should it be *they*?'

'The police don't know.'

'It's got to be a gang, hasn't it? Only a gang could have cleaned out the antiques and pictures in the drawing-room. The same thing happened to friends of mine. They live on a remote farm in East Anglia. One night a gang came along with two big lorries.

They apologised. Said they had understood my friends would be out. They tied them up and cleared the house. Halfway through, they shared their flasks of tea with them. Left them their tooth-brushes and some loo paper and that was about all.'

'There were no flasks of tea this time.'

'No. Look, now that we've met and talked, would you do an interview for me?'

'Absolutely not.'

'Why not?'

'Well, I . . .'

'It'll be a serious documentary. I promise you that.'

'I don't think so.'

'That's better.'

'Better than?'

'Better than absolutely not.'

'It means the same thing but only more politely. You see, Mr Wylie, you want to exploit the boy. I want to help him.'

'I hope you don't always sound like that.'

'Like what?'

'So damn smug.'

After he had gone she stood by the window. The area under the streetlight was clear. She wondered if she had imagined the man.

The phone rang. It was Mrs Brind. 'You told me to phone you.'

'Yes, of course. Has something happened?'

'He started crying.'

'What?'

'After we got home and I put him to bed. I saw tears in his eyes. Just a few, but they were tears.'

'Did he make a noise? Did he sob?'

'No.'

'I wonder why. He's never cried before.'

She thought of Tom. He hadn't cried either. Not sentimentally, anyway. Tears had come from frustration or anger.

TWELVE

Peter Ferry found his house in darkness. It was unusual now and projected him back into that best-forgotten period after his wife had left him and before his father had arrived to take her place. He hated even to think about that time.

Gradually the house had become dirtier and more untidy until he began to abandon rooms. The kitchen was the first to go. He could not cope with the cooking and the washing up. He had closed the door and lived on takeaways.

Then the sitting-room. He could not bear the dark, empty spaces when he came home. Now her chair had been taken over by his father but during the interim it had stood bleak and empty and accusing.

Finally, by the time he had invited his father to come and live with him, he had retreated to the bathroom and his bedroom. He'd had to hire a firm of professional cleaners who'd charged him triple the normal price because of the state of the house.

So this evening he found his spirits dropping to zero when he switched on the lights in the empty rooms. Even though the heating had come on, the place looked and felt cold.

He went into the kitchen. The stove was not on. He looked in the oven. Nothing.

'Jesus Christ!' he said out loud.

Even as he said it he knew it was not the lack of a cooked meal that was bothering him. The thing was: he'd got used to his father being there. And this time he wasn't.

He went down the street to the Black Ox and looked into the four-ale bar. It was nearly eight o'clock and the place was crowded.

He pushed his way through the scrum and saw his father standing near the darts board.

'Dad?'

'Son.'

'Your throw, Bert,' a voice said.

'Dad!'

'Hang on, hang on.'

Albert put down his pint pot and took his place on the rubber mat. He threw one dart.

'Eighteen,' the voice said.

He threw another. It stuck in the double nine.

'You lucky bugger!' a voice said. There was laughter.

'Mine's a pint,' Albert said, draining his mug.

'Dad!'

'You see that?' Albert said. 'See that double nine?'

'Yeah, I saw it.'

It was hot in the pub and his father was sweating.

Ferry pulled at his father's shirt. 'I want a word.'

Albert turned to his mates. 'Just a sec.'

'What are you doing here?' Ferry said.

'What d'you mean what am I doing here?'

'I mean you're supposed –'

'I ain't *supposed* to be anywhere!'

'Listen, Dad, come home and we can talk.'

'Can't you see I'm enjoying myself for once?'

'The house was dark. There wasn't any food.'

'You think you can come home any time and I'll be there with the plate of hot grub? Why don't you get something here? A pork pie, a ham sandwich.'

'For Christ's sake, I eat that sort of stuff in the canteen. I want something decent when I get home. Anyway who the hell are these people? You didn't tell me you knew people around here.'

133

'Pensioners like me. Men who've lost their wives. Men who don't work no more, who've got nothing to do and all day to do it in. I meet them in the shops and in the Pop-In Club and at the post office getting their money. We look at each other and we recognise each other. We're a tribe, see.'

An impatient voice called him to play. 'All right. I'm coming.' To Ferry he said, 'Have a pint. Relax. Enjoy yourself.'

Ferry had four pints before his dad was prepared to go home and by that time he was half pissed. On the way he bought a doner kebab.

'I dunno how you can eat that stuff,' Albert Ferry said. 'Stinks to high heaven.'

'It isn't only the meal,' Ferry said, returning to his theme.

'What then?'

'It's just that I . . . well, I had a bad day.'

'With Mr Begg?'

'Yeah.'

'Whenever you have a bad day you want me here so you can complain.' He rolled a cigarette and lit it.

'You used to have Mum to complain to.'

'I'm listening.'

'I told you about the psychiatrist and the drawings. She said she thought there could have been another kid. Maybe earlier.'

His father switched on the TV set.

Ferry was incensed. 'You want to watch the box or listen to me?' He switched it off.

'Well, anyway I had to check it out. I mean, there was a possibility. If the women had done it once they could have done it twice. You know how many children go missing every year in Britain? Hundreds! Thousands!'

'So?'

'So I organised a search. In the house and the garden.'

'You got that special equipment now, haven't you, that can look into the ground?'

'Not in a suburban garden. Waste of time. No, we used the old methods.'

*

134

The old methods were like an engraving from a Victorian novel. Mist hung over the Vale of Health, falling softly on the dead leaves. Men dug in the flowerbeds.

'Sir, it's like one of those horror movies,' Holder said to Ferry, looking round the garden. 'You know, when the vampire's dug up.'

It *was* a bit like that, Ferry had thought. He had six detectives each with a shovel and a pick and a long metal probe. First they'd gone through the house looking for disturbed floorboards, then they'd gone into the garden. They'd roped off the stone terrace and the paths as nonstarters and then they'd gone over the flowerbeds. Wherever there was a suspicion of soft earth they had dug or probed.

But how could you ever tell, Ferry thought. A child's body was so small. It could be anywhere. And the whole of the Heath was just around the corner.

They worked all that morning and afternoon, even probing under the hedge.

And then, as the misty day darkened to dusk, Begg had arrived.

He had stood at the garden gate looking at the activity and raised the index finger of his right hand and curled it slowly at Ferry. They walked down the lane out of earshot.

Begg turned. His glance lingered on Ferry's clothes. 'What the hell's going on?' he said.

'Searching the grounds, guv'nor.'

'What for?'

Ferry told him what Hannah had suggested.

'Who gave you permission?'

'No one, guv'nor.'

'No one? You take six men off duty and use them for some bloody silly scheme like this and you don't check with me first?'

'I looked for you,' Ferry lied.

'Who do you think you are?'

Ferry stared at him. It was like being scolded by his old headmaster.

'No, I mean that quite seriously. Who are you supposed to be? Steve McQueen? You're not on the bloody ranch now. Look at you! With your boots and your denims. For Christ's sake, man, this isn't a fancy-dress party. Nor is it the East End. You're not some macho street kid. You're a detective inspector in Her Majesty's Constabulary. And you're at London North not bloody Shoreditch or Bethnal Green. Am I getting through to you?'

'Yes, guv'nor.'

'You come here from your East End streets and you think you're Jack-the-lad. Well, let me tell you something: I've worked with people like you before. You don't last. Not with me. My advice to you is to ask for a transfer. Because if you don't I'm going to and that'll go down on your record. And I want a report on my desk by tomorrow morning. Subject: why Detective Inspector Ferry took six men off duty to dig in a local garden when A: there's an acute manpower shortage allowing the villains on the streets to have an even easier time of it; and B: just because some silly woman psychiatrist suggested it. You understand?'

'Yes, guv'nor.'

'And, Ferry, have you found a body?'

'No, guv'nor.'

'Have you found anything?'

'No, guv'nor.'

Begg turned and walked back to his car.

As he told it to his father, Ferry was still shaking.

'Make me one, Dad.'

His father rolled him a cigarette.

'It's been like that ever since I went to London North. They've never taken to me.'

'Don't start feeling sorry for yourself, son. Don't give them the satisfaction. Give them two fingers instead. They're only jealous.'

Ferry laughed harshly. 'Jealous of what?'

'Listen, you did well on that last murder case. Commendation. That can't be bad. They know you're good, son.'

'I *am* good. Bloody good. But he wants me to get out of the force altogether. Almost said as much with his talk of a transfer.'

'Well, you're not going to let him push you anywhere, are you? You've always wanted to be a policeman – though God knows why. So stick to it.'

'I will, don't you worry. What I really need is a break on this one.'

'Is that why you went ahead on your own?'

'Yeah. He's an old woman. He'd probably have said no. The thing is no one's got an idea. If I could bring it in, slap it on his desk and say this is how it was done and this is who did it – well, he could go and screw himself!'

'Two fingers to Begg,' Albert said, sticking his two fingers up in the air and taking a mouthful of Scotch.

'Two fingers,' echoed Ferry.

Dear Dr Wilton,

I always seem to be apologising to you. And I'm about to do so again. It was quite wrong of me to become obnoxious in the way I did. Put it down to frustration. This is the best documentary subject I've ever had and it looks like slipping into limbo. Still, that's not your fault.

I'm sorry for being rude.

But there is a caveat. I can't help feeling that you're on the wrong track with the boy. I know that sounds presumptuous for a layman but you didn't see him as I did when he thought he was unobserved. I have something to show you if you're interested, but I'd need a quid pro quo.
Sincerely, Duncan Wylie.

She looked at the address. There was a telephone number. She dialled.

When he answered she said, 'Thank you for your apology but there was no need. It *was* a rather smug thing to say.'

'So why don't we start over?'

'That depends.'

'On?'

'The quid pro quo.'

'Okay, I'll show you something that may give you a different slant on the boy. In return, you reconsider your stance on the documentary.'

'That's all I have to do? Reconsider?'

'Yes.'

'All right. How do we start over?'

'Meet me this evening at –'

'I'm sorry, I don't go out in the –' She stopped herself. This was just ridiculous. 'Sorry. Forget what I just said.'

He gave her the address of Wilderness Films. 'It's just behind Marks and Spencer's Marble Arch store. There's a small alley. About seven thirty?'

'Make it seven forty-five.'

The Christmas rush was in full swing when she reached Oxford Street. She parked under Selfridges. Some stores were still open and the Christmas lights were on all the way down to Tottenham Court Road. She rang the street door and identified herself and he let her in.

'I've never heard of Wilderness Films,' she said.

'Only people in the business have. It's a facilities house. They've got everything a film maker needs. And it's all for hire.'

He led her up a narrow flight of stairs and into a warren of corridors. 'In here.'

It was a small room with metal filing cabinets against one wall. 'This is a cutting-room.' He offered her a chair and she sat down in front of a small monitor. Wylie unlocked a filing cabinet and brought out a roll of film.

'It looks like the kind of console Dr Strangelove would have used.' She pointed at all the knobs and dials.

'This is where movies are really made. And that', he pointed underneath his chair, 'is the cutting-room floor as in "The best part of the movie was left on the cutting-room floor."'

He threaded the film into the machine.

'I can run it back or forward frame by frame so ask me to stop at any time. There isn't much so watch carefully.'

'What am I watching?'

'You'll see.'

He was being mysterious and she felt a slight frisson of expectation. There was a blurred flicker of images, then the film settled down.

'This is Hampstead Heath at night,' Wylie said. 'I'm using an image intensifier, which is why the picture's so fuzzy. I'm in a hide about two hundred yards from the Vale of Health. That brown thing is the path.'

He stopped the film on the litter basket. She could see some paper on the ground. It looked strange, unearthly, as though she was viewing something in the barren tundra by sunless light.

'Look at three o'clock from the litter basket. See those shadows?'

'Yes.'

'Okay, watch them.' He let the film go forward slowly. The shadows jerked into view closing on the basket.

'They're dogs,' she said. 'No, foxes.'

'Right.'

'I didn't know there were foxes on Hampstead Heath.'

'They're in quite a few cities. Bristol's another. Very successful at living with man. I'll let the film run. See, it's a vixen and cubs. Watch how she goes for the food in the basket. I put some meat there.'

Hannah watched fascinated while the vixen pulled out the bag of meat.

'Now go left,' he said. 'About ten o'clock. See anything?'

'A darker area. Is it a bush?'

'I'll move the film forward slowly. See it?'

'What?'

'What you thought was a bush.'

'Oh yes . . . it's moving towards the basket. It's . . . what is it? Some sort of animal?'

'Look at the foxes.'

'They're frightened.'

'Sure. Now the figure again.'

'It's a chimp, isn't it?'

'Good girl.' He gave a slight smile. 'Sorry. That just slipped out. I'm so used to Ellie sitting there.'

'Who?'

'Doesn't matter.'

'Oh look, it's going to the litter basket. It's taking something out.'

'Pizza box.'

'How do you know?'

'Checked afterwards.'

'Do chimps eat pizzas?'

They watched the figure open the box.

'It certainly knows how to –' She stopped suddenly. 'It isn't a chimp, is it?'

'No, it's not.'

'Oh, my God, it's the boy!'

'Yes. It's the boy.'

'But you never . . . The police never told me you had him on film.'

'They don't know.'

She leaned back in the chair. *They don't know?*

'They'd have confiscated it.'

'But it's evidence!'

'Of what? No one's investigating The Case of the Child on the Heath.'

After a moment she said, 'I suppose not.' She sounded doubtful.

'It might take months, even years to get it back.'

'Could I see it again?'

'As many times as you like.'

He ran it twice more.

'What do you think now?' he said.

'I don't know what to think.'

'Have you eaten?'

'No.'

'I know a Lebanese place round the corner that's –'

'I'm sorry but I –'

'Oh, yes, I forgot. You don't go out in the evenings.'

She ran her hand through her hair, brushing it away from her eyes, and smiled at him. 'Sorry. Yes, of course. I'd love to.'

They walked the few hundred yards. The place was warm and the waiters welcoming. 'Do you know Lebanese food?' he said.

'No, you order.'

'The best things are the starters, the *mestes*. I usually make a meal of them.'

'Fine.'

He ordered eight dishes between them and a bottle of white wine.

'I've got a problem,' she said.

'I thought you might have once you'd seen that.'

'It concerns you too. Let's take it in order. The police think they might have a child witness to two killings but the witness is totally silent. There is a suggestion that the witness is autistic. I'm hired to find out if this is so. My first reactions are that the child could be; he shares some of the characteristics. But he doesn't share others. I'm ambivalent. Then you show me a strip of film which indicates that the child is *not* autistic.'

'What d'you base that on?'

'The way he opened the pizza box.'

'That's what I thought the moment you told me you considered he might be autistic. It was the box.'

'Tom would've –'

'Who's Tom?'

'A child I treated once for autism. He would have ripped open the box. Torn it to pieces and the food too probably.'

'So what's the problem?'

'If he's not autistic then he's in shock. That means his mind is available.'

'Or he might be a wild child. Simply deprived of human speech.'

She frowned at him. 'You used that phrase before. What exactly did you mean?'

'Well, you get them occasionally. I mean the Wild Boy of Aveyron, Kaspar Hauser, the Wolf Children of Midnapore –'

'Back to Mowgli.'

'Sure. Why not? There have always been kids like that. I was going to do a documentary on one in the Kalahari. A Bushman child who was thought to have been brought up by baboons. I did a lot of research but by the time I found the place, he'd died. I interviewed the people in Botswana who had found him. They

141

thought he was about ten or eleven. Couldn't speak a word. He seemed deaf to speech but he could hear other sounds. Just like this boy.'

'As I remember it, the Wild Boy of Aveyron appeared out of a French forest in the early nineteenth century,' she said. 'We have no wild places left like that.'

'You haven't told me yet what the problem is.'

'It's simple: I've got to tell the police.'

'Tell them what?'

'That they may have a witness. And they'll ask how I know. I'll have to tell them about the film.'

'You can't do that.'

'But I have to.'

'That was privileged information. I thought you knew that.'

'But don't you see my dilemma?'

'I'm sorry, but no!' His voice was angry now. 'All I wanted was to help you and the boy.'

'Help us? If you only wanted to help then there would be no problem. But in fact you want a quid pro quo.'

They paused.

'We started over and it still didn't do much good,' he said.

She felt suddenly guilty. 'Look, there is a way. I could simply say I'd conducted some tests and found it was unlikely he was autistic.'

'What sort of tests?'

'He was hungry. I bought him a pizza in a pizza box and he opened it.'

He leaned back in his chair. 'Brilliant!'

The food came. They were both hungry and they ate in silence.

'These are good,' she said, nibbling at a small round ball. 'What are they?'

'Falafel. A kind of chick pea fritter.'

When they had finished she said, 'I really began to wonder after he'd smashed the TV. Mrs Brind phoned me and told me he had cried. Not hysterically, more like weeping.'

'What do you think triggered the incident? Something on the screen?'

'It could have been anything.'

142

They drank thick Turkish coffee and picked at sweetmeats.

'Who is Ellie?' she asked. He frowned and she said, 'You mentioned her name earlier.'

'A friend. What about the documentary? Have you reconsidered? It's a better story if the boy *isn't* autistic.'

'Is that how you think of him? A story?'

'In a way. I'm also sorry for him.'

'So what makes it a better story now?'

'Now the police may have someone who saw something. You said so yourself. His mind is "available", you said. What if the killer were to discover that piece of information?'

THIRTEEN

Sophie was just skin and bones, Hannah thought. She spent most of her day in bed now. A woman came in to help in the house but since there was no food to prepare she left in the middle of the afternoon. It was now early evening and the house felt cold and damp.

'You've got to stop this,' Hannah said, switching on lights and fan heaters and generally trying to brighten the place up.

'Why?'

'Because it's not sensible.'

'I feel fine.'

Sophie was like a statue in white bone china. She looked almost transparent.

'Well, you don't look fine. You're much too thin now.'

Sophie ignored her. She was sipping from a glass of hot water. She said, 'I've been hallucinating. It's quite fascinating. If I had the strength I'd make notes. Everything's much sharper than dreams. I had one this morning. We were all having a picnic. You and Tom and Richard and me. We were in a forest. In the dark. Or that's what I thought. Then when the sun rose I found we were actually sitting in the middle of a deserted motorway. What do you make of that?'

'I don't think one is supposed to make much of hallucinations, darling. Dreams are different.'

Hannah rose and went to the window and looked out onto the

144

road. It was dark and a cold north-west wind was blowing a veil of rain past the streetlights.

'I've got something interesting to tell you.'

'I knew you had. You look . . . wound up.'

Hannah told her about the film and her conversation with Wylie. About her own reactions and her own feelings now.

'Well, if anyone should know what autism *isn't* it's you.' She paused. 'The Wild Boy of Aveyron? He's knowledgeable, your Mr Wylie.'

'He was going to do a documentary about "wild" children and read up on the subject.'

'I like the idea of Mowgli on the Heath. The foxes. We yearn more and more for that kind of thing in our society. Lost innocence. There was a time when scholars thought of these "wild" children as tabula rasa, blank tablets on which they could write their version of human behaviour. But that's changed. We would hope to learn from them now, I think. Truffaut made a film about the wild boy.'

'I saw it years ago.'

'I think it's a blind alley in this case.'

'I'm not so sure.'

Suddenly Sophie said, 'Genie! That's it. That's the name I've been trying to think of.'

'The bottled sort?'

Sophie did not smile. 'In America – California – in the sixties or seventies there was a child locked away. I can't recall much about it except that there was a lot of publicity and so they never released her real name and called her Genie instead. I should have thought of it before except we were hung up on autism. It led us astray.'

'It was only natural after Tom. Specially as Sidney Rosenberg thought so. He's seen quite a few cases.'

'The trouble is everything begins to look familiar. You see what you want to see; hear what you want to hear. If you go into my study . . . on the shelves on the right of the window . . . I'm sure I've got something about the case.'

A few moments later Hannah came back clutching a book.

'Here it is. *Genie: Psycholinguistic Study of a Modern-day Wild Child.*'

'That's it. The whole of the second half is about linguistics but the first part might spark something in you.'

'I'll read it tonight.'

Sophie had put her head back on the pillows and closed her eyes. Her breathing was so faint that for a moment Hannah thought she had died.

Then she opened her eyes and said, 'It's Christmas next week.'

'I was going to talk to you about that.'

'I knew you were, that's why I got in first. You'll want to decorate the house and come here and spend the day with me.'

'How did you guess?'

'Because I know you.'

'And that's what I'm going to do.'

'No, you're not. I've got another twelve days to go on this diet. I don't want to be tempted. And Christmas Day . . . well, I don't want to celebrate anything this Christmas. I just want to get it over. Ignore it. Pretend it isn't there. And then, when I come out of purdah, I'll have my Christmas with you.'

'You're just being silly. You know you can't ignore Christmas. I tried to last year. It's far worse. Celebrate it. Pretend you're part of the world. Then you get through it.'

'Are you worried about me or yourself?'

'Both of us.'

'Well, let me worry about me and don't worry too much about yourself.'

'I wanted to bring him here,' Hannah said.

'Who?'

'The boy.'

'I didn't know he was spending Christmas with you.'

'Of course he is! Where else?'

'The Brinds?'

'No, no, they see him all the time. I want him on Christmas Day. I've bought him clothes and toys and games and . . . You know, I'm actually looking forward to it this year.'

Sophie did not reply and Hannah rose, crossed to the window and looked out.

'Why do you keep doing that?' Sophie said.

'Doing what?'

'Peering out of the window. You're as nervous as a kitten. Don't worry, no parking warden is going to come round at this hour or in this weather.'

'It's not the car. It's . . . I've had a feeling someone's watching me. And then Duncan Wylie said something that didn't help.'

'What?'

'Well, if the boy isn't autistic, and the killer finds out . . .'

She left the sentence unfinished.

Sophie said, 'Have you told the police?'

'I want to speak to someone called Ferry but he's been out. I will tonight.'

'Then I shouldn't worry. Only you, Wylie and the police will know.'

'And you.'

Sophie gave a slight rattling laugh. 'I'm not likely to murder the boy.'

Hannah smiled. 'Of course you're not.'

But she hadn't been thinking of that.

On the way home from Sophie's, Hannah shopped at a deli in Heath Street then drove to her apartment block. About a hundred yards from home she pulled into the side of the small street. This was where she had seen the figure before.

On such a cold, rainy night, few people were about, and certainly there was no one standing and watching the apartments; it was far too unpleasant for that.

She drove on down the street and turned into the underground parking beneath the flats. There was a small room where an attendant had once sat, but he had long since been made redundant.

She hated underground car parks. Nothing had ever happened to her in one but she was always expecting the worst. It was a case of conditioning, she thought. Almost every thriller on TV had a scene of terror or violence in a basement car park. With their echoing floors and dank, grey walls, they lent themselves to the creation of fear. Now she was conditioned. It was a clear case of behaviour modification and Pavlov would have loved it: *see a car park, freeze in terror.*

It was not a big parking area. There were forty apartments and forty spaces and each space was numbered. She parked. The air down here seemed colder than outside. Rainwater was running into the garage from a blocked street drain.

She fetched her parcels from the back seat and put them on the roof of the car while she locked it. She thought she heard a noise, a shoe scraping on concrete. Her parking space was an end bay and she was between the wall and the car. She stood quite still, listening, but the noise did not come again.

She was afraid now. Her brain was racing and she was talking silently but speedily to herself. There was only one way into the garage and one way out of it. You parked and then walked back up the small ramp to the front door of the apartment block. Once there had been a back entrance, a flight of stairs leading up from the garage into the flats, but when the attendant had been made redundant, the door had been blocked off for security reasons.

She gathered up her parcels. She would have to walk past at least a dozen cars to reach the entrance. Whoever had made the noise — if there had been a noise and it hadn't just been her imagination — might be behind any one of them. She pushed her parcels into the wide top of her handbag and slung that over her left shoulder. Then she held her bunch of keys in her right hand so that several sharp ends protruded between her fingers. It wasn't much but it was something.

The cars were parked on either side of the walkway so that by trying to keep as far from one line as possible she would inevitably move closer to the other.

This was when she wanted a car phone. She could hear her voice deriding them in the past. But who would she phone? Sophie? The police? ('I thought I heard a noise, Sergeant.')

She walked down the aisle between the parked cars. Six on each side, one covered in a dusty plastic cover looked more menacing than the others yet she knew it quite well. It belonged to an elderly doctor who was off on a round-the-world trip.

Now, in her imagination, almost anything could be hiding beneath that cover.

Her high-heeled shoes made a clacking noise on the concrete. That was another TV cliché: *hear a footstep, freeze in terror.*

She tried to tell herself that she was within a few yards of a well-used suburban street but it didn't help. If no one was in the street it didn't matter how near you were.

She passed the cars and started up the ramp. Wind blew drizzle into her face.

Nearly there.

She came up into the wet night air and into the haloed light of the streetlamps. Her front door was a matter of a few yards away. She ran up the steps, opened the big glass security doors, darted inside and leaned on the door as it closed.

She felt a flood of relief. Home. Safe. Two of the most important words in a woman's lexicon. Somewhere in the gloom behind her a man cleared his throat. She whirled, holding the keys up in a bunch, forgetting how she had planned to use them. The figure came forward.

'Hannah!'

'Oh God, Mitchell, you gave me the fright of my life! What are you doing here?'

'Waiting for you.'

'How did you get in?'

'Mrs Levinson let me in. She wanted me to wait in her apartment but I said no.'

He looked large in his heavy coat. He'd removed his cap and his thinning hair was pressed onto his skull in untidy waves.

'Happy Christmas.' He thrust a package at her.

'But, Mitchell, it isn't Christmas yet and anyway I wouldn't take –'

'Please.'

She took the gaily wrapped box. 'Well, thank you very much.' He waited. She wanted to get to her apartment and be by herself. 'Would you like to come in for coffee?'

'I'd love to.'

*

He came into the kitchen with her. 'Instant?' she said.

'Fine. I'll have it black.'

They sat – in Hannah's case, perched – in her sitting-room. She needed a drink but then she would have to offer him one. Coffee was all he was going to get.

'I came last night,' he said.

'I was out.'

'You don't often go out at night.'

'No, I don't. This had to do with my work.'

Why am I explaining things?

He watched her over the steaming rim of the coffee mug. 'You're very attractive,' he said.

'Thank you.'

'I really mean it. You know it was me who found you first.'

'Found? You mean like some lost creature here in the Hampstead jungle?'

He had a habit of flicking his nail against the coffee mug. Flick . . . flick . . .

'A joke, Mitchell.'

'Yes, I know. But don't you remember? I met you at the Newbolds' party. You were only about twenty-one.'

'No, I'm sorry, I don't remember.'

'Surely –'

'No, I don't.'

'And I introduced you to Dick.'

'I don't think so. I met Richard at North London General.'

Flick . . . flick . . . went the finger.

'No, I remember it clearly. It was at the tennis club in Frognal.'

'Please, Mitchell. If I thought we had met socially I would never have taken you on as a patient.'

She saw his eyes go cold. Mitchell Bourke, star of the silver screen, did not like going unremembered.

'I just wanted to remind you that I knew you before you met Dick and –'

'For God's sake stop calling him Dick! No one ever called him that.'

He shook his head stubbornly. 'I introduced you.'

'If you say so.' It seemed appropriate to agree and then he might leave. 'If you did I'm very grateful.'

'I don't want your gratitude.'

She was becoming irritated now.

'What *do* you want?'

'I want . . .' he paused.

Flick . . . flick . . .

'I want you to *know* . . .'

'Know what?'

'How I feel about you.'

'Mitchell, you've recently broken up with your wife. You feel lonely. Bereft. You'll get over it. You have in the past.'

'We didn't "break up" as you put it. She left me.'

'It's always damaging to the ego when a wife or a husband prefers someone else.'

'But she didn't prefer anyone else. There wasn't anyone else.'

'I see.'

'No, I don't think you do see. It's shattering. You can just live with the fact that she leaves you for someone else. But, Christ, if there's no one . . . No, you can't know what it was like to be someone like me. To have any woman I wanted. Yes, that's true. I could have had thousands. They couldn't wait to get into bed with me.'

Flick . . . flick . . . flick . . .

'Mitchell, this isn't really the time to –'

'I pay you to listen. I'll pay you to listen now if you like. But I thought you were a friend as well as a therapist.'

'Look, I have a lot on my plate just now and –'

'What? Tatting? Macramé? You never go out at night. I've watched. I know what you do. You're in bed by eleven and sometimes you read till two and three. You know what you need?'

'I'm sure you're going to tell me. You're going to say I need a man. That's what all men say about women who live alone. And the man you think I need is you. Right?'

'Are you seeing anyone?'

'That's none of your business.' She rose. 'Now if you don't mind I've got a great deal of work to do.'

'I'm sorry. I didn't mean to upset you.'

He did not rise and his apology did not sound sincere.

What was Mitchell up to?

'It's not the policeman, is it?'

'Is what?'

'Ferry. Are you seeing him?'

'I'm working with the police on the Vale of Health murder. I can't discuss it.'

'He told me you were but I didn't believe him at first.'

'You've seen him?'

'He brought me in for questioning.' He looked up at her and she thought his expression had become . . . sly? 'That was your fault.'

'How mine?'

'You spoke to me outside the house.'

'What was I supposed to do? Ignore you? And why do you say "fault"? You said you knew the women. It's only reasonable he should want to know more.'

'Maybe he thinks I did it.'

'Did you?'

'What do you think? You're my shrink, do you think it's possible for me to have murdered them?'

'I suppose it's possible for anyone to murder anyone.'

'That's not the question. What do you think?'

'Why do you want to know?'

'Oh Christ, not that. That's what we keep for the sessions. Every time I say something you repeat it; make me analyse it.'

'You brought it up, not me. When did you see Ferry?'

'Yesterday. He wanted to know where I got the money to buy a new car – since I'm out of work.'

'And where did you?'

'A legacy. An aunt in Australia.'

'I see. You didn't mention that.'

'I don't mention *everything*. He also wanted to know if I knew anything about antiques.'

'And do you?'

'Oh, yes, quite a lot. I used to do a bit of buying and selling to keep the wolf from the door. That was before I became a success. He thinks I'm lying. I can see that.'

'Are you?'

'I said stop that!'

He rose to his feet and without thinking she stepped backwards.

'I must be off. Oh, yes, there was one other thing. Christmas Day. What are you doing for Christmas? I thought we might do something together. We're both alone.'

'I'm going out to So — I'm sorry, Mitchell, but I'm booked up.'

'Oh. Okay. Well . . . goodnight, Hannah.' He paused at the door. 'I'll be seeing you.'

FOURTEEN

Hannah stood at the window, hidden partly by the curtains, and watched Mitchell go back to his car. It was a large Jaguar, just the kind of status symbol he would have bought, she thought. With the legacy? From the aunt in Australia?

There was something off-key about him she had not noticed before. A sly confidence. Up to now he had just been Mitchell Bourke the has-been leading man who was in need of an ego massage. Not any longer.

She phoned London North and this time she got through to Ferry.

'I've just had a visit from Mitchell Bourke.'

'I've had him in and we had a little chat.'

'What did you make of him?'

'Difficult to say. I don't meet actors much. They're strange. He seemed to be talking to someone over my shoulder.'

'He does the same with me.'

'Have you changed your mind?'

'About what?'

'You said what was between you and him was privileged.'

'It is.'

'Could you answer one question? This is just an opinion: do you think he could have killed the women?'

'That's exactly what he asked me. Almost the precise words.'

'And what did you tell him?'

'I told him anyone could kill anyone.'

'Well, that's the truth.'

'The real reason I called is that I've carried out more tests on the boy and I think it possible we were wrong.'

'We?'

'Me, then.'

'About what?'

'About him being autistic.'

There was a pause and then he said, 'I thought you were so sure. I thought you said –'

'I know what I said! But one can never be positive in a case like this. I'm telling you that he probably isn't.'

'Then, doctor, if I may ask, what the hell have you been doing all this time?'

'Finding out precisely that!'

'Why is he like he is then? I mean he's a bloody zombie as far as I'm concerned.'

'There could be several reasons and I'm working on them, but the point I'm making is that I think it's possible to get into his mind and if he did see something, it's possible we can retrieve it.'

'You make it sound like a computer.'

'It is in a way. It's like a limbo file. We have to find the code to bring it back.'

Ferry's voice suddenly became animated. 'Do you think you can?'

'It might take some time but at least there could be a reward at the end. Whereas if he is autistic there is no way we could trust whatever he said even if he could make himself understood.'

'Does that mean you'll have to change your methods?'

'Somewhat.'

'But you're reasonably certain?'

'Yes.'

'Terrific.'

Ferry put down the phone with a rush of elation. He pulled a memo sheet from his drawer and began to write a note to Begg. This was what he had wanted; something to show the bastard he was on top of the case.

'Inspector Ferry,' a voice said.

He looked up and saw a short, bespectacled, plain-clothes officer standing at his desk.

'I'm Bainbridge. Forensic. What d'you want done about this?'

He placed a silver cigarette box on Ferry's desk.

'What is it?'

'It's from the Vale of Health house. One of your officers said there was a stain underneath. Might have been blood. We brought it in for testing.'

'Was it?'

'Red wine.'

'So?' Ferry was trying to maintain his train of thought.

'It's got to go back.'

'Okay, leave it with me. I'll see it gets back.'

Bainbridge stood by the side of the desk for a moment and then said, 'That's the second time it's been out for testing.'

'What? . . . Yeah, okay . . . Just leave it.'

Bainbridge shrugged, put the box on Ferry's desk, and went out. Ferry locked it in his drawer and went back to composing the memo to Begg. It was giving him a great deal of satisfaction.

The phone call to Ferry helped Hannah. At least she had shared her unease about Mitchell without breaching the doctor-patient relationship.

She paced the apartment, tried to settle to her journal but couldn't. Finally she picked up the phone and dialled Duncan Wylie's number. His voice sounded slightly blurred.

'I've been thinking about the documentary,' she said.

'And?'

'I've decided I'll do it.'

'That's great.'

'But I'd like to see the interview you did with the old lady in Wales. The one you told me about. Just to get some idea of how you'll go about it.'

'Gladly, but I don't want to do another like that. It was formal. I'd want something more relaxed. With you and the boy. And not in your office.'

'That makes things difficult. Where?'

'I don't know off-hand. I'd have to think.'

'I'm going to have him for Christmas Day. If you have a free hour –'

'Christmas Day.'

'I realise it'll be difficult. It was just a thought. You're probably going to friends.'

'No, I'm not. Is it just you and the boy?'

'Yes.'

'Look, why don't we spend the day together? I know! Let's have a picnic, the three of us.'

'In midwinter?'

'Why not? In the old days people used to go to Box Hill on Christmas Day. And if there was snow they'd toboggan. Now the whole country closes up. It's the dreariest day of the year.'

'I don't think it's a good idea. Not with a small child.'

'Listen, we'll have a barbecue, a proper one. The boy will love it and it'll make wonderful pictures.'

'I've got a better idea,' she said. It had come bursting out before she could stop it. 'We . . . I mean, I've got a boat in Suffolk. It was my husband's really. Why don't we drive up there instead?'

'Brilliant! We can have the barbecue there. Marvellous backgrounds for the camera.'

'And a different set of stimuli for him.'

When she put down the phone the expected reaction did not come. She thought she would have been frightened. The boat was something she had put off and put off. Several times she had had phone calls from the man who had looked after it when Richard was alive, telling her that this had to be done or that. And she had said just do it. The boat was a minefield. It still contained clothing that had belonged to Richard and Tom. With Wylie and the boy there she could sort everything out without so much pain. It was often the case that a stranger was better company in a situation like that than a friend.

She felt a sudden surge of optimism. A month ago she had been dreading Christmas. Now it had all moved into a different dimension.

As she lay in bed that night she began to plan the food. She'd ring Wylie in the morning and ask him what he needed for a barbecue. In her mind's eye she saw the three of them in the car travelling to Suffolk, then on the boat, then walking along the beach at Dunwich. But the images in her mind were of Richard and Tom and she smiled to herself.

She woke once during the night and thought: the police will never let me do it, the social services will never let me do it. And then she thought: they'll never know if I don't tell them.

'Christmas Day?' Mrs Brind said when she brought the boy for the next session. 'Well, I don't know.'

'It'll be a break for you and someone to keep me company. I'm alone this Christmas.'

'Yes, I . . . well, I didn't like to say anything but . . .' There was relief on Mrs Brind's face. 'We've got a horde of family coming, some of them not much older than the boy. And I've been worried about him. I don't know how he'll take to a crowd.'

Hannah turned to the boy, 'We're going on a picnic. I wonder if you've ever been on one.'

Mrs Brind was surprised. 'In midwinter?'

'Not an outside picnic. I've . . .' It slipped out more easily this time. 'I've got a boat in Suffolk. It's on the Blythe at Holness.'

'Oh, I know it! It's beautiful up there. We used to go to Southwold for our holidays when I was little. He'll love it. But what about social services? Do you think they'll agree?'

'Can you imagine Ms Challis agreeing to anything like this?'

'No, I can't.'

'Well, then, I don't think social services need to know, do you?'

'River buses!' Albert Ferry said. 'They didn't have no river buses in my day.'

It was a cold Sunday morning and Peter Ferry and his father were waiting for the river bus at Charing Cross Pier.

Peter rubbed his hands and stuck them in his pockets. The river bus was late.

'Six quid each,' the old man said. 'That's what he charged us, didn't he? Six quid just to go down to Greenwich.'

'It's an "explorer" ticket, Dad. Not just a straight ticket. We can stay on the river bus all day if we want to with this ticket. And we can go up and down as often as we like. If we want to we can go to Chelsea Harbour.'

'It's all Arabs.'

'What's all Arabs?'

'That live at Chelsea Harbour. They're the only ones with enough money.'

'You know this for a fact, do you? I mean, you go visiting there? Know the people?'

'I read it.'

'Jesus, you got out on the wrong side of bed this morning.'

The river bus arrived and they started down towards Tower Bridge. They were the only two in the fast catamaran. It was a sentimental journey which Ferry had promised his father; now he was regretting it.

The river was grey under a cold grey sky. They entered the Pool of London. Two barges were moored in the stream.

'It's dead,' Albert said. 'When I worked here there were ships lying two abreast waiting for an unloading berth. Progress!'

'Well, what can you do if the ships don't come any more?'

They stayed on the river bus as far as Greenwich, had a drink at a pub in the High Road, and then caught another river bus to the old West India Docks.

'This is where I came every morning for all my working life,' Albert said. 'Don't even recognise the place now. It was all cranes. Now it's all blocks of bleedin' flats.'

They wandered round the old docks. It had been transformed, but not well transformed.

'The old life's gone,' Albert said. 'But what have they put in its place?'

It was true, Ferry thought. He'd grown up half a mile from here. He didn't recognise it either. It was part yuppieland, part building site. There were no corner shops, no old-fashioned pubs, nothing that made it a community as it once had been. He had to remind himself that it had stood vacant and derelict for years and years while the planners made up their minds – but even so it still looked dead.

They wandered around it for an hour, Albert trying to find landmarks that would give him some link to his early life, and failing.

'Let's go and have a drink somewhere decent,' he said.

They walked back towards the commuter pier through deserted streets and between vast new blocks of luxury flats, half of which were empty.

They turned the corner of one such block and walked straight into Begg and a young woman.

''Morning, guv'nor,' Ferry said, embarrassed.

He introduced his father and waited for Begg to introduce the woman, but Begg, looking impatient, made no move. Instead he said, 'Sight-seeing?'

'Bringing my dad to see his old haunts,' Ferry said.

'I'm Mandy,' the young woman said.

Ferry had been taking covert glances at her. She was one of the most sexually attractive women he'd seen for a long time; tall, with a white sweater that showed off her breasts, a leather jacket slung over her shoulders and long leather boots.

'My father used to work on the ships here,' Ferry said.

'When there was ships,' Albert said. 'It's all . . .' he indicated the blocks of flats, '. . . all City gents now.'

Mandy watched them with a half-smile on her lips. Ferry noticed that her eyes were slightly watery. The four of them stood uneasily for a second then Begg said, 'Well, don't let us –'

'We was just going to find a place for a pint,' Albert said. 'All the old pubs are gone.'

'Come up and have a drink with us,' Mandy said. 'The sun's over the yardarm, as we say in these parts.'

Her voice was thick, Ferry thought, and sounded as though she'd had a few.

Begg frowned, looked at his watch and said, 'I don't think we have time to –'

'Of course we do, darling.' She put her hand on Begg's arm and smiled at Ferry. 'Your father can see everything from our balcony.'

They went up in the lift, the men looking at their feet.

Ferry was struck by the modern furniture, the yellow and

browns of the curtains and carpets. He wondered if she worked in the City. They paid women enormous salaries there, he'd been told.

Begg took them out onto the balcony pointing out where the old docks had been.

Albert was speechless. To him it was devastation on a grand scale. 'Looks like it was bombed and rebuilt,' he said.

Mandy came out with a jug of martinis and gave them each a glass. Albert drank his suspiciously.

'It's a damned sight better than it was,' Begg said.

'I grew up only a few streets away,' Ferry said. 'You couldn't bring up kids here any more.'

'But you got out,' Begg said. 'I mean before all this building started. Don't you live in Holloway?'

'We were kicked out!' Ferry said. 'Our house was torn down to make room for all . . . all this.'

'But they must have offered you alternative accommodation.'

'On a council estate?' Ferry said scornfully. 'We could never live in one of those.'

'Families go up and they go down,' Mandy said, and smiled to herself as though at a private joke.

They finished their drinks and left. Begg came to the lift with them. 'Anything new I should know about? I mean about the boy. Is he talking yet?'

'Not yet. But soon, they think.'

Albert and Ferry walked down to the pier and waited for a river bus. Ferry turned and looked back at the block of flats.

'The dirty old bugger!' he said out loud.

FIFTEEN

Christmas Day was crisp and sunny. Hannah had gone to see Sophie the night before to take a present and to check that she was all right. Then she had come home and prepared the picnic basket. Wylie was at the apartment by eight o'clock on Christmas morning and they had picked up the boy twenty minutes later.

London was like a city of the dead. There was hardly a car moving in the streets, even the M25 was empty. In less than a couple of hours they were up on the Suffolk coast. They didn't speak much on the drive, for Wylie's big camper was noisy and in any case Hannah, for the first time in weeks, felt herself relaxing.

She had become used to having the boy with her; the solemn, still face and empty eyes no longer disturbed her as they had in the beginning. But each time she saw him she longed to find the key that would unlock his mind.

The village of Holness lay off the main road and they were there soon after eleven. The North Sea was less than half a mile away and the village nestled on the edge of marshy land and was surrounded by creeks and thick reed beds. A great church, built of flint, occupied its centre, below which was a creek which joined up with several others linking it to the sea.

Hannah's boat was moored below the church and they made their way down to it past the old gravestones.

The sun was intermittent. Every now and then the village and the reed beds were engulfed by banks of sea fog rolling inland on a north-easterly breeze.

'We've got it to ourselves,' Wylie said as they reached the boat. 'Or almost . . .' He paused and they heard shots in the distance.

'Wildfowlers? On Christmas Day?'

'Doesn't make any difference. If mallard and teal are flighting there'll be poachers.' He indicated the creek. 'Have you got the whole mooring stretch?'

'The other boats are laid up for winter. I should have got round to it.'

'I'm glad you didn't.'

The boat was tied up to a high, reedy bank and they could step down onto her deck.

'Nice,' Wylie said.

'I'm afraid she's very neglected.'

She was a forty-foot auxiliary sailer built more for comfort than for speed. 'We really use her – used her – as a houseboat,' she said. 'I'm not much of a sailor.'

'Nor am I. The sea scares me.'

'It was rather like having a country cottage. And we chose Suffolk because Richard liked to look at birds.'

Wylie looked around him and said, 'The fog's complicated the filming a bit. I think I'll shoot atmosphere footage of you both and then later we can do an interview in your consulting rooms. If that's okay?'

'Fine.'

She unlocked the boat and they opened it up. It smelled musty and damp and there was mildew. She found herself suddenly tense. Every view brought back memories of Richard and Tom. There was a large saloon with a table in the middle and bunks on either side. Further on was a galley. She began to open ventilators and hatches.

'I haven't been near here for eighteen months,' she said.

'Is that when it happened?'

She opened lockers in the galley and looked in. There was rust everywhere.

'When what happened?'

'I looked you up. There was an accident.'

'Yes. About eighteen months ago. No, not "about" – exactly eighteen months and two weeks and three days.' She turned to the boy. 'Come on, darling, we'll help Duncan. May I call you Duncan? Mr Wylie seems a bit formal for Christmas Day in the Suffolk marshes.'

'Of course.'

He built a fireplace on the bank out of large stones, then took the boy by the hand and they walked along the creek picking up driftwood. Wylie would pick up a piece and give it to him to hold. At first the boy dropped it but Wylie said gently, 'No, don't do that. Look. Hold it like this.' After a while he held the pieces of driftwood but Hannah couldn't tell whether it was purely rote or not. All the while, Wylie was using the lightweight video camera.

Hannah watched them for a few moments. They looked so like Richard and Tom going off along the bank that a lump came into her throat. She began to go through the lockers making a pile of clothing and blankets to be carried back to the car.

When they returned she had a dark blue Guernsey pullover in her hands and held it against the boy's chest. He took several shots of her doing that.

'It'll fit perfectly,' she said. 'Would you like it? Okay, it's yours.'

'How old was Tom?' Wylie said.

'Six.'

He lit the fire and soon flames were leaping up. Hannah cut up tomatoes and buttered bread. The boy sat watching.

'We're going to have a barbecue,' she said to him. 'A real barbecue like Duncan has in Africa.' She took his hand and they stood in the warmth of the fire as it burned down to hot embers.

Wylie went on filming, then let her use the camera. Finally he said, 'That's enough for the time being. I'll give you a break.'

He had brought champagne in a cool bag and the bottles were beaded with moisture. When the sun was out it was almost warm enough to be autumn; brilliant, bright weather, then as the fog rolled in it would grow dank and cold.

He grilled chops, spicy Cumberland sausage and hamburgers, which Hannah had made because she thought the boy might prefer them.

'I haven't done this for a long time either,' he said. 'Ready?'

He gave them sausages and a hamburger each. She watched the boy eat. He seemed to get on all right.

'Was it with Ellie?' she said.

He was standing across the fire from her, the smoke blowing past him. In his heavy sheepskin coat and untidy hair he looked like a nomad at his campfire.

'The night before she died.'

'I didn't realise. I'm sorry. You mentioned her name the other day.'

'We were filming elephants in south-east Africa. There's a sub-species there, survivors of the nineteenth-century holocaust when most of the elephants were wiped out for their ivory. They live in bush near the coast. It's so thick you can hardly see a yard ahead of you. The only way to get in is to use the logging tracks.

'There aren't many elephants left. Maybe a couple of dozen. No one really knows for sure.

'We'd been trying to film a lone bull for a couple of days and he'd been getting increasingly irritated with us. They get like that in old age: infested by parasites, some with injuries to their feet, most of them with osteoarthritis.'

She looked surprised.

'Oh, yes, animals get that too. Anyway we'd been following him all morning. He kept on appearing and reappearing and flapping his ears and pretending to charge and then not charging. And I'd just said to Ellie that elephants didn't charge vehicles, when he came out and turned us over and one of his tusks went through the open window and killed her.'

She stared at him, not knowing what to say. He threw a chop bone onto the fire.

'That's a terrible story,' she said.

She excused herself and went to fetch the pudding. She wanted to be alone to adjust to what he had told her. It had been so starkly told she had not known how to reply. He seemed not to need or want sympathy. After a few moments she returned.

'It wouldn't be Christmas without proper pudding.'

She cut slices and fried them in butter. They ate them with cream.

'Now your turn,' he said.

'I don't talk about it. Anything else but that.'

'Why not?'

'I just don't, that's all.'

'Isn't it your job to expose what others want to bury? To bring it all out into the open?'

'Probably.'

'But not for yourself?'

'Probably not.'

'Let me say one thing more: how the hell are you going to treat someone like the boy if you can't treat yourself?'

'Very good. Physician heal thyself. You're not the first to suggest that, by the way.'

'They died in France; it said so in *The Times*.'

'You know, Duncan, parlour psychiatrists are clichés. You really shouldn't –'

'"Noted psychiatrist and son die in boating accident." The headline was something like that. But it was only a small story, short on detail.'

She said, 'And even then they got it wrong. They said there was a boat. There wasn't a boat. They said it was the Lot. It wasn't the Lot, it was the Dordogne. They said Tom was seven, he was six. They even managed to get the names of Richard's books wrong.'

She seemed to be standing outside herself, looking at herself. She was talking about the one thing she never talked about. Never! She had begun even before she realised it.

Ever since they had spent the winter in France while Richard wrote his first book, it was the country they loved most for holidays. But because of Tom they had to plan carefully. There was never any question of taking him to a hotel so they usually rented a cottage. They had been several times to Brittany, and the South of France. But on the final holiday they took a *gîte* on the middle Dordogne near the Crusader village of Carriac. They knew nothing about the place when they arrived but almost instantly Richard discovered something that he wanted to pursue.

In the 1960s the village had been struck by tragedy. It lies under high yellow cliffs, a triple row of houses occupying the space between the cliffs and the great green river. After weeks of rain the cliffs above the central part of the village collapsed, killing a dozen people and knocking half a dozen houses, their contents and their gardens, into the river.

The village still contained relatives and friends of the dead and Richard, whose French was excellent, began to interview them: what did they remember? how had they suffered physically and mentally? how had it changed their lives emotionally?

She had been delighted he had found an interest because he was a restless holidaymaker. So in the cool of the mornings he would go off with his notebook and pencil while Hannah spent a couple of hours working with Tom. Then in the noon heat they would meet on the little beach that lay just below the village. This was no more than a large sandbank but summer traders had colonised it. There was a stall selling merguez sausages, another pancakes, and a third cold beer and fruit drinks. Hannah usually hired deck chairs and a sunshade and they had their lunch there.

Tom was not a bucket-and-spade child. They had tried it once on a Brittany beach and he had used his bucket to attempt to brain another small boy. He couldn't and perhaps might never swim, but he loved the water once he had made up his mind that it was not dangerous.

Soon Richard found a way of entertaining him. He would walk upstream along the bank carrying him on his shoulders, then wade in until the water grew deep and, keeping Tom where he was, float down on the swift current.

Hannah would sit in her chair and watch them come sweeping down a long bend towards her, the small boy on his father's shoulders.

'I watched them go up along the bank as usual,' she said to Wylie. 'Tom on Richard's shoulders. It was the first swim of the day. Then I bought the lunch and carried it back to the chairs. It took me about five minutes, and they should have been coming out of the water.

'But they weren't. And I thought: they must have gone further downstream. But I couldn't see anyone. I mean, all the French people – and there weren't many at the little *plage* – all of them were eating their lunches. No one was in the water.'

167

She and Wylie and the boy went back into the boat and she made coffee. She did so like an automaton, never stopping in her detailed recollection. Everything was in her story, weather, time of day, colour of water, temperature. To Wylie it sounded obsessive.

'I thought they must have gone into the village. But it didn't seem logical. They would have done that *before* entering the water. The current was far too strong to swim against.

'After about ten minutes I began to get really worried. Then I heard people shouting.' She paused. 'When something is affecting you or your family, you *know*. I knew that the shouting had to do with Richard and Tom.

'A Dutch tourist driving along the river had seen Tom's body being washed into a little backwater. It was only once we managed to get Richard out that we were able to piece everything together.

'The police thought that when the rockfall swept the houses into the river it also swept in their fences. And lying on the bottom, just waiting for someone like Richard, was a snarl-up of barbed wire. It caught his dangling legs, held him and the current instantly pulled him under. He must have released Tom hoping he would get to the shore. And then he drowned. Both of them drowned.'

She stared down into the mug of coffee and swirled the last of it round and round.

'Tom just looked as though he had gone to sleep,' she said. 'There were no marks on him. But Richard was badly torn. Long gashes in his legs, holes in his feet, as though the struggle caused the wire to work deeper and deeper. He wasn't bleeding any more by the time they managed to release him.'

She began to shake and hastily put the mug down on the table top.

'It's difficult to describe just what it felt like then,' she went on. 'We'd gone down there on holiday, three of us, a family, and in less than five minutes there was only one of us. I wished for a long time that I'd died with them.'

'Do you still?' Wylie said.

She sat down on the bunk opposite him.

'Sometimes I do. Did you?'

'For a time. But the will to live is powerful. Anyway, you're doing something useful. That must help.'

'Yes, it does.'

'I don't quite understand about Tom. It sounds as though there was something wrong with him. You mention the fact that he couldn't go to hotels, that kind of thing.'

'Tom was autistic. Really autistic. No question about it.'

He paused. 'So because of Tom the social services asked you —'

'No. They never knew about Tom. They asked my mother-in-law to look at the boy. She's a child psychiatrist. But she's very ill so she passed him on to me. I'm something of an expert, you see.'

She put her hand up and brushed back her hair. 'God, I must stop this! And why to you? I haven't even told her all the details and Richard was her son.'

'People often tell strangers more than they would their friends. Haven't you found that?' She nodded. 'And I had shared Ellie with you. Maybe that had something to do with it.'

He rummaged in his bag and brought out a bottle of whisky.

'No, really —' she said.

'Medicinal. I'll have one too.'

She sipped the whisky and felt its warmth and said, 'But all that detail. The wounds. I never thought I'd ever speak about those.'

'Do you feel better?'

'Not just at this moment. I feel raw, as though someone had rubbed my psyche with a cheese grater. Wouldn't it be lovely if catharsis was instant and reliable.'

The whisky put colour in her cheeks and she said, 'I feel like I'm waking up after dozing. Maybe that's how my patients feel sometimes.' She looked around. 'Where's the boy?'

'Jesus, I was so riveted I didn't even notice him go!'

Wylie ran up on deck, Hannah followed.

The boy was in the cockpit. It had seats on three sides. The bulkheads were painted white. Next to the boy, on the white paint, was a drawing.

Hannah looked at it in amazement.

169

Wylie said, 'It wasn't there when we came down for coffee!'

There was no doubt that with its circles and curlicues and squiggles it was the same kind of drawing she had seen in the house.

She bent and held the boy's hands. 'That's wonderful,' she said. 'It's marvellous. Won't you do another?'

But the boy, if he understood or even guessed at what she was saying, sat like a rock, his eyes blank.

'Why?' she said to Wylie. 'Why now?'

'Maybe he just felt like it.'

'And what did he use? Did you give him a pencil?'

'No, and anyway that's not been done with a pencil.'

She looked more closely. 'It's a ballpoint of some sort. Did you have one?'

'I usually carry one.' He pulled a bright green Pentel from his pocket.

The boy turned suddenly, his eyes quick and alive.

'Duncan, give him the pen!'

Wylie held it out to him. 'It's yours.'

As though fearing reprisal, the boy hesitantly put out his hand, and took the pen. Hannah dashed down into the cabin and came back with a notebook. 'Here, darling,' she said. 'Take it. Draw!'

He would not take the notebook. She held his hand. 'Come down into the cabin and draw there. It's warmer.' As she led him away she said softly to Wylie over her shoulder. 'See if you can find the other pen.'

She settled the boy at the table. 'You can draw now. As much as you like.'

Wylie followed them down. He held up a second green Pentel. 'It was under one of the cushions where he was sitting. He must have hidden it there.'

The boy had turned. His eyes were fixed on the pen.

'Give it to him,' she said.

Wylie passed him the pen. In a flash it was gone.

'He's sitting on both,' she said.

'I think I know where he got it. He was in the back of the camper when we drove here. It must have been lying around. I usually have one or two.'

'It's the trigger,' she said. 'Or, I should say, another trigger. It must have been the same as the pens he had in the house. Green Pentels. He hasn't been interested in anything I gave him, not pencils, not crayons, just this.'

'If he wanted to draw, why hide it?'

'He'd hidden it from *us*! Don't you see? The women must first have given him the pens to keep him quiet. Then maybe if they thought he was being – in their eyes – naughty or intransigent they'd take them away . . . And they were all he had. Day after day, month in and month out . . . all he had were the pens. They let him draw. That was the one thing he could do. All over the walls, all over everything . . . Then – bad boy! And they took them away. And now he's found them again. Bright green. Distinctive.'

'And he thinks we may take them away again like the women did!'

'Triggers,' she said. 'That's what it's all about. Something on TV triggered the attack. A bright green pen triggers a drawing because that's the pen he's used to.'

'And so when he finds a pen he hides it.'

'Absolutely. Tom used to hide things too. I think if it hadn't been for your film this behaviour would have strengthened my belief that the boy was autistic. But as it is it shows he's thinking, planning.

'If only we knew how long he'd been locked away. I've been checking on a child they called Genie in California. She'd been locked away for years and was thirteen when she was found in the early seventies. Thank God the boy's so young.'

He frowned. 'I should have thought that would make it worse.'

'Not if he was exposed to language before he was locked away. Language is acquired early. If for some reason – like your Wild Boy of Aveyron who wasn't in contact with human beings because he was in a forest, or Genie, who was purposely kept out of human contact – a child is prevented from learning to speak, then there comes a time around puberty when it may be difficult, if not impossible, to learn a first language at all. It has to do with the hemispheres of the brain and it's called

171

lateralisation.' She smiled. 'You probably think that's just psychobabble but it's a fascinating subject.'

'So what can you do now? I mean, now you think he's not autistic.'

'Try to adapt for him the process of learning they developed for Genie. She'd been locked away by her father because he thought she was retarded. She was tied naked to a potty-chair and left like that, even at night. When she was found at thirteen she couldn't chew food, stand upright or control her functions. Mrs Brind says the boy won't chew unfamiliar food and —'

'My younger brother wouldn't eat unfamiliar food when he was a child. He'd spit it out. But he hadn't been locked away or lived in a forest. He was just bloody-minded.'

'There are other similarities like —'

'I seem to recall you found similarities between him and autistic children; now you're doing the same thing with wild children.'

'All right! You tell me!'

When he didn't reply she said, 'Psychiatry isn't an exact science. We're groping in the dark. That's all we can do. But we've made some breakthroughs: we know that with the boy there are triggers that set off behaviour patterns; we know he can understand certain things; we know he can see and hear and feel and plan; now it's a question of finding out if he can bring out what language he may have known.

'Look, in a few years they taught Genie to speak. It wasn't very sophisticated, about the level of a five-year-old but they did teach her. And remember this was a really terrible case of deprivation. I came across another case, this time of a mute child of six who lived in isolation with his mute mother. He was taught to speak normally in two years. So you see the boy is the right age, thank God, and anyway he may not have been deprived totally of human speech.'

'Aren't you being optimistic? The Wild Boy of Aveyron never spoke even though Dr Itard worked with him for years.'

'How else can I approach it? Of course I must be optimistic. What the boy needs is sympathy and love and care — lots of it. And I can give him all of those things.'

'What about the Brinds?'

'What about them?'

'They're already giving him love and sympathy.'

'I know . . . I know . . . Yes, of course they are.'

He waited for her to continue but she did not say anything more. 'What about a walk before it gets too late?' he said.

She took off the boy's pullover which had been supplied by social services and put on Tom's Guernsey. As she was adjusting it she felt his body. He'd put on weight. His head no longer seemed too large for his neck. Surreptitiously she felt for the green pens but could not locate them.

The three of them walked along a path through the marshes. 'You know, this Christmas has been far better than I could ever have expected,' she said.

'Maybe it's because you've stopped holding everything back.'

'Maybe.'

They were soon surrounded by high feathery reeds and there was water on either side of the path, which had become more like the flat top of a dyke. She had not exaggerated. The day *had* been much better than expected. Certainly a different Christmas from the last, when she had driven aimlessly around the Home Counties until nightfall.

They came to a shingle beach. Others were out walking off their Christmas dinners and she thought how well the three of them fitted into the family atmosphere. The boy looked just like any other small boy.

'I wish we knew his name,' she said to Wylie. 'Dr Itard called the wild boy Victor. The trouble with a nameless human being is that it's difficult to empathise.'

'You seemed to have overcome that.'

'What do you mean?'

'Only that you're showing him the kind of warmth he needs.'

'I wonder what his name really is, and if we'll ever find out.'

'Probably John. That's the most popular, isn't it?'

'He doesn't look like John to me.'

On the beach there were dogs. One particularly big one with an unmistakable Rottweiler face came bouncing towards them. He wasn't much more than a large overfriendly puppy but the boy was instantly afraid and for the first time he put his hand in hers.

'It's all right, darling, we won't let him hurt you.'

The dog bounced on past them chasing a tennis ball.

They walked for a mile in the deep slithery shingle watching the North Sea beat itself into brown froth on the beach. When the sun broke through they could see the fog banks. Apart from the hissing of the water, the only other sounds came from the wildfowlers and the mournful foghorn at the lighthouse on Holness Point.

They took a different way back to the boat. This was wilder, with denser reeds and long tunnels of water.

Wylie said, 'They used to say that in the old days people who lived in marshy areas like this had webbed feet.'

They started to see birds: avocets, shell duck, and dunlin with the last of a red sun glittering on their plumage.

Wylie said, 'I want to go ahead and get the camera. I'd like a couple of shots of you and the boy coming to the boat.'

She pointed him in the right direction and told him to keep the church on his left. It towered over the countryside, seeming to rise out of the marsh itself.

One moment Wylie was there, the next he had vanished through the wall of reeds.

'I wish you had a name,' she said to the boy. 'What about Matthew? Or Christopher? Look! There's a duck.'

She pointed to the water almost at their feet. But when she looked more closely she saw it was a lifelike model of the kind hunters set out as decoys.

She heard the noise of water lapping. Then, like something from Arthurian legend, a punt slid quietly into view. It was empty. It came on silently towards them. There was something frightening about it that froze her blood.

A man seemed to materialize out of the water and the reeds. He rose up. He turned. He was wearing chest waders and a shooting coat and cap. As he turned she saw his face was covered by a woollen balaclava. Only his eyes and mouth were uncovered.

She stared, transfixed.

He had a shotgun in his hands. He put it to his shoulder. It seemed to be pointing at them. She opened her mouth to scream. Fog engulfed them. She grabbed the boy and threw him to the ground. The gun fired. She saw flashes from its barrels and heard the shot roar into the reeds behind her. Then she had caught the boy's hand and they ran towards the boat.

They were almost there when the figure reappeared.

He was standing on the pathway in the swirling fog. Waiting for them.

She turned and, pulling the boy with her, found another path.

'Come closer,' Wylie's voice said. 'I can hardly see you from here.'

SIXTEEN

Hannah let her head sink back against the seat of the camper. They were on the motorway heading for London and night had come. She was exhausted. It should have been the simple tiredness of childhood after a day in the open but it was complicated by several things, especially The Incident of the Man with the Gun.

That was how she was to think of it, according to Wylie. An incident. An accident. They had been over and over it. From the moment she had run to him and blurted out what had happened they must have been over it five or six times.

Wylie had gone instantly into the reeds to search for the duck hunter, while she locked the boy and herself into the boat. Twenty minutes later he had returned. He had seen no one. If it hadn't been for the decoy duck in his hand she wondered if he might not have put it down to imagination.

'You'll find fifty of these in the marshes,' he'd said, holding out the decoy.

He made her tell it in detail: the fog, the empty punt, the man rising from the water.

Couldn't he have been straightening up from a bending position? And wasn't he several feet lower than she was? And could he not have seen *something* – perhaps a duck – for a fraction of a second before the fog closed in again?

Every winter wildfowlers were injured in shooting accidents, he'd said. So were grouse shooters by idiots firing down the line of butts, so were hunters in America at the opening of the season who mistook donkeys and sheep for elk and bighorns.

Anyway, why would a duck hunter have wanted to kill her? Because she was involved in a murder inquiry, that's why.

But only the Brinds knew where she was. Ralph Brind? In disguise?

When you were hunting, Wylie said, you saw what you expected to see; what you *wanted* to see. The man was hunting duck. There had been a movement in the fog. He'd seen a duck.

She thought about that. Grudgingly she came to the conclusion he might be right. Hadn't it happened recently in her own treatment of the boy? Hadn't she expected to see something and *had* seen it? Erroneously, as it turned out.

But still it nagged at her. She didn't like it happening there, in the place she had been so happy with Richard and Tom. Perhaps she should sell the boat.

The boy was sitting between Wylie and herself. He had fallen asleep and his head had come to rest on her shoulder. She sat very still in case he woke and removed it. She knew it was sentimental, but she was moved nevertheless.

Ralph Brind was still wearing his paper hat. She looked past him and saw the decorations in the hall. She had not put up any this year.

'My wife's taking a nap after all the festivities,' he said. 'Would you like to come in for a drink?'

'No thanks. We've had a long day too.'

She had her arm round the boy.

'He's got a couple of pens,' she said. 'I'd be grateful if you'd give him notebooks or a ream of paper. Just save everything for me.'

'He's never drawn before.'

'We didn't give him the right pens.'

She bent down and kissed the boy and then Ralph Brind said, 'The police phoned this morning. My wife took the call.'

'What was it about?'

'I don't know. We haven't had time to talk. Fifteen for Christmas lunch. They've only just left.'

When they got to her flat, she invited Wylie in for a drink. Gave him a whisky, poured a glass of wine for herself and checked her answering machine.

The first message was from Mitchell Bourke with Christmas greetings. There was something strange about the way he said it, the tone more than the words. The sly expression she had seen on his face seemed to have shifted to his voice. He ended by saying 'Have a good day, darling.'

It was the way he said it that made her uneasy – as though he knew she was *not* going to have a good day. And calling her darling. It was probably only actorspeak but she could not recall him using the term before.

The next message was from Ferry. 'I've got some news,' he said. 'Please phone me when you get in.'

She phoned London North but Ferry wasn't in. 'This is Detective Constable Holder, Dr Wilton. Inspector Ferry said I was to give you his home number. He's expecting your call.'

At Ferry's house the Christmas dinner was not ready.

'We should have gone out,' Ferry said, lifting the turkey onto the kitchen table and putting a skewer into its breast. Blood seeped from the hole.

'*Out?*' His father sounded indignant. 'You can't go out on Christmas Day. We've *never* been out on Christmas Day. Think what your mum would say.'

'Mum's not here any more.'

'Don't speak like that.'

'Well, she's not.'

'The only places open are your Chinese or Indian. You can't have Christmas dinner at one of them.'

'It'd be better than this. Look at that blood.'

'Try the other side.'

He put the skewer into the other breast.

'See? That's done. Let's eat that side.'

Albert was drinking a mixture of whisky and ginger wine and had been for many hours. He was unsteady on his feet. Ferry was drinking straight whisky.

'Jesus, what a bloody waste,' Ferry said. 'Look at the size of the thing. We'll never eat a whole turkey. Never. Not if we eat from now till Easter.'

'Turkey. Stuffing. Sprouts. Roast spuds. That's Christmas dinner. And I've got a proper tinned puddin'. I mean, if you'd told me you were working Christmas Day I'd have made different arrangements!'

'I didn't know, did I? Okay, I'll slice from this side. But don't blame me if we get salmonella. You're supposed to eat turkeys well cooked through. Same as chickens.'

The phone rang.

'Who'd that be on Christmas bleedin' night? If it's the station I'll –'

'I think I know.'

He went into the next room and took the call. 'Dr Wilton? Yeah . . . it's me. I left a message. Yeah. I got news. We found the kid's family.'

'What!' Hannah could not keep the excitement from her voice.

'Grandmother. There's no one else. Just the old lady.'

'Where . . . ? How . . . ?'

'Southsea. A neighbour phoned the police. Thought she recognised the boy from the newspaper pictures. We did the DNA grouping on the grandmother and got the mother's blood group from her medical records. It's within the main spread. The old lady says the boy would be six. Except she doubts he's alive. Doesn't understand about DNA – never heard of it, and wouldn't believe it if she had.'

'When did you hear?'

'Late last night.'

'But that's marvellous. Can you give me the details?'

'That's the problem. The old girl, well, she's . . . she's pretty depressed. Doesn't talk much. Influence of the Christmas season more than likely. She's in one of those nursing homes, you know, for the elderly. I'd be depressed if I was in one of those at Christmas time. Any time for that matter.'

He had dropped his voice so his father would not hear talk of nursing homes for the elderly.

'I went down this morning. Grotty sort of place. Everybody in paper hats, half of 'em asleep. The other half staring at the television.'

'Are you sure it's her? I mean the blood grouping isn't absolutely positive, is it?'

'All the other things fit. Her daughter was a single parent. She's dead, by the way. Brought the boy up to London. They were in Morgans, the big department store in Oxford Street. It was having a sale. She left him in the toy department while she went to buy towels. When she came back he was gone.'

'How terrible for her!'

'Yeah. Well, anyway, the old girl doesn't want to talk about it. That's where you come in.'

'How?'

'She might talk to you. I mean, you know the boy. You're treating him. You'll probably know how to talk to her.'

'I'm not sure about that.'

'The point is you're more likely to get something out of her than we are.'

'What sort of something?'

'Something to unlock the boy's brain, doctor. I'll give you the address.'

She wrote it down. 'I'll ring the matron and make an appointment.'

'The matron? Places like that don't have a matron.'

'Well, whoever's in charge.'

'Yeah. Do that . . .'

Just then his father shouted from the next room.

Ferry said to Hannah, 'I better go. Haven't had my own meal yet.'

'Did she tell you his name?'

'I'm coming!' Ferry said, holding his hand over the phone. 'What was that?'

'His name. Did she tell you his name?'

'David. David Haynes.'

Ferry put the phone down and went into the kitchen.

'I carved from the part that's done,' Albert said. 'It's getting cold. Here, pull.' He held out a Christmas cracker. They pulled that one, then a second. Albert unwrapped the hats that fell from the open crackers.

'You're not wanting us to wear them are you?' Ferry said.

'We always wore hats when your mother was alive.'

They put them on. Albert raised his glass and said, 'Merry Christmas, son.' And then, 'Absent friends.'

Ferry saw that he was crying.

'Come on, Dad. None of that.'

They ate in silence for a while then Albert said, 'Who the bloody hell was that?'

'The psychiatrist. I asked her to phone.' He gave his father brief details.

Albert began to munch on the Brussels sprouts. 'That Mr Begg phoned while you were out this morning.'

'What? Why didn't you tell me?'

'He just wanted to know if you were home. I said no. He said not to worry. He'd get you at the station.'

'The bastard! You know what that's all about? I told him I had to go to Southsea. Told him about the old lady. So he rings here, checking up!'

He got up, poured himself another whisky, sat down.

'He's really riding me, Dad. Waiting for one mistake before he puts the boot in. I've got to have a report on his desk every morning. Every bloody morning. Where is the boy? What's he doing? Every bloody detail. I said let's put a team on the Brinds' place. They can watch him night and day, even when he goes to the bleedin' toilet. Haven't got the manpower, he says. Christmas holidays. Flu. Too expensive anyway. But that's crap. He wants me on the job twenty-four hours in the day. Wants me to cock it up!'

'Eat up, son, it's Christmas dinner.'

'His name is David,' Hannah said to Wylie. She lingered on the name, tasting it.

She told him the substance of Ferry's call. Instantly Wylie said, 'I'm coming too. If that's okay?'

'Well, I –'

He had not been expecting the doubt in her voice. 'Why not?'

'I don't know if the police would want you to.'

'Did they say you weren't to take anyone else?'

'The subject didn't arise.'

'Well, then . . .'

'But if it had I don't think —'

'It didn't. End of story. Look this is a *must* for me. If you won't take me with you I'll find out some other way.'

'How?'

'I'll follow you.'

'Really?' She was icy.

'Hannah, don't object to things you don't have to object to. There's no reason why I shouldn't interview her too. If I found her and didn't tell the police, that would be different. But they've seen her. They've had first crack.'

'If you want to follow me there's no way I can stop you.'

'Oh, Jesus, I didn't really mean that. I wouldn't, and you know it.' He was becoming irritated too. 'You know you accused me, or suggested anyway, that I was exploiting the boy. Don't you think that you —'

'Don't call him that! He's not "the boy" any longer.'

'All right. David.'

She waited for him to continue. 'You were going to say something.'

'Nothing.' He rose. 'I must go.' At the door he said, 'Thank you for letting me come to the boat. It was a marvellous day for me. I'm sorry about the accident though.'

She recovered and smiled. 'Yes, it was a lovely day. Particularly for David. I don't think he even knew what was happening with the hunter.'

'You decide.'

'Yes, I'll be in touch.'

She stood at the window and watched him drive away. She realised, to her annoyance, that she was hiding behind the curtains, as though this had become a natural part of her life.

As she turned away the phone rang. It was harsh and strident in the silence and gave her a start.

'Hi,' the voice said. It was Mitchell.

Had he been out there watching and waiting? Had he seen Wylie come out of the apartment building and drive away? But where could he have got to a phone so quickly? And then she thought: a car phone? Part of the legacy?

'Did you have a nice Christmas?' Mitchell said.

'Yes. Very. I went on a picnic.'

'That's original. Especially in midwinter.'

'It was good. We had a barbecue. What about you? Did you have a nice day?'

The moment she asked she regretted it.

'A nice day? Oh, yes I had a lovely day. I spent it by myself, just as I'd planned. You know how it is, you really need to have some time to yourself and Christmas is it. I bought a lovely package dinner and a tiny plum pudding. Did you know you could buy tiny Christmas puddings? For people who live alone. I'm told it's a growth industry. And I went for a walk on the Heath and –'

'Don't, Mitchell.'

'And I'm now going to have a nice Christmas drink by myself unless you were to invite me over to have one with you.'

She did not answer. He waited.

'I'm tired, Mitchell. I'm going to bed.'

'Is it that wonderful outdoorsy feeling we used to have as kids? Or is there something not quite right about it?'

'What do you mean?'

'Why does everything have to *mean* something? See you Wednesday.' He put down the phone.

Hannah had a bath and got into bed. She found she couldn't sleep. She kept on seeing, in her mind's eye, the figure of the man rising out of the misty water. It was like a Pre-Raphaelite painting. Some lines of Keats' entered her mind: *The sedge is withered from the lake,/And no birds sing.*

Suppose Wylie was wrong?

But who would want to kill her?

Perhaps ... perhaps he didn't want to kill her; *perhaps he wanted to kill David.*

That was nonsense! These were the late-night horrors. You're an analyst, she told herself, analyse it.

The fact was that no one, apart from the Brinds, herself and Wylie, knew where David had been all those Christmas hours. And only they knew about the boat. There was no one else.

Was there?

SEVENTEEN

Southsea in the rain.

Hannah had finally agreed to let Wylie come with her to see old Mrs Haynes. She had no background for this kind of interview; it wasn't her normal session; it was more of a journalist's interview. She thought that in his job he must be used to knocking on doors and extracting information from reluctant subjects.

She and Richard used to play a game dividing the sexes into women he thought attractive enough to take to Monte Carlo and men she would go up the Amazon with. Wylie was that sort of man; the kind of man you would be pleased to have sitting next to you in an aircraft when the captain announced that they were having engine trouble.

Once they had left the motorway in mid-afternoon he said, 'I'll show you something.'

He had taken her on side roads until they came over the Downs. In the distance they could see squalls coming in across the Channel but the great Portsmouth naval base, which unrolled before them, was like a bronze engraving tinged with copper. An aircraft carrier was at her berth and there were more than a dozen frigates.

'My grandfather used to bring me here when I was a kid,' he said. 'He loved ships. He always used to imagine three-deckers sailing into harbour in line astern – home from blockading the French.'

The romantic image did not last into the streets of Southsea where the wind was whistling along the old terraces of red-brick Victorian villas and cat's paws of rain were bursting against the bow windows of parlours.

The Bella Vista Nursing Home (Prop: Beryl Spong, NNC) lay in a narrow back street, a stone's throw from the seafront. It consisted of two terraced houses knocked into one. Wylie had telephoned Miss Spong the day before. At first she had been cold and unwelcoming.

'I don't like my ladies disturbed,' she said. 'We had the police on Christmas Day. We've never had the police before.'

Then Wylie had mentioned the documentary.

'Did you say television, dear? What time would be convenient?'

Now he rang the bell and Miss Spong came to the door.

She was a short woman in her sixties, with close cropped hair parted on the side like a man's. She wore a nurse's uniform with a pencil and thermometer in her breast pocket and a clipboard in her hand. They looked to Hannah like stage props. Her face was round as a ball and her cheeks were ruddy, with the look of someone who has been in cold winds for long periods.

'What a day!' she said. 'My guests don't like it when it's like this. Do come in, dear.' Her manner was gracious but her voice, as her eyes, was like iron. 'I call them guests because that's what they are and that's how I treat them. Honoured guests in my home.'

Wylie introduced Hannah.

The cold eyes drilled into her. 'Good day to you, doctor. What a pleasure.'

They followed her down corridors that smelled of stale cooking and old age. They passed rooms where senile women were asleep in sagging armchairs, the rooms made bleaker by the cheap Christmas decorations hanging from the ceilings.

'I've put Mrs Haynes in my own private quarters,' said Miss Spong. 'You won't be interrupted there.'

Miss Spong's flat was in great contrast to the rest of the place. Money had been spent on it. Her sitting-room was bright, fluffy, extravagant. Like a child's room for the middle-aged. An elderly woman sat on a hard chair staring at nothing.

'Here we are, Cynthia,' Miss Spong said. 'Here's the gentleman from the television. He's going to make you a star, dear. And this is Dr Wilson.' She turned to Wylie. 'Where would you like us? On the sofa?'

It took some moments for Wylie to convince Miss Spong that there was to be only one star in this film. She left the room with a bad grace to see to her other 'guests'. All this time Mrs Haynes sat staring into space.

Wylie set up his equipment and the lights, checked the amount of tape he had and then said to Hannah, 'Okay.'

'My name's Dr Wilton,' she said. 'Not Wilson. But it doesn't matter. We've come to talk about David.'

Mrs Haynes was small and thin and sat erect, her hands in her lap. She was wearing a dull brown frock and her hair had been set in steel waves – almost certainly, Hannah thought, by Miss Spong for the great moment.

Hannah moved her chair to the left so that she could look directly into the old lady's face. The mauve eyes stared at her vacantly.

Hannah said, 'First of all I want to say how sorry I am about your daughter and about David.'

There was a slight rustling, like leaves blown on a paved terrace. It was Mrs Haynes speaking. She hardly seemed to move her lips and Hannah had to strain to hear her.

'Carol's dead,' she said. 'So's David.'

The sibilants hissed out through badly fitting teeth.

'Yes, we know that Carol's dead.' Hannah had turned to Wylie to bring him into the conversation, but he shook his head. This was to be her interview.

'So's David.'

'No, Mrs Haynes. David is alive. I know David. I talk to him. He's a lovely boy.'

The mauve eyes focused on her. 'He's dead. God's told me. He took him. He took Carol too.'

'Mrs Haynes, will you tell me what happened?'

'Why are you doing this to me? I want to die.'

'I'm sure that's not true.'

'They steal here.' She pulled out a small key on a piece of string she had hung down the inside of her dress. 'I lock things away. But when I'm asleep they take the key.'

'Who steals?'

'The nurses. I was a nurse once. They're not nurses.' She paused and said, 'They took my rug. They took my dressing-gown. When I came here I had rings on my fingers. I had a gold brooch. Everything's gone. They say I've lost them. How? I never go anywhere.'

She looked about as though afraid Miss Spong might have heard her.

'Mrs Haynes, can we get back to your daughter and your grandson? The police say your daughter took David up to the sales in London. How long ago was that?'

'Two years come January.'

'And David was how old then?'

'Four on the twelfth of January.'

'So he's nearly six.'

The old woman began to shake and her voice rose. 'Don't you hear me? Can't you understand? David is dead!'

'If David was dead why did you identify the newspaper picture?'

Mrs Haynes sat without answering, grinding her dentures.

'I think you *hope* he's dead, don't you Mrs Haynes? You hope he's not suffering. You'd rather he was dead than suffering. Isn't that so?'

'She telephoned Carol.'

'Who?'

'The woman. The woman who took him. At first she said *she* was his mother now and he loved her more than Carol. But later she said he wasn't a good child. He wouldn't talk to her. Wouldn't be her little boy. She said she was going to teach him a lesson. She was going to lock him away. She said the world would never see him again. That's why my Carol . . . why she . . . She couldn't stand it. Not the calls. It was bad enough David disappearing. She was looking everywhere. Used to go up to Oxford Street every day. She'd go in and out of shops and pubs and restaurants. I went with her some days. "Have you seen a little boy?" she would ask. "Have you seen my child?"'

'And then the woman began to telephone. I took a few calls. She was always angry, swearing at us down the phone. We told the police. They were London calls. But from phone boxes all over. That's when Carol knew she'd never find David again. She began to pray. She wasn't religious. But she prayed and prayed. And then she killed herself. Carol's dead. And so's David.'

Hannah was on the point of giving up but she had in her mind what Ferry had said: the boy was a possible witness; there *had* to be a key.

She began again: she asked at what age he had started to talk, how his speech was when he was four, had he been interested in drawing; could he make out words; was he advanced or average or backward in other things; how long had it been before he was toilet trained . . .

Mrs Haynes answered briefly. According to her answers the boy was normal, average.

Hannah asked every question she could think of about his young life and behaviour. But after a while the old lady lost interest. She began to talk about food. About her dressing-gown that had been stolen. About how rude the staff were to her.

It was early evening when they drove back to London.

'We're going to get caught in the traffic,' Wylie said. 'I know a pub in the Meon Valley. Would you like a drink?'

'I need one.'

They stopped at the Cricketers' Arms, a traditional pub of dark mahogany and rich ale smells. They were the only customers in the snug. There was a good log fire and Wylie drew up a table and two chairs in front of it.

'Not very nice out,' the landlord said, throwing another log on the fire.

They ordered and Wylie stood with his back to the flames. 'What do you think about Mrs Haynes?' Wylie said.

'Poor old thing, she's been wrecked by it all. I suppose we were lucky to find out anything.'

'I didn't think we *had* found out anything.'

'We know he was normal, average. That's a plus. He could

have been backward, he could have had half a dozen syndromes that would have made my job much more difficult. As it is he developed as an ordinary little boy; he would have been able to point to words, to write or at least draw letters even though he might not have known what they were. He would have been able to speak, to understand when spoken to. He would have been starting to take his place in the world of communication.'

'Do you think you'll get him to talk again?'

'Oh yes. If he could talk before, if the trauma hasn't been too great, then he'll talk again. I need time, that's all.'

'Those are pretty big "ifs".'

'Of course they are; this is a pretty nasty case.'

The landlord put his head round the door. 'Everything all right?'

'It's lovely,' Hannah said. 'Like having our own sitting-room.'

'Could we order some food?' Wylie asked.

The landlord rattled off a list of sandwiches.

'Anything cooked?'

'I could do you a steak.'

'Sounds good. Hannah?'

'A steak would be fine.' Then, after the landlord had gone, she said, thinking of Mrs Haynes, 'Food's all the old ever talk about in places like that.'

'It's all they've got to look forward to. Eat, drink and be merry . . . for tomorrow we grow old. That's why the phrase was invented.'

'Well, we're drinking and we'll be eating in a minute, but I'm not very merry, are you? Not after seeing that place and that Spong woman.'

'Not very.'

There was a pause, then Wylie said, 'Being merry means different things to different people. It's difficult being merry alone.'

'It's difficult being merry period.'

'For merry read happy. What makes you happy?'

'Well . . . I don't know . . .'

'Come on. One thing.'

'I'm not sure you can just point to something and say that's happy-making. Happiness is usually recognised retrospectively. I

190

mean we think back and say to ourselves, "Yes, I was happy then."'

'With Richard?'

'Yes, with Richard. Not every minute, but enough minutes.'

'And Tom?'

She hesitated. 'Yes . . . there was a certain happiness.'

'You're qualifying it.'

'I have to. Nothing was simple with Tom. All my emotions had to be analysed.'

'You analyse too much.'

'That's my job.'

'It may be your job, but you're doing it to yourself all the time.'

The food arrived. The steaks were good and came with chips.

'Have you got a man?' he said, his mouth half-full of chips.

'What?'

'A man. A fella, as they gruesomely call them. A companion.'

'I don't see that it's any of your affair.'

'Okay, let's analyse it.'

'Let's not.'

'A: you haven't got a man. Reason: you're still carrying a torch for Richard. B: you have got a man but you don't want to talk about it. Reason: you're ashamed because you think you *should* still be carrying the torch for Richard.'

'C: I don't want to talk about it because it's none of your bloody business.'

'You know, that's the first time I've seen real emotion in you. You're cool. Laid back. You were scared when you thought that duck hunter was out to get you but that was pure reaction.'

'Don't spoil –'

'I know what fear is. I've been scared out of my wits in my time. And I know what depression is and what living alone is. And I'll tell you something: it's no bloody good. Neither Richard nor Ellie would want us to go on doing what we're doing. Richard died eighteen months ago, didn't he?'

'Yes.'

'Ellie was killed a year ago. Don't you think the mourning should come to an end?'

She finished her meal and drank some wine. 'If I say no you

191

say what I'm doing is masochistic and self-indulgent on the one hand, or unhealthy and self-destructive on the other.'

'Or words to that effect.'

'And if I say I think it's time to come out, you say why don't we come out together. Yes?'

He threw back his head and laughed. It was an expansive, all-embracing, unself-conscious noise and she realised she had not heard him laugh before.

'Well, doctor,' he said. 'As a psychiatrist you're great, why don't we see what you're like as a woman?'

She had had just enough to drink to find the exchange amusing.

'What's your suggestion?'

'There's a romantic little hotel near here. Why don't we go there?'

'Thanks but no thanks.'

'Are you going to be chaste for the rest of your life?'

She smiled. 'Probably.'

He leaned back. 'Well, I thought I'd ask.'

'I think we should be getting back to town.'

They argued about the bill and he finally won. As they were leaving he said, 'You know, you won't find Tom again in the boy.'

'David! His name is David! And what I find or don't find is my business!'

EIGHTEEN

The important thing is to discover the triggers to David, *Hannah wrote in her journal.* We have already discovered two. The first is obvious, the pen. Even though drawing must have been his salvation locked away in the room, he would not draw unless he had the one pen he wanted, the green Pentel.

He has continued with his drawings. He does them at the Brinds and here in the sessions with me. At the moment he seems to be obsessed with one kind of drawing.

At first it seemed like the ones in the house: spirals and whorls of the kind that two-year-olds do. Even Tom was able to draw better.

But when I showed these to Duncan he saw something I had missed. According to him, David is drawing a wheel. At the centre is a large black dot, the hub. Several spokes radiate outwards to the enclosing circle. There are variations on this theme but basically that is the drawing. However, it is not as simple as that or I would have seen it. It is covered by other lines almost as though there are two drawings. Of course, once you have seen the wheel you wonder why you missed it earlier.

Duncan said he might be trying to hide the drawing with the other lines and, given his fear of the two women and the fact that he hides things naturally, this is a possibility.

I want to go back to the house and see if there is a pattern in the drawings on the walls that I missed earlier.

The second trigger has something to do with TV. I have let him watch programmes when he comes but he seems indifferent to most of it. There was one programme where the presenter drew figures of cartoon characters and I thought this might interest David but he preferred to do his own drawings instead.

I have taped a six o'clock news programme and will watch it with him. I know the Brinds watch *Channel 4 News* at seven because Ralph Brind told me.

Mrs Brind has given me some interesting information. She often takes David shopping with her in the high street where they live. They go regularly to a greengrocer. The woman who serves them always gives David an apple.

Yesterday she said to Mrs Brind, 'He's autistic, isn't he?' She explained that her nephew was autistic.

I asked Mrs Brind whether she mentions the word 'apple'. She does. I want to carry out an experiment the next time he is due to come to me.

Her telephone rang, it was Ferry.

'Anything new?' he said.

'In what way?'

'Well . . . with the boy?'

'He has a name now. David. No, nothing new.' She was about to mention the drawings but held back in case both she and Wylie were wrong.

'You said he wasn't autistic, that he'd probably talk again. I want to know –'

'Inspector, this is a damaged child. How damaged I don't know. He may start to talk in a week, in six months, or in six years. I just don't know!'

'If it was possible I'd leave you to get on with it. But it isn't. Two dead women and what are the police doing about it? That's the question. We haven't located any of the paintings or any antiques. So you see the boy – I mean David – is our only hope.'

'I'm sorry,' Hannah said. 'I'd like to be able to help you, but helping David is just as important. In any case, if I can help him then he may be able to help you. It's a question of one step at a time.'

Ferry put down the phone. How the hell was he going to convince Begg that they should take one step at a time? He reached into his drawer for a memo sheet. It was the same every day now, memos to Begg that said damn all. And he sensed that Begg was watching and waiting. If he didn't come up with the goods his life at London North would be made untenable.

His hand touched something unfamiliar and he drew it out. It was a silver cigarette box. He frowned, trying to identify it. Then he remembered that several days before someone from Forensic – Bailey? Binstead. No, Bainbridge – had stopped at his desk and told him about it. But what was it he'd said?

Ferry had been in the middle of something else at the time and he hadn't paid much attention. But he recalled that the man had said something about it being the second time the box had been brought in for testing. He picked it up and went to look for the exhibits officer.

'Forensic says this came in once before for checking.'

The exhibits officer was in the Begg mould; neatly dressed, neatly trimmed. You could see the sort of people Begg wanted round him.

'Look through the crime sheets. Go back about a year. Let me know if you find when it was out and why.'

A couple of hours later the exhibits officer phoned Ferry. There was no record in the crime sheets of the cigarette box having been brought in earlier for checking.

'Okay. Leave it with me.'

Ferry then rang Forensic. He spoke to Bainbridge. After he had identified himself and the subject he said, 'You said the box had been in for checking before.'

'That's right.'

'It's not in the crime sheets. We can't trace it. Do you keep a record?'

'It should be on the computer. But I'm tied up now. I'll check when I can. Is it urgent?'

'Everything's urgent.'

'Okay, I'll get back to you.'

Hannah arranged to pick David up herself for the next session. Mrs Brind had him ready and they met at the door. He was wearing the Guernsey that had once been Tom's. Mrs Brind pulled out the points of his shirt collar and straightened his clothing and it seemed to Hannah that she was looking at a prototypical mother-child scene and for the moment she felt a tug of wistfulness and longing. It was as though she were a visiting aunt come to take out her nephew for a treat – and she didn't want to be an aunt.

She realised then how lucky Mrs Brind was. She had had a normal family, normal relationships with her children. That's why she was so normal and down-to-earth herself. But Hannah had never had a normal relationship with a child of her own; such a simple thing to have missed but so precious.

They went to a greengrocer's in Hampstead. It was a large and expensive shop with much of its produce out on the pavement. There was fruit from all over the world, including apples. Hannah let David go first. There were other people being served and they had to wait. Hannah steered him towards the boxes of apples. Then she said softly, 'Would you like an apple?'

He swung round suddenly and looked into her face. The reaction was so swift she felt a beat of excitement. She reached into the box and gave him one. He stood for a moment as though disorientated, then he put it into his pocket. She paid for the apple and they left. She felt elated. It was another small breakthrough.

They walked from the High Street to Haverstock Hill. At this time of the afternoon the streets were crowded. People glanced at them as though they were a natural part of the scenery. She loitered in front of shop windows looking at their reflections. Some were unclear, only silhouettes. They could be any mother and child.

She took him into several shops, drifting past the counters, enjoying herself. They went into a branch of British Bazaar. It was like a Woolworth's with dozens of counters containing thousands of items.

'Have you ever been in here?' she said as they walked up and down the aisles. 'What would you like if you could choose anything? I bet you'd choose something special.' She talked continuously as a way of maintaining a level of communication. After a while they went slowly to the door.

A young man in a neat suit stopped them as they were leaving.

'Excuse me,' he said. 'But you have something you haven't paid for.'

'What?' Hannah said. 'I don't think so.'

'Your little boy took something. Would you please come with me.'

'Now, just wait a minute,' she began, but he moved off without listening.

She followed him with David past other fascinated shoppers. A voice at her elbow said, 'Hannah, is there anything I can do?'

It was Mitchell Bourke.

'No thanks, Mitchell. Nothing. There's been a mistake.'

But in the assistant manager's office she discovered that there had not been a mistake.

A woman detective, dressed in mini-skirt and T-shirt, said, 'I watched him. I saw him take it.'

The young man moved forward as though to search David. 'You're frightening him,' Hannah said. 'I'll look.'

In his jeans pocket she found not one but two green Pentel rollerballs.

'I'm sorry,' she said. 'I didn't realise.'

'It's our policy to prosecute shoplifters,' the young man said.

'A six-year-old?'

'Well . . .'

'What court would you bring him into? Infants' court? Is there such a thing?'

'You're taking the wrong attitude,' the woman detective said. 'If every little boy was like yours there'd be no stock left.'

'Spare me the lecture,' Hannah said. 'If you're going to arrest us, then do it. But before you do I'm offering to pay for the pens

and I suggest you take a minute to telephone Detective Inspector
Ferry of London North and tell him that Dr Wilton is in your
shop with David – and you are going to have us arrested.'

'Now, I didn't say I was going to have you arrested –'

'And I'll phone the Press Association and they can release the
story to the national papers. Think of the headline: *British Bazaar
prosecutes Six-Year-Old Child.*'

They looked at each other in silence and then the assistant
manager said, 'Please pay on your way out.'

After dropping David, Hannah went round to see Sophie. She
had started eating again, but it didn't seem that the fast had done
anything other than cause her to become emaciated.

'Stop fussing,' Sophie said to her questioning. She was using a
stick now to move from one room to the next.

Hannah told her about the shopping expedition but Sophie did
not seem to be able to concentrate. Her drawn face gave Hannah
the feeling she was in pain.

To try and take her mind off it even a little she brought out
David's drawings. Sophie glanced at them briefly.

'Yes, I can see what you mean about a wheel.' She lifted several,
dropped them on the pile. 'On the other hand it might just be a
collection of lines that he's become used to drawing. I doodle
when I'm taking telephone calls. I always draw boxes.'

'That sounds very nasty,' Hannah said. 'I'd see someone about
it if I were you.'

They both laughed but there was little mirth in it and soon
afterwards Hannah left.

Wylie arrived that evening with the VHS tapes of Christmas Day.
Hannah had installed a new TV set. They watched them together.

'I'd forgotten how beautiful the place is,' she said. 'Especially
in the sunshine.'

He had gone for backgrounds: the church, the village, and the
reed beds, which were bathed in sunlight one moment, engulfed
by fog the next.

She sat entranced as the film showed the three of them, Wylie
and David picking up driftwood. Then her pictures at the

barbecue with the smoke drifting past Wylie, and making him look, in his heavy sheepskin coat, like a Central Asian nomad.

'Watch David when you hand him the food,' Wylie said. 'There.'

On film Hannah was giving him a hamburger. He opened the bun and looked at the meat before he began to eat.

'It's so natural,' she said. 'He would never have done that a few weeks ago. These are marvellous pictures.'

As she watched she began to realise she was no longer seeing Richard and Tom in the figures of Wylie and David. There had been a sea change since Christmas.

Wylie said, 'The other day you were talking about happiness only being perceived retrospectively. You look happy there. I mean, if these were strangers you were looking at wouldn't you say they were happy?'

'Yes, I would. But I can't remember feeling happy at the time. There were too many memories in the boat.'

As they watched she told him about her afternoon with David.

'No wonder he was grabbed for shoplifting. He saw you pick up an apple. So he picked up a pen. It doesn't prove anything.'

'I don't think that's the reason. He's getting used to words. To cause and effect. He heard the word "apple" and reacted to it.'

One of the tapes contained some of the earlier material he'd shot. She looked again at the Brinds' garden path and the early pictures of David. Again she thought how much he had changed. Then there were the shots of Ferry talking to someone on the steps outside London North police station.

She rose and crossed to the window.

'Is there something wrong?'

'Why?'

'I thought you might be expecting someone. You've gone to the window a couple of times.'

She frowned. 'No. I'm not expecting anyone.'

He leaned back in his chair. 'Have you thought about my offer?'

'What offer?'

'Well, proposition. The small country hotel. Hot muffins for breakfast. William Morris wallpaper.'

She smiled. 'I know those hotels. They have beds that damage your spine.'

'And dining-rooms where no one talks.'

'And plumbing that keeps you awake. I think for what you're proposing you want one of those big commercial hotels where everything works and no one comes knocking on the door saying breakfast's ready.'

'I know several of those if you're interested.'

'Again, thanks but no thanks.'

He rose and picked up the tapes. 'You can't say I don't try.'

They stood looking at each other, knowing what they wanted, but unable to express it.

Then Hannah said, 'Let me get you another drink.'

He put down the tapes. 'Sure.'

She gave him a whisky on the rocks. 'What about here?' she said quietly. 'It's not a hotel but it's just as comfortable and no one will come to the door asking about breakfast.'

They made love in her big double bed. No one had shared it with her since Richard had died. Several men had tried: colleagues, friends of Richard's who were divorced and some who weren't. Most thought it would be therapeutic for her. She had easily been able to disabuse them.

She was glad it had happened at last and glad it had happened with Wylie. As he had said at Christmas, some things were better done with comparative strangers. And this, this breaking of her fast so to speak, was one of them.

Afterwards he fell asleep with his arm over her. Even though in his dreams he probably imagined she was Ellie, it still felt good.

Another voice inside her head, the voice of the doppelgänger who so often stood beside her, said it wouldn't, mustn't last.

She hadn't planned it, but her subconscious must have accepted that this was probably going to happen from the time they had gone to Suffolk on Christmas Day. Seeing the videos had only hastened it.

Fine, she thought, I've done it. I'm in control. She slept.

The following morning they made love again. This time her body was soft and relaxed and it was not so much a self-conscious act of reaffirmation as one of passion and enjoyment.

When it was over, he raised himself on his arm and looked down at her. 'Good morning,' he said. 'That was very nice.'

'Good morning yourself. Yes, wasn't it?'

She gave him bacon and scrambled eggs. It was strange cooking breakfast again. She usually only had yoghurt and toast. But she was hungry and she joined him.

'Was that a one-night stand?' he said.

She sensed what would come next.

'Let's not plan anything,' she said. 'Why don't we let things happen?'

After he had gone she remained in the kitchen in the winter sunshine and had a second cup of coffee. She felt a sense of freedom she had not had for a long while.

NINETEEN

On the way to work Ferry stopped at a tobacconist's shop near London North and bought a pack of cigarettes. He was ashamed. He and Alison had given up together three years before. When the tobacconist asked him what brand he wanted he said, 'Oh, any kind,' as though they were not for him. 'And a lighter.'

He looked at the display drawer and shook his head. Begg used an expensive lighter. It wouldn't be in character, at least Ferry's character, to do the same.

'Just something cheap.'

'These are the cheapest. You throw them away when they run out of fuel.'

'That's fine.'

When he had used the fuel in the lighter he would stop smoking again. It would be his target.

He had just reached his desk when his phone rang.

'Ferry.'

'This is Bainbridge in Forensic. You asked me about a silver box.'

'Oh, yeah.'

'I've checked on the computer. We had it the first time last July. Brought in by a DI with the initials MS.'

Ferry jotted it down, then went through to the desk sergeant and said, 'Is there a DI here with the initials MS?'

The desk sergeant shook his head. 'Not that I know of.'

'Well, was there one? I mean in the past six months?'

The sergeant stared at Ferry while he thought. He knew his reputation as a Cockney hard lad. He knew that neither Begg nor the other brass cared for him much. He was too much on the defensive, too aggressively down-market. He remembered, with an inner smile, the incident of the black tie. The desk sergeant did not take sides. He bent gently with any wind blowing. 'MS. Could be Stacey. Mick Stacey. He went to Paddington. Okay?'

'Thanks.'

Ferry phoned Paddington. Stacey was out on a job. He left a message for him to call back.

It was late afternoon and Hannah was trying to teach David the names of objects and also to react to commands. She was convinced, after the scene in the greengrocer's shop when David had reacted to the word 'apple' that he could learn and absorb. What he had not shown any inclination to do was communicate.

She had a series of objects on her desk and was naming each. Then she would take one, a ball, and put it on the floor.

'Ball, floor.' She said, 'Put the ball on the floor. Look, I'm doing it. I'm putting the ball on the floor. Put . . . the . . . ball . . . on . . . the . . . floor.'

She indicated the ball to David. He ignored it. He was drawing again.

'It isn't drawing time now,' she said. 'Let's do something else. Let's play with the ball instead.' She picked up the ball and held it out to him. 'David!'

He did not look at her.

'David, you're never going to talk if you just go on drawing. Give me the pen.'

She held out her hand. He paid no attention. His body was bent over the paper and he went on with his squiggles, which now seemed to her to represent nothing at all.

She was working with him every day and she was not making any progress. Ferry was pressing her. She was beginning to feel frustrated. What she needed was time to take things slowly, to let David make the pace, but she was not being given time. Even the social worker, Ms Challis, had sounded a warning note about the money that social services were paying. It was as though she had a deadline to meet – and that was not how things should be done.

'David!'

Sometimes he responded, sometimes not. Now he did not.

He looked so much like a normal little boy. He was lying on the floor on his stomach, drawing. Tom used to do this. So did most kids. This was how kids *were*.

'David! Would you like to give me the pen?'

She got down onto the floor beside him.

'Darling, you can't learn other things if you go on like this. There's a whole world waiting for you. And there's more to it than drawing. You've got to learn and I've got to teach you.'

He turned away from her.

'David, listen to me! Once upon a time, long ago, there was a boy just like you but a little older who lived deep in a forest in France. He lived all alone with no one to talk to. And when he came out he couldn't speak or walk properly or do anything that human beings do. But he met a kind doctor called Dr Itard and he and the doctor lived together for many years and Dr Itard taught him many things. But he never taught him to speak. David, you've *got* to speak. That's what most distinguishes us from animals. So why not give me the pen and let's try again.'

She put out her hand.

'David.'

She was on his level and tried to make him meet her eyes. He did this often now, but not today. Instead he looked over her shoulder as he had when she had first been introduced to him.

She felt tired and sad and defeated.

She touched the pen. 'Pen,' she said. 'Give it to me.'

He shrank away from her.

'David, if I could only explain. If I leave you like you are you may come out of it in your own time but time's against us. You know what will happen? They'll take you away from me!'

He bent down and began to draw again.

The frustration of the past weeks boiled over. She leaned

forward and reached for the pen. She had meant the gesture to be firm but not so sudden as to startle him. But he jerked back and she was forced to snatch it away from him. His reaction was sudden and frightening. He threw himself at her and bit the hand holding the pen. She dropped it with a cry and he scooped it up and retreated across the floor on all fours to a corner where he sat hunched up. He began to rock from side to side.

'Oh David!' Her remorse was devastating. She felt as she had sometimes felt when, worn out, she had lost control of herself with Tom. She caught David in her arms, pressing him to her chest. She felt tears come to her eyes. 'Oh God, David, I'm so sorry!'

That was how Mrs Brind found them. She had come in to tell Hannah — as she had been asked to — that the BBC news was just beginning.

'I wanted to make him concentrate,' Hannah said. 'I tried to take his pen.'

She released David. Mrs Brind was about to step forward to pick him up when she sensed this was not the time. Instead she took his free hand and said, 'Come on David, let's see what's on TV.'

They sat through the news: it was the usual mixture of politics and violence and David was uninterested. As though using it as a defence he went back immediately to his drawing, shutting out both the women and the TV.

Mrs Brind and Hannah watched him surreptitiously. He drew and drew, one drawing after another, flicking over the pages of the notebook.

Mrs Brind said, 'It's always the same drawing. It's always that cap.'

'I thought it was a wheel,' Hannah was only half listening to Mrs Brind. She was still seized by guilt.

Mrs Brind seemed less affected. 'A wheel? Oh, yes, I see. Ralph thought it was a cap.' She pointed to the drawing. 'He thinks that's the peak. But I'm sure you're right. It's more of a wheel.'

'That's if it's anything.'

Nothing about the newscast or the weather forecast that followed seemed to touch David, and when they left Mrs Brind said,

'I shouldn't be too upset. He recovers much more quickly these days.'

Hannah felt angry with herself for what had happened and angry for putting herself in a position where Mrs Brind could sympathise. She liked Mrs Brind, but she didn't want sympathy from her.

As she returned to her consulting room to tidy up and put away the toys the phone rang. It was Ferry.

She could visualise him in his bomber jacket and his trainers, his short cropped red hair and his white, freckled skin. She did not want to talk to him just then.

'If it's about David then I must insist you stop telephoning me,' she said, releasing her anger.

He sounded surprised and hurt. 'No, I haven't phoned about David. You said you'd let me know the moment you had something definite and I agreed to wait.'

'Well, what is it, Inspector?'

'It's about Mr Bourke,' he said. 'You said he'd been married three times.'

'You know I can't answer questions about a patient. I told you that.'

'I've checked on the ethical side. You're not obliged to tell the police anything you are told in confidence.'

'That's correct.'

'Were you told in confidence, in a direct session with Bourke, that he had been married three times? I mean, is that what he said to you? Is it part of the confidential discussions you have?'

'No, of course not.'

'Then please, doctor, don't make problems that don't exist.'

The quality of her anger changed. She took a grip on her emotions and said, 'I'm sorry, Inspector.'

'Okay. Let's start again. You say he's been married three times. It's actually four. The first was in the sixties.'

'He never mentioned that one.'

'To a Phyllis Bacon, an actress . . .'

'I had no idea.'

'And so he didn't mention he was widowed?'

'No.'

'Is he normally secretive?'

'Just the opposite. I know more about his emotional hang-ups than . . . well . . . I thought I did.'

'Sins of omission?'

'I'd hardly call not telling me about his first wife's death a sin of omission.'

'Not if it was a natural death.'

She felt a jolt. 'What precisely do you mean by that?'

'You see, doctor, you want me to give you information but you don't want to give me any in return.'

'You know my position.'

'As I understand it, *you* have the responsibility. It is up to you what you divulge. Isn't that so?'

'Honestly, Inspector, I haven't checked with an expert in medical ethics lately but –'

'I have. You can break the confidentiality if you have to. And I'm putting it to you that there are a dozen or more situations where it would be your duty to break it. What if you had a terrorist as a patient, and he let slip or you found out he had planted a bomb, and that it was due to go off in forty-eight hours and would kill scores of people?'

'That's an extreme case!'

'Murder is murder, whether it's by bomb or strangulation. Only the numbers vary, the principle is the same.'

'I'm not a fool, Inspector! And anyway you haven't told me much. Only that he had a first wife I knew nothing about. You're making it sound like a crime.'

'You're his psychiatrist, don't you think it's odd you know nothing about the first wife?'

'People don't disclose everything, not even to their psychiatrists. We all reserve something.'

'Like the fact that you had an autistic child?'

She felt breathless for a second. 'How dare you pry into – ?'

'You're involved in this case. We pry into everyone who's involved. We ask questions. We look up things. We've got a Holmes computer that's one of the most powerful in the world. We looked up your Mr Bourke.'

'And?'

'There you go again, doctor. It's something for nothing. It's one-sided. But I'm going to take a chance on you. First of all, this is highly confidential. If my guv'nor found out I was giving out this kind of information he'd have my ba– he'd have my neck in a noose.'

She couldn't stop herself. 'Or your balls for braces? I'm a big girl, Inspector. I'm familiar with the patois.'

She had expected him to laugh but the silence on the line was one of embarrassment. He wasn't as sophisticated as she had thought.

'Okay, Inspector, I'll make a deal with you. Tell me what you think I should know and I'll pass on what I think I morally can.'

'In the sixties he was into the drug scene.'

'Good Lord, is that all? I thought everybody was into the drug scene in the sixties. Marijuana was as common as ordinary tobacco if you believe what you hear.'

'This wasn't marijuana, it was heroin. And his first wife died from an overdose.'

'Oh. But that still doesn't mean –'

'He was suspected of dealing but nothing could be proved. That's not so funny, is it?'

His voice had become hard and she said, 'I didn't mean to make light of it. No, heroin isn't funny.'

He paused again and then said, 'Murder is like throwing a stone into a pond. You never know where the ripples will stop, what they'll touch.'

'What about the legacy? That would give you some sort of lead, wouldn't it?'

'We're still checking that out.'

'There's something else. How could a man who was so well known in the seventies as an actor hide that kind of background?'

'Easy. Different name. His real name is Mitchell. And he might be dealing in drugs again.'

She absorbed this new information then said, 'I'm pretty sure he's not using them. One can usually tell.'

'I don't think he ever used them. Just dealt. His wife wasn't an addict either, according to the coroner's report. Don't you think that's odd?'

'She might have OD'd *because* she wasn't used to it.'

'Everything's possible.'

'But what's this got to do with the two women in the Vale of Health?'

'What it has to do with is Mr Bourke's attitude to, and relationship with, women. I was hoping that's what you might discover.'

'He doesn't have lasting relationships. That's one thing.'

'Thank you, doctor.'

'Don't be so touchy! I didn't mean it ironically. Look, there's something that could help us both: I've come to a kind of cul-de-sac with David. I need to stimulate his mind. Can I take him to the house?'

'Isn't that a bit extreme?'

'I don't think so.'

'Okay, you're the psychiatrist. I'll organise it.'

'Oh, and one other thing –'

'There you go again. Asking, not giving.'

'This is a small thing. Were there any marks on either of the women's hands? I mean bite marks, or scars that could have been made by teeth?'

'Hang on, I've got the pathologist's report here somewhere . . . Let's see . . . Yeah, on the younger woman's hands . . . Hilda's.'

'I thought there might be.'

'David?'

'I think so. He likes to draw. I took the pen away from him and that's how he reacted. I think that's how Hilda must have punished him.'

'It's a wonder she didn't get blood poisoning with the state of his teeth.'

'He's been to the dentist. You wouldn't recognise them now.'

'Remember what Mum used to say?' Ferry said to his father. 'About sins of omission?'

'What?'

'Don't tell me you've forgotten. I remember from the time I was a kid. She always used to say that sins of omission were just as bad as sins of commission.'

They were finishing their supper in the small kitchen. Albert had served up something new from his cookbook and Ferry had eaten it without comment.

'Did you like it?' Albert said.

'Oh, yeah. Very nice.'

'Well, say so then.'

'You're becoming like a . . . like I don't know what with your cooking. Prima donna. Yeah, that's it.'

'I like to be told.'

'Great. Fantastic. You want a tailor-made?' He offered his father a cigarette from his pack.

'I prefer my own.'

'Don't be huffy. I enjoyed it. Really. Anyway this bloke Bourke's got secrets. I never trust people with secrets.'

'We never had secrets,' Albert said, rolling a cigarette in his docker's fingers. 'We lived too close for that. In the old days people never had secrets.'

'Sins of omission. I remember once on a hot day I went for a swim in the river. I knew Mum thought it was filthy and dangerous so I never asked her. When she found out she was livid. Said I never asked because I knew she'd say no. Same with this geezer Bourke. Keeps all his past – the nasty bits – under lock and key so no one will know.'

'Be reasonable. Wouldn't you?'

'He used to deal in drugs. His wife died of an overdose. What if she was given it by Bourke?'

'That'd be murder, wouldn't it?'

'She's an actress, right? Good in the fifties. Gets some marvellous parts and has good reviews. That kind of thing. Marries Bourke. He's good-looking. Thinks she's terrific. Probably thinks he can hang on to her and she'll pull him up with her. Trouble is, all this praise goes to her head –'

'You know this or are you just making it up?'

'Some and some. Just listen, okay? So she's in the newspapers and on the telly but she's difficult to work with. Won't do this part, won't do that part. Starts telling the directors and the producers what they should be doing. So pretty soon they don't want to work with her. Can't blame them. No parts for her.'

'Does she know this geezer Bourke spent some time in the nick for drugs?'

'Maybe. Maybe not. I dunno. So anyway, Bourke starts getting parts. Soon he's got more work than he can manage. But she hasn't. It's like a seesaw, he's going up on one side, she's coming down on the other.'

'You don't knock someone off for that.'

'She's ten years older than him. It's okay when she's having this terrific success, but not when she isn't. He starts having it off with younger birds. She makes a fuss. Won't give him a divorce. He says why don't you try this nice medicine, make you feel better.'

'The heroin?'

'Why not? Bingo, she shoots up enough to kill an elephant and that's that.'

'You should've been a writer,' Albert Ferry said. 'Writing for the TV. Those police programmes. Jesus, son, you'd never prove any of this.'

'I know. I know. So listen to this. He's finished now. They don't want actors like him any more. Drugs again? But he's been in the nick once for drugs. Now he's met these two women in the Vale of Health.'

'How? You said they was recluses?'

'Hilda's got to go shopping. He meets her at the shops, okay? They get friendly. He sees the goods in the house, paintings and antiques. He promises to marry her. The mother's bedridden upstairs. They clean out the lot, then he kills them both.'

'You said the old lady fell. You said that's what killed her.'

'Yeah, but after a struggle. Bruises on her arms. It's still murder.'

'So how do you prove it?'

'I dunno, that's why I'm hoping that psychiatrist might help. She could find out stuff in the sessions she has with Bourke. It's all pressure, Dad. Begg's putting pressure on me, I'm putting pressure on her.' He lit another cigarette. 'I don't think I like her. She's too — what's the word? — too aggressive for a woman. Always arguing. Putting her point of view. And too much money. You want to see her place.'

'That's no reason to dislike her.'

'You know something? She had an autistic child. Never said a blind word. Secrets . . . By the way, what was that we had for supper?'

'It's Spanish. Rice and stuff. I didn't put any prawns or mussels in. I don't care for those. And I didn't make the rice yellow like they said. Just rice and chicken.'

'You mean that was supposed to be paella?'

'Well, sort of.'

'In the old days in Spain they shot people for making paella like that.'

TWENTY

'My name is Begg, Detective Superintendent Begg.' He showed Hannah his warrant card and she let him into her consulting room.

'If this is about the Vale of Health murder, I've spoken to your Inspector Ferry and, really, my time is limited.'

'Yes, it is, and I'm sorry to take up more of your time but we all have a public duty.'

She bit back her reply. She was becoming tired of being wrong-footed by the law.

The difference between the two policemen was marked. Where Ferry was the tough, aggressive East Ender, Begg was more polished. There was still a trace of accent but his clothes were conservative and looked good and he was wearing a club or society tie.

'I wanted to hear about the boy.'

'Everyone goes on calling him "the boy". This isn't going to help him find a personality.'

'David.'

'But I've given Inspector Ferry detailed reports on what I'm doing and how we're coming along. There must have been some breakdown in police communications.'

'Not at all, doctor.' Begg had walked to the windows and was standing with his back to the light and she could not see his face sharply but there was something familiar about it. 'There is a necessary doubling when we want to get our facts precisely right. Inspector Ferry tells me that the . . . that David is not autistic and that there is a chance he may be taught to communicate in the near future, is that correct?'

'Well . . . yes, I suppose you could use that kind of shorthand.'

'How soon?'

'It's not that simple. I don't think David is autistic but there is a huge difference in making that assumption and going on to suggest that he may be talking soon.'

She described the Genie case briefly and told him she had considered the various tests the Californian authorities had given the girl.

'What sort of tests?'

'Do you really want to know, Superintendent?'

'I wouldn't be wasting your time if I didn't.'

'All right. They were mainly Gestalt: the Harshman Figures test, the Thurstone, the Mooney Faces.'

He held up his hand, but she went on remorselessly. 'They were all tests for someone whose attention could be focused, who was willing to participate, who had some communication. David doesn't yet.'

Begg looked irritated. 'What is Gestalt?'

She smiled slightly. 'Superintendent, you've just asked me to define a whole school of thinking.'

'Try.'

'Well, it has two meanings. One has to do with shapes and form, the other, the psychological one, postulates that we are more than the sum of our parts. That we can't just be analysed by analysing each part.'

'Oh.'

'And while we're using big words I must tell you that I think David will eventually have to see someone who is an expert in neurolinguistics. I'm not and this is the next stage for him.'

'Neurolinguistics!' Begg tasted the word and did not seem to like it.

'Babies listen to and copy adults. If you say, "Hello, how are you?" to an autistic child he will probably reply, "Hello, how are you?" It's called echolalia. But when a normal child wants a biscuit he doesn't say, "Do you want a biscuit?" Yet that's what his parents say to him.

'There are people like Noam Chomsky of MIT who have done a great deal of work on the subject and it can be used to help children like David speak again.'

'So what will happen?'

'Social services will find an expert to take him on. But it might not be necessary. There are triggers that stimulate memory. I've seen that with David already. He was about four years old when he was taken from his mother so he'd have been talking and been part of the human communications network. We need something to kick-start speech memory.'

She looked at her watch but Begg was impervious. He began to walk slowly backwards and forwards near the window.

'That's all very interesting, doctor, but it doesn't help much.'

'Well, I'm sorry about that!'

Begg was impervious to irony too.

'While I'm here I'd like to ask you about something else. We try to build up a profile of a wanted murderer. What exactly is a psychopath? We hear the word often enough but few of us really know what it means.'

'Are you suggesting this was the work of a psychopath because – ?'

'I'm not suggesting anything, all I want is information.'

'Well, it could be, I suppose. Except that there were more than one and you'd be unlikely to get two psychopaths working together.'

'Who said there were more than one? Ferry?'

She remembered Wylie talking about a gang. 'It seems logical, doesn't it?'

'We don't make assumptions. There are no fingerprints; nothing to tell us how many there were. But you haven't answered my question.'

'A psychopath is someone . . . well, he or she could be your next-door neighbour and you wouldn't know it. They look normal and act normally until they want something. Then they take it, because morally they can't tell right from wrong. And if they have to kill to obtain whatever it is – and I don't mean only material things, it could be achievement of a state of mind – then they kill.'

'So a psychopath who kills would have no feeling that he or she had done wrong?'

'That's right. And you wouldn't be able to convince him. In fact psychopaths can become dangerous if they're criticised or contradicted.'

'Would a psychopath steal for gain?'

'Yes. Certainly.'

'And kill anyone – like our two dead ladies for instance – who got between him and his goal?'

'Yes.'

At that moment the phone rang. Hannah spoke for a few moments then said to Begg, 'I'm sorry. I must go. My mother-in-law has been taken to hospital.'

She was at North London General in fifteen minutes. At the desk they told her that Sophie had collapsed the previous day and her cleaning lady had phoned for an ambulance. She was on the third floor in a private room.

Hannah braced herself. Sophie was propped against the high pillows and looked old and drawn. Her hair was loose and there was more white in it than Hannah could remember. She had clearly been given a painkiller but was fighting the drowsiness.

'I phoned because I'm sick of this place already. I've no one to talk to, and when the nurses come they don't listen. I want some company, I need someone to stimulate me.'

'Tell me what happened first.'

'I don't know what happened. I woke up in this bloody place.'

'It's not a bloody place and you know it. You've worked here for years and you've always said how good it was. I'm glad you're here.'

Sophie gave a kind of snort and said, 'I was getting along just fine.'

'No, you weren't, you collapsed. They told me down at reception.'

'Now they want to do all sorts of tests. I said I know exactly what's wrong, you don't have to do anything of the sort. Try telling them! That's the problem these days, forty years or whatever it is of the Welfare State and individuals are no longer allowed to make up their own minds. Nanny will tell you. Nanny knows best!'

'Sophie, you'll tire yourself.'

'And the next thing they'll want to do is explore. And I don't want to be cut about. I want to be left alone and I want you to get me out of here.'

'You know I couldn't, even if I wanted to.'

'Well, I'm not signing any permissions. They can't operate or give me anaesthetics unless I say they can. And I'm not going to.'

'You're being stubborn.'

'I explained it all once. Don't make me explain it again. I didn't ask you to come here for that. I wanted you to take my mind off things, not burden me with doubts. So ... tell me ... what's been happening in the big world? Especially to you and David?'

Hannah caught her up on her treatment of David and what they had made of the drawings.

'Did you let him watch the news?' Sophie said.

'There was no reaction, he just went on drawing. I'm taking him back to the house to see if that triggers anything. The policeman was surprised. Do *you* think it'll do David any harm?'

'No, it's what I would have done. I think it's what you have to do, but only as long as you're there with him so that he's reassured.'

'There's something I wanted to ask you, it's about the secrets of the confessional, so to speak. Ferry wants me to pass on to him anything I think germane to the case in my sessions with Mitchell.'

'Good God, do they think he's mixed up in it?'

'Did you know he'd been married four times?'

'I'm afraid I didn't keep score with Mitchell. I've never been particularly interested in him.'

'Nor me. She was an actress in the sixties. She died of a drugs overdose and the police think he might have had a hand in it. They also think he may have been dealing in drugs.'

Sophie shifted on the pillows. 'And?'

'The problem is how far do I go in telling Ferry? He says I have the responsibility. Now that I think about it I can't remember exactly the ethical guidelines, can you?'

'No, of course I can't. These things are enshrined in committee morality, like encyclicals. What we, the ordinary humans, have to do is use our commonsense.'

'That's more or less what Ferry said.'

'Then I'd go along with that. You have to play God either way so you might as well try to preserve rather than destroy society. What do you think about Mitchell? Is he the sort who could commit murder?'

'It's possible he could have killed the two women for money. That would buy back his self-respect. It's been eroded badly by his wife leaving him and his acting career being in the doldrums. Money helps self-esteem, so does a big new shiny car.'

'When is he due to see you again?'

'Tomorrow.'

'Be careful.'

'Ferry's promised he'll have someone at the apartment.'

But Bourke was waiting for her when she got back from the hospital and there wasn't a policeman in sight. As she approached the front door of the block of flats she saw him get out of his Jaguar about a hundred yards up the street.

'Hannah! Hannah!'

There was nothing she could do but wait for him to join her. It was mid-afternoon and a bitter wind was blowing powder snow across the pavement. Bourke looked huge in his coat and cap and scarf.

'I can't make it tomorrow. Can you see me now?'

'No, Mitchell, I can't. I've got a lot of work to do. We'll have to postpone.'

He took her keys from her hand. 'Let me.' He opened the door and followed her inside. 'Hannah, I need to see you. Things aren't good.'

'I'm sorry, Mitchell. I just can't break up my day like this.'

'Have you got someone booked?'

'Yes . . . I have.'

He pressed the elevator button. It was already on the ground floor, the doors opened instantly, and before she could react he was in it with her and they were going up.

'Mitchell, it's no use, I simply can't –'

'Ten, fifteen minutes, that's all. Your next patient may not come in this weather. If he does I'll leave.'

He opened her door.

'Please don't –'

But he was in.

He handed her the keys and took off his outer clothing. He rubbed his hands. 'God, it's cold.'

'All right, go into my room and sit down. I'll be with you in a minute.'

In her bedroom she closed the door and phoned London North. As the phone rang she held her breath, listening for either his footsteps or the click of the phone in her consulting room being picked up.

Ferry wasn't there, nor was Holder. No one knew where they were.

Her hands felt clammy. She phoned Wylie's flat. No answer.

'Hannah.'

Bourke was at the bedroom door. She opened it.

'I won't be a moment. Why don't you make yourself some tea? You know where everything is.'

'I've had tea, thanks.'

He followed her to the hall. She hung up her coat and went into her consulting room.

'I have to make a call. Would you mind going into the waiting-room for a moment?'

She closed the door, looked up Wilderness Films, dialled and asked for Wylie.

The receptionist said, 'He *was* here. He's just gone out.'

She thought Bourke might be listening against the door and said, 'Would you tell him that Dr Wilton rang. He has an appointment with me in a few minutes and I want to know whether he is going to keep it or if he is just going to miss it as he did last time.'

'Oh. I see. Yes. I'll tell him.' The receptionist sounded taken aback at the chilly note in Hannah's voice.

She called Bourke in and said, 'I can give you fifteen minutes.'

'I looked in your book. You don't have another appointment this afternoon.'

'You had no right to do that, Mitchell. Anyway I don't write down every appointment.' She sat at her desk. 'Please sit down if you want to talk to me.'

Keep cool, she told herself. Act naturally. You're in charge here.

For a moment it looked as though he would not sit, but she began to fuss with files and paper, and at last he did.

'Why do you think you looked in the book, Mitchell? I think that's a good place to start, don't you?'

'There's a better place,' he said. 'Why are you making my life a misery?'

'What do you mean by that?' Her tone was professionally uninvolved.

'You know exactly what I mean. You started a witch-hunt, Hannah, with me as the witch. You brought me into this mess and now my friends are being rung up by the police and so are my ex-wives: "Who is this monster? Tell us about him!"'

'I didn't bring you into anything. You were at the house. All I did was say hello. I think you have yourself to blame –'

'Don't say that!' It came out like a pistol shot. 'I'm not to blame for *any*thing!'

He was sitting on the edge of the chair and she noticed that he was flexing his fingers. This was something he had done when he first came to her.

'How's your head?'

'What?'

'Early in your treatment you said you were having severe headaches.'

'They're okay.' He rubbed the back of his neck and she guessed he had one at that moment.

'Why don't you relax? I can't be any use to you if you don't. Push the chair back.'

Reluctantly he moved the recliner and settled himself in a semi-recumbent position.

'Tell me what's brought this on, I mean this sudden need to see me.'

'Who's Mr Wylie?'

He made no pretence about not having listened to her conversation and this worried her. 'Why, Mitchell?'

'Why, Mitchell?' He mimicked her in his actor's voice. 'Because I want to know. That's why.'

'It's not your business.'

'I'm making it my business.'

From his position in the chair he looked past her at the mirror, but every few seconds his eyes switched to her and she felt them almost as a physical presence. As though a laser was focused on her.

'Mr Wylie is a patient. He's been coming regularly. That's why he's not in the book.'

'You're lying. You've been seeing him. You spent Christmas with him.'

'So you've been snooping! You've been following me and watching this apartment. What if I did go out with Mr Wylie? There's no law against it.'

The recliner came down with a crash. 'Yes, there is! Your own law. Rule of the house, remember? You wouldn't go out with me!'

His face was sweaty and mottled by small red patches.

'Mitchell, have you had your blood pressure checked recently?'

He said angrily: 'Don't change the subject.'

'I'm quite prepared to go back to the subject. After all you're paying me to listen, but I must tell you I think you look as though you need a medical.'

'Rubbish! I'm as fit as I was thirty years ago.'

He lay back and seemed to make a conscious effort to relax. 'The worst thing a shrink can do is lie to a patient.'

'That's the second worst. The worst is becoming involved with a patient.'

'But you've become involved with this man Wylie!'

'He's not a patient.'

221

'You said he was.' There was a triumphant note in his voice.

'He's actually a documentary film maker and I'm helping him with some work. We had a loose appointment this evening. It just seemed easier to call him a patient.'

'A documentary about what?'

'I'm afraid that's confidential. At his request. But it has −'

He leaned forward again. 'It's about the case, isn't it?'

'Only tangentially. It's about autism.'

'Wait one minute! The papers said a child had been found in the house! That's it, isn't it?'

He was becoming excited but it was the edgy excitement of hysteria.

'I told you, I can't discuss it.'

'They said the child might have witnessed the killings!'

She heard the slam of a car door in the street and it gave her courage.

'Does that bother you?'

'Why shou − ?' He laughed harshly. 'So you think so too? You really think I put my fingers round her throat and smashed the hyoid bone and strangled her?'

'I never said that.'

'No, but that's what you *think*. You and this Mr bloody Wylie. Is he your lover?'

'That's enough! I'm not going to −'

'You're in it together: the police, Wylie, you!' He rose and came towards the desk.

'Please sit down!'

The moment she said it she knew it was a mistake.

'Don't tell me what to do! It was you who told them about my first wife!'

'I didn't know about your first wife!'

He wasn't listening. 'You told them about the overdose.'

'Mitchell, *they* told *me*.'

'It's a bloody conspiracy! I trusted you and −'

The buzzer sounded.

Bourke was between her and the entry phone.

'I have to answer it.'

'No. We have to talk.'

The buzzer sounded again.

'Mr Wylie knows I'm here. He won't go away.'

They stared at each other. She moved round him and lifted the phone and heard Wylie's voice with enormous relief.

'I'll be seeing you, Hannah.' Mitchell went out into the hall. It sounded like a threat.

The two men met as he was getting into his coat.

'Excuse me,' Wylie said, as they shuffled round each other.

Hannah was childishly pleased to see that Wylie, in his sheep-skin, was even bigger than Bourke.

Wylie said, 'Sister Anne, Sister Anne . . . do you see anyone?'

Hannah was at the window watching Bourke go up the street to his car.

'This is becoming a bad habit,' she said. 'There was a movie once called *Woman in a Dressing Gown*. They could make a sequel: *Woman Behind the Curtain*. Anyway, I'm very glad you got my message.'

'A little bit obscure, but I thought, what the hell, better get out there and see what the good doctor wants. The receptionist was all agog. She was wondering what was going on. I was, too, for that matter.'

'He was listening. I had to be obscure.'

'I think what particularly interested her was that I'd broken an appointment before. Confirmed that all the people who use the cutting-rooms are a bit like that.'

'Anyway, you came. That's the important thing.'

'I thought modern women were past needing men for . . . well, for anything.'

'There are times when no woman feels particularly "modern", as you put it. Though most of us would never admit it.'

'I don't think you'd better see him again, or at least not by yourself in the apartment.'

'I wasn't *supposed* to be by myself! The police were supposed to be looking after me.'

She gave him a glass of wine and told him the background and what Ferry had discovered about Bourke.

Wylie frowned. 'That's bloody irresponsible of them!'

'That's what I thought. I'm damned if I'm going to help them again.'

They walked up to a Greek taverna in Fitzjohn's Avenue. There was bazouki music and the place was cheerful. They ate a feta salad, dolmades, and drank a bottle of Apollo. But she could not relax. Reaction hit her and she spoke obsessively about Bourke.

'How would he have known about the hyoid bone?' she said, referring to his comment on strangulation.

'He may have read about it in the papers. It's not all that arcane, I've heard of it too, though I'm not precisely sure what it is.'

'It's a little bone in the neck. It's often fractured in strangling cases. When it fractures you die. Duncan . . . do you think he could have come up to Suffolk? Do you think he could have fired the shots?'

'Is he a hunter?'

'He's never said so, but that doesn't mean he couldn't pretend to be. He's an actor, don't forget. And what was he doing outside the house in the Vale of Health? Don't they say murderers often have a compulsion to revisit the scenes of their crimes?'

'You're a psychiatrist, you should have the answer.'

'I've never dealt with anything like this, but I was explaining what a psychopath is to Superintendent Begg, Ferry's superior, a little earlier and God, Duncan, it seemed just as though I'd been describing Mitchell.'

'What did Begg want?'

'I think he wants to check that Ferry's doing his job.'

The waiter gave them more coffee.

She continued where she had left off. 'Mitchell's been following me, watching the apartment.'

She told him about the time she had become frightened in the underground garage.

'But he only came to give you a Christmas present. There's nothing very criminal about that.'

'Why is it that every time I voice a suspicion you try to knock it down?' Her voice had risen.

'Because this case is complicated enough without adding to it unnecessarily. Someone kills two women in a secluded house. It's possible a boy saw the murder, that he's a witness. Wouldn't the murderer be following the boy?'

'Yes, he would, but not exclusively, not if he thought I had extracted – or could extract – the information from David.'

But Wylie was doubtful. 'He fancies you. He's jealous, sure, and he's probably unbalanced, but that doesn't make him a killer. If everyone who fancied you was under suspicion it'd be tough on a lot of us.'

She smiled at him. 'Thank you for that. But I wish it was that simple. You've never sat across the desk from him and listened. He's . . . well, he's been sexually impotent for years. I shouldn't be telling you all this but I want you to understand him. I'm not sure how it started, perhaps with his second wife. It might even have been his first.'

'The one he doesn't talk about.'

'Right. He boasts about the hundreds of women he's had. Now he can't make it. His wives divorce him. It haunts him.'

'But you're his mother confessor – if there is such a thing. You've listened to him sympathetically. You know his problem. He's shared it with you. So . . . if only he can get you into bed . . . bingo.'

'It all sounds too predictable. The human psyche doesn't always work the way you want it to.'

'Women are said to fall in love with their male psychiatrists, why not the other way round?'

'It can happen.'

'What if he tried the same thing with the younger woman, Hilda? Just one more female in his search for the one who is going to release him. And then discovered the haul of paintings and furniture? Listen, he was a soap idol. She may have seen him on the screen. He could make that sort of woman fall for him easily enough. You'll have to tell Ferry.'

They walked back to her apartment in silence. It was snowing more heavily and the winter trees were outlined in white.

'Would you like a brandy?' she said.

'I'd love one.'

225

She gave him the drink and said, 'I want to check my answering machine.'

When she returned she was smiling. 'We may get a move on now. I asked Ferry if I could take David to the house to see if looking at the drawings would trigger anything. He's left a message saying it's okay for tomorrow afternoon about three thirty.'

'The house? The Vale of Health house? The murder house? I'm coming too!'

'I'm not –'

'For Christ's sake, I'm not going to pass up a chance like that.'

'Duncan, going down to see the old lady was one thing, but I don't want anyone else at the house. It's going to be difficult enough just the two of us. Having you there may distract him.'

'Why? I know him and he knows me. We got on like a house on fire at Christmas. How do you know that my presence there won't be a help?'

'I can't take the chance. I'm sorry.'

He threw back the brandy. 'What if I were to ring Ferry? What if he said okay?'

'You don't understand, it's got nothing to do with Ferry. This is my decision for David!'

He frowned, nodded, 'Okay, fine. Thanks for the drink.' He picked up his coat, gave a small wave, and left.

She felt irritated at his irritation. She picked up his glass and was taking it to the kitchen when she heard a violent bang down below. She ran to the window. The street was empty. Her buzzer sounded and she answered.

'Yes? Who is it?'

Silence.

'Duncan?'

She thought she heard a groan.

'Duncan, is it you?'

She put down the phone and ran for the lift. She was clutching her bunch of keys in her hand as a weapon.

She waited for the lift doors to open, standing as far back as she could with her finger over the Doors Close button just in case.

The foyer was all glass and mirrors and potted plants and there was no one in it. But out on the top step she could see the figure of a man in a sheepskin coat slumped against the toughened glass door. She ran to the door and opened it. Wylie stumbled in.

He had a head injury and blood was running down his cheek and neck.

She got him into the lift and into her flat. He was swaying like a tree about to fall. She removed his coat and helped him to the bathroom. The wound was above his right ear and towards the back of his skull, more of a graze than a cut.

She bathed it and he began to regain his senses.

'Someone hit me from behind,' he said.

'Mitchell?'

'God knows. I never saw a thing. But whoever it was had let down one of my tyres so I'd bend down to check. When I bent down, bang!'

'I heard the noise.'

'Whatever he hit me with bounced off my head and cracked into the mudguard. That's what you heard.'

'Keep the towel against it,' she said as they went back into the sitting-room.'

She held up a finger. 'How many do you see?'

'One.'

'What's your name, age and address?'

He gave them correctly.

'At least you're not suffering from concussion.'

'Can I have another brandy?'

'I'm afraid not. But I'll make you some tea. Go and lie down on my bed and I'll bring it to you.'

He pulled her duvet up and sat propped against the headboard drinking the tea.

'Thanks. I'll be going in a minute. I'll get a cab.'

'Don't be absurd. You're not going out in the freezing snow. Whoever it was may still be there. Could it have been a mugger?'

'My wallet is still in my coat.'

'I suppose it had to be Mitchell.'

'You must let Ferry know. It shows he's got the nerve to kill.

If whatever he hit me with had been a little nearer the front he'd have got me on the temple.'

'Thank God he didn't. Listen. I'm going to leave you here. The bedroom's yours, I've got a put-you-up in the sitting-room. There's a bottle of aspirin in the bathroom. Take two and try to get some sleep.'

'Yes, doctor. Anything you say.'

She kissed the tips of her fingers and touched his cheek. 'Good night.'

She woke about three. There was bright moonlight reflected from the snow and the whole of Hampstead hill was soft and white and quiet. She went through to her bedroom and stood at the door. His big frame almost filled her double bed. She had often stood like this and looked at the sleeping forms of both Richard and Tom. It seemed a long time ago.

TWENTY-ONE

Evening came to the River Thames. It was the time Begg liked best. He could stand on the balcony of his flat with a drink in his hand and look out over the darkling water to the lights on the southern bank. That was the side he knew best, where he had spent part of his childhood.

The January night was cold and Limehouse Reach was like a wet, black street. He lingered, remembering his mother and the 'uncles' he had grown up with. He'd hated that at the time. Now, he understood. She'd needed someone, everyone did.

Even Mandy.

He went back into the sitting-room and closed the sliding glass doors behind him. She was in her usual place on the sofa watching TV. She seemed to watch it all day. When he went to work in the morning she was often watching the breakfast shows, when he came back in the evening, there she was, still watching. As well as BBC and ITV, they had satellite and cable, and the movie channels.

But then, he supposed that if what had happened to her had happened to him, he'd also be watching TV twenty-four hours a day – so he wouldn't have time to brood.

This would be one of his problems in the future; as it was he had his job to keep him sane.

He poured himself another whisky and said, 'What're you watching?'

'Nothing much.'

'You want to talk or watch?'

'I can do both.'

It was true, she could. He remembered his kids. They could read and talk and play and eat – all with the TV on. She was closer to his kids' age than his. He, on the other hand, couldn't concentrate on more than one thing at a time.

'Did you go out at all?' he said.

'Of course not.'

'You'll have to sooner or later.'

'You say the same things every evening when you get back: Have you been out? Have you had anything to eat? Has anyone come about the flat? No . . . No . . . And no . . .'

He sat down on the big sofa beside her. In the soft light of a tablelamp she looked stunningly beautiful, a thin, almost perfect face, short, cropped hair and grey eyes. He'd never seen anyone before with grey eyes.

And there was her body.

And her voice.

She had a low-pitched voice that came straight out of the top drawer; the best schooling money could buy; the best in everything. And here she was on his sofa. Sometimes he couldn't believe it.

He looked at her as closely as he dared. After nearly a year the scars were fading. Soon they'd be gone. Then she wouldn't need to feel ashamed any longer. Though he didn't think that was the reason she stayed in the flat all day long. That was simply fear.

And you couldn't blame her. When he'd found her in her apartment in North London she'd been very close to death. Blood all over the place. It looked as though someone had taken an iron bar to her head and shoulders.

They'd never found the weapon, nor the man. That was part of the reason she was afraid: he was still out there somewhere.

Begg had told her over and over that whoever had done this to her would never find her in Docklands, but she'd taken no notice. She still wouldn't go out unless he came with her.

'The word is symbiotic,' she had said to him once. He didn't know what it meant. 'You need me and I need you. We have differing reasons. One day I won't need you any longer and then I'll leave you.'

'Perhaps.'

'I'm telling you that's how it'll be.'

He remembered the time she was in the hospital. Apart from the reporters and photographers marooned outside at the gates, he was the only one who had visited her. At first the visits had been purely professional but then he had been unable to stop himself and he had made excuses about checking this fact and that fact. He had tried to shield her from the world but he couldn't keep out the tabloids with their glaring black headlines: *Army General Shoots Himself After Call Girl Daughter Survives Murder Attempt.*

Why? That's what the press wanted to know. Why had this beautiful girl from an up-market background become a call girl in London?

The Mandy he had found in hospital had been a different woman from the one he knew now or the one he imagined before the assault. In hospital she was alone and for the first time was realising what fear was. She was vulnerable. He supposed she was still vulnerable, but the hard outer layer was beginning to reform.

He had taken her grapes and flowers. She'd looked at the flower card, registering the name of the shop. 'You're a snob,' she'd said.

'I suppose I am.'

'It's your background,' she'd said. 'Some of us try to escape our backgrounds, become something else.'

'Why would you want to escape yours? I mean, it's an –'

'Up-market one?'

'Sure.'

She twisted away on the pillow without answering. Then she said, 'Families go up and they go down. It's what always happens. You've gone up and I've gone down and we've met in the middle.'

She didn't talk like that any more. She wasn't as soft now as she'd been then.

They both knew what was happening. The visits became more

frequent. She didn't try to stop him for he was her shield. Anyway, he wouldn't have stopped.

'I want to disappear,' she had said to him one day when she was convalescing. 'You're a policeman. Can you make me disappear?'

By that time he was infatuated with her. 'I can make you disappear. But you'll have to come with me.'

She'd shrugged. 'You're the boss.'

He'd taken leave and smuggled her out of the hospital, driven to Manchester, taken a flight from there to Munich, changed planes for Madrid, rented a car, driven through Estremadura, and finally reached the coast. He'd stopped on the big new corniche and looked at the lovely, blue, polluted water and said, 'Home.'

That had been the beginning of everything, of his life, really. And now, if he wasn't careful, it would mark the beginning of the end.

He poured himself another drink and saw her eyes on him. She didn't drink, didn't smoke, just went to bed with people for money. He'd never asked her why.

He'd taken her to Gibraltar and shown her the bar his father had owned. Now it was called Dixie's.

'Let me guess,' she'd said. 'I bet your father called it the Britannia.'

'How do you know?'

'Because there's a Britannia in all these grisly tourist traps. A Britannia bar or restaurant or café or tea-room or fish-and-chip joint.'

He'd thought it romantic; she'd made it sound seedy.

He took her to the house his father had bought after he'd sold the bar. It was in the hills above Torremolinos.

'Really?' she'd said. 'That's original.'

They'd looked down at the smog and the traffic and the concrete and he'd said, 'It wasn't like this when I was little. It was beautiful then.'

The house was gone, instead there was a development round a swimming pool and tennis courts.

'God, I hate these places,' she'd said.

But Spain was all they had. Then, and for that matter, now.

They'd stayed at a hotel for two weeks. She was frightened all the time.

'Look,' he said, 'he was a foreigner right? Probably a business-man. I'd bet he flew out that night or the next morning, before you were found. He'll never come back. Too dangerous.'

She didn't believe him and he didn't really want her to. But she panicked when their time was up.

'I want to stay,' she'd said.

But he had his job. 'I'll hide you so well no one will find you.'

He was able to borrow enough to put down on the flat in Docklands but he knew he could never support her there indefi-nitely in the way she wanted. She'd got used to it, but she wanted Spain, which was why he was taking early retirement.

He put his hand on her leg. She went on watching TV and at the same time began to unbutton her blouse. There was something so mechanical about it that he stopped.

'You want to?' she said.

'Mandy . . . I . . . No, not now.'

She did up the buttons again.

He rose and began to pace. 'We'll never sell this bloody place at the moment.'

'You're like a caged tiger,' she said.

'Funny how life turns out,' he said. 'After my father died, all my mother wanted was to come back to England. You get like that when you live overseas. When something goes wrong you want to run for home. And things went badly wrong. He'd never told her about his debts. She had to find out the hard way.'

She did not reply.

'Can you imagine what Rotherhithe was like after that?' He paused. 'We'll have a terrific time. You'll see.'

'So you keep telling me.'

'I've got enough in the Banco de Vizcaya to live ten or fifteen years or longer if we're careful. This place will sell eventually and we'll have that money as well.'

'You really think we'll be together in ten or fifteen years?'

'Yes.'

For once a look of compassion entered her grey eyes. 'You've been good to me. But I'm a shit. Just remember that and don't say I didn't warn you.'

'I'm a shit too. So was the foreign businessman. There're a lot of shits about, especially men who buy it.'

The compassion vanished and the fear came back.

The phone rang. 'Yes?' Begg said.

'Guv'nor?'

There was something in the voice Begg recognised.

'Who's that?'

'Mick Stacey, guv'nor.'

'Thought I recognised your voice. How the hell are you?'

'Great.'

'How's Paddington?'

'Not as good as London North.'

'We miss you. What's the problem?'

'You got a new DI called Ferry?'

'That's right. Came a few months ago from the East End.'

'He came to see me tonight. Asking questions.'

'What about?'

'You remember that attempted break-in at a house in the Vale of Health about six months ago?'

'Hang on a sec, the TV's on.'

He went into the bedroom to the other phone and spoke for five minutes. When he came back Mandy was watching him. He lit a cigarette and poured himself another drink. He suddenly looked old, she thought.

'What is it, Harry, work?'

'Yeah. Something's come up.'

She looked back at the screen. She'd made her conversational effort for the night.

Albert Ferry woke up in his living-room. The TV was on with the sound turned down and he had no idea what time it was except that it was late. He was stiff and cold for the central heating went off at ten.

He clambered up the stairs and looked in at his son's room

234

but the bed was empty. He thought he heard a noise and went down again.

'Peter?'

'I'm in the kitchen, Dad.'

Albert found his son sitting at the kitchen table, a bottle of whisky to hand and a large notebook in front of him. He was writing busily.

His skin was very white and the freckles stood out like small blobs of mud.

'You look terrible,' Albert said. 'You been on the booze?'

'Give us a break, Dad.'

'When you were a nipper your skin went white when you were sickening for something.'

'Well, I'm not sickening for anything, okay?'

'You had something to eat?'

'I don't want anything.'

Albert opened his mouth and then saw the expression in his son's eyes and the faint tremor of his hands.

'What is it, Peter?'

Ferry leaned back in the kitchen chair and swirled the whisky round and round in his glass. 'You want one?'

'Might as well keep you company.'

'Roll me a fag then.'

The old man rolled a cigarette and gave it to him to lick.

'I'm writing it all down,' Ferry said.

'All what?'

'Everything. So I'll know and you'll know and anyone else will know and they won't be able to say I got it all wrong. Because this is the big one, Dad.'

'I'm listening.'

'Did I mention an actor called Bourke?'

'Yeah. He was on the box in the seventies and early eighties. I remember seeing him.'

'Okay, well we've done some digging, talking to actors who were with him in his series, we've found his ex-wives. That sort of thing . . . And he is not a very nice person. In fact I would go further: he's a very dodgy character and may even be an outright villain.'

235

'You told me about his first wife, the one he doesn't mention.'

'Yeah. But what I've found out now is what one of his other wives says. First of all he can't make it in bed. Impotent. And second of all he blames his women. This ex of his is called Sandra. Lives in a hostel in Maidstone. You want to see her, Dad. I mean she's only about twenty-eight but looks fifty. Dyed hair, smoking all the time, always looking over her shoulder. Seems that our Mr Bourke used to beat her . . . batter her . . .'

'I hate that sort of thing! I never lifted a finger to your mother in all our married life!'

'Of course you didn't. I know that, Dad. Now the thing about this woman is that she's willing to talk. I mean, I could hardly stop her. It's the kind of place where other battered wives fetch up, a refuge I think they call it, and they tell each other the details over and over.'

'Like Alcoholics Anonymous.'

'Right. It's part of the therapy. Talked about the most intimate things. Seems he became impotent while he was married to her. Said it was her fault, said she'd faked all her sex with him, I mean the good parts.'

Ferry was always embarrassed talking sex with his father and tried to avoid it.

'I know what sex is,' Albert said.

'Okay, well she faked her orgasm. I mean right from the beginning. Must have been a kind of pattern. Because one night she got drunk and he had her and this time everything was okay and she really did have one. But, of course, her reactions weren't the same as what he was used to. And he thought she was faking it.'

'What? She comes for real and he thinks – ?'

'Yeah. Bit ironic, don't you think?'

'So?'

'Well, he gets in a terrible rage and hits her in the face. Damages her right eye. And that was the start of it. The more she was afraid of him the less she was able to cope and the more he hit her. Kind of a vicious circle.'

'Poor bloody woman.'

'Yeah. Not very nice, is it? Anyway, he threatens her. He says that if she goes to the police he'll kill her. Says it right to her face. So I went to see another of his ex-wives and asked if he'd beaten her. But she wouldn't talk. And I thought: why won't she even deny it?'

'Sins of omission.'

'Absolutely. So here's this Bourke – I told you his real name was Mitchell – who was doing drugs in the sixties, meets the younger of the two Hampstead women, Hilda. She's rich. Lives with an invalid mother. Whole house is stuffed with expensive pictures and furniture. Now he's someone with experience of women, right? So he tells Hilda he loves her and wants to marry her. Tells her any story you like. There're women like Hilda all over the country; women who don't know they're born.'

'Especially when she's living with her mother,' Albert said. 'Just the two of them.'

'And he promises to take her away and stick the old lady in a home. Hilda must have jumped at it.'

'And then he takes the stuff –'

'– and murders the two women.'

'Christ!'

'Good scenario, isn't it?'

'Marvellous!'

'Except that it's all bollocks. He might have done all sorts of things but I bet he didn't do in the two women.'

'Who did then?'

'Begg.'

Albert, who had been leaning against the wall, sat down abruptly at the table as though his legs had gone. 'What're you saying, son?' It was almost a whisper.

'You heard me.'

'Christ almighty! Are you sure? Can you prove it?'

'I'm ninety-eight per cent positive but I don't know whether I can prove it or not.'

'Is this what you been on this evening?'

'Yeah, I went to see someone at Paddington. A DI who used to work with Begg at London North.'

*

He'd met Stacey at a wine bar near Paddington Green police station. For a moment he thought it was Begg standing at the counter. He was dressed like Begg, in a good grey suit with a waistcoat and tie. The London North 'look' as he had come to think of it. All Begg's team dressed as though they were businessmen. Ferry, in his bomber jackets and Levi's and Nike running-shoes, had not fitted that image. He was a cop not a bloody yuppie.

Ferry introduced himself and Stacey said, 'Have a glass of wine. They do a rather good Côtes du Rhône here.'

Ferry had never heard of Côtes du Rhône and resented Stacey's casual expertise. Instead he had a glass of lager and studied Stacey over the rim. Dark hair modishly long and looked after by a hairdresser, sharp face, university tie, up-market accent, reasonably good-looking with blue eyes as cold as ice-chips.

He was aware that Stacey was examining him too, and judging him, and that his mouth was turning down in distaste.

Stacey was everything that Ferry hated. But he controlled himself. All he wanted was five minutes of chat and then he'd be gone and he wouldn't have to clap eyes on Stacey again.

'On the phone you said something about a Vale of Health break-in,' Stacey said.

'Yeah, you were the DI in charge. Whoever it was didn't get away with anything.'

'Why should I remember it?'

'There was an invalid in the house at the time. She and her daughter. Valuable paintings and furniture. A silver cigarette box was brought in to see if there were any prints and to have a stain analysed. You remember it now?'

'Vaguely.'

'Forensic said you signed for the silver box.'

Stacey sipped at his wine. His eyes had clouded with suspicion. 'What's this all about?'

Ferry realised that Stacey was worried he might have been derelict in his duty and hastened to reassure him. 'Nothing, only we got the box in for examination again and I was wondering about it. The original crime sheet is missing.'

'Missing?'

238

'Yeah, it's not on file. I mean you'd have filled in a sheet, wouldn't you?'

'Of course.'

'I thought so.'

'I remember now. Yes, I filled in a sheet all right. I remember the house too. Overloaded with pot plants.'

'That's it.'

'Why are you interested in it all of a sudden? Hey. Wait a minute, it's not the . . . the two women? Those two?'

'The same.'

Stacey began to look more than uneasy. 'Listen, Ferry, take my word for it, I put in a crime sheet.'

'Sure. I believe you. And you took the silver box back to the house?'

'Yes . . . no. Wait. Let me think . . .'

'My turn,' Ferry said, ordering two more drinks. 'There's no hurry.'

'I'm just going back in my mind . . . Oh, yes . . . I remember now. I was going to return the box to the house. We'd tested it for prints and the stain. No positives and the stain was . . . can't remember . . . some sort of – yes, it was red wine, I think.'

'That's it.'

'Anyway, I was going to take the box back and I met the guv'nor on the way out of the station and –'

'Who was your guv'nor?'

'Begg.'

'I see.'

'He asked me about the box and I told him about the house. About it being filled with paintings and valuable furniture and he said he'd like to see the stuff and the women, perhaps advise them on security because there were a lot of tearaways working Hampstead at the time. He said he'd return the silver box and that's the last I heard of it.'

'When were you transferred to Paddington?'

'About a month later.'

'Were you expecting it?'

'Christ, no. It came out of the blue.'

'Were you happy about going?'

'Not at all. I liked it at London North. We were a team, we had style.'

Ferry stared at him and thought: yeah, you ponce, I bet you did.

'Anyway, what's this all got to do with you?'

'That's my business.'

Now, in Ferry's kitchen, Albert said, 'that doesn't mean he did it.'

'Hang on. After I left Stacey I went to the Yard and checked up on Begg. Know what I found? He'd worked in the Antiques Squad for nearly five years. How about that?'

'Can you prove it, though?'

'It'd be easier if I had a mate at London North, but who's going to help me there, who's going to take my word against Begg? I'm going to have to do it my own way.'

'How?'

Ferry's eyes slid away from his father. 'If I told you, you'd want to stop me. It's better for both of us that you don't know.'

'Son, you're not going to do something stupid, are you?'

'Don't ask, Dad. I'll tell you when it's all over.'

TWENTY-TWO

Hannah picked up the key of the house from the desk sergeant at London North police station. With it was a note from Ferry which she read in the car.

Dear Dr Wilton,
  In letting you take David to the house by yourself I'm putting my neck on the line. I understand why you don't want anyone else with you but it is most unusual and I'm only agreeing to it because you say it is the only way you think something will be jogged in David's head that might lead on to him giving us a picture of the night in question.
  I must ask you not to touch anything. The house is exactly as we found it and it must stay that way until the case is closed or at least until we admit defeat – which we aren't going to do.
  Please let me know as soon as possible if anything happens.
                    Yours sincerely, Peter Ferry
                    Det. Insp. London North

She put the letter in the glove compartment and drove off to pick up David. She always felt a lifting of her spirits as she turned into the Brinds' street. It came on two levels: one was the professional excitement of David's case; the other was the simple pleasure of seeing him.

It wasn't an ideal situation taking David back to the Vale of Health house but what else was left to her? So today was important. It was her best chance of breaking the deadlock. In fact, she did not see any other way except the field of neurolinguistics — and there, as she had told Begg, she was out of her depth.

She had decided not to tell Mrs Brind about the experiment, but as soon as she had David in the car she began to try to communicate with him as she usually did.

'We're going on a special outing today,' she said. 'First we're going to Hampstead Heath. This was where Duncan saw you. And we're going to let you see the place he photographed. I don't expect you to recognise it because it was dark when you went there but there are parts of your mind that may remember something. Anyway, it's the place to start.'

David stared out of the window. He did not react to what she was saying; it was as though he were deaf. She did not mind, she had not expected reaction; that would come, she hoped, in the next hour or so.

The day was gloomy. The wind lay in the north and the snow had packed down solid along the pavements. Its pristine beauty had vanished; now it was spattered with frozen mud.

She parked at the top of the Heath and they walked down hand in hand into the trees whose black, leafless branches shivered and clashed in the wind. It was almost empty except for a few people walking their dogs.

They reached the path that Wylie had described to her. It was slippery with snow. She saw a litter basket attached to a pole. Was this it? It looked quite different from the film.

'This was probably where he had his hide, don't you think? I seem to remember the bush on the left. That's where you came from.' She held David with her right arm, pressing him to her legs and pointed with her left hand. 'Do you see, darling, that's where you found the food. Come on, let's go and look.'

She took him to the litter basket.

'You took something out of this,' she said. 'Duncan says it was a pizza box. And you opened it very cleverly. Do you remember?'

Today it contained only a few empty beer cans.

The grass, the path, the basket – nothing seemed to get through to him. When she turned him this way or that he simply stood and looked until she moved him to another position.

Ferry had called him a zombie and yet Hannah knew that inside his head there was a working brain. It wasn't simply in chaos. There were thoughts and processes, there was cause and effect. From the moment she had seen him open the pizza box she had known that.

She had not really expected him to react to the litter basket so she was not disappointed. What she was doing now was a kind of mental lacquer work, painting on layer upon fine layer of experience and memory, so fine that David might not even recognise the individual layers, but when it was all there, it would give him a picture from his past; hopefully one he could link with the present.

'Come on,' she said. 'It's too cold to hang about. Let's go to the house.'

The Vale of Health reacted on her in the way it had done before: it did not seem to belong to the city around her; it had its own brooding personality.

The lane was empty now. It was too cold for pensioners and even the police guard had been withdrawn. She and David walked past the hole in the hedge that he had used as his entrance and exit to the gate that led up to the front door. All was still, all was as she remembered it.

As they walked she watched David carefully but he showed no signs of emotion.

Hannah paused on the front step and took out the key. When she had first asked Ferry if she and David could have the house to themselves, he had smiled and said, 'Won't you be scared?'

It had raised the hackles of her feminism and she had answered him with a sense of her own superiority. 'No, Inspector, I won't feel scared.'

Now, as she put the key into the lock, she felt, if not scared, distinctly uneasy, not only because of what had happened in the house but because the experiment with David was just that, an experiment. She knew she was taking a chance, one she would

243

not have taken if there was any other way and certainly only because he now seemed so much more in control of himself even though he was mute.

The lock was stiff and did not turn. She looked at the key. It was bright gold in colour, clearly one that had been recently cut. She tried again. This time it worked and the door swung open.

Even after all these weeks there was still a faint smell of burning in the front hall and the chalk marks were white and glaring on the floor.

She was holding David's hand and she closed the door. Immediately the hall grew dimmer.

'We could do with a light on,' she said, 'but they told us not to touch anything, so better not.'

They went first into the drawing-room.

'Once upon a time, a little boy called David lived in this house. It wasn't his house. It was one he was brought to . . . when . . . well, after his mother died. I wonder if he ever saw this room. It used to have furniture and pictures in it but now it doesn't have anything. Look, you can see where the pictures hung.'

She took him to the kitchen. Here were the dead plants but here also were the cupboards in which he must have searched for food and found only tins, which he could not open.

'Do you remember this room, David? Do you remember being hungry here?'

It was an extraordinary sensation; she knew and he knew in some part of his brain that he had been here before yet he was not reacting.

'Let's go upstairs before it gets too dark.'

They stepped over the chalk marks at the bottom of the stairs and she had the sensation of stepping over dead bodies. She tried to banish the feeling but it persisted. The whole house was infused with a scent of death.

'One . . . two . . . three . . . four . . .'

Still holding his hand, she counted each step as they went up. 'Five . . . six . . .'

She felt a slight jerk on her hand when she reached the word 'six'.

'Does it bother you? Okay, don't worry about it. Seven . . .

244

eight . . . nine . . . ten . . .' She went on counting as they climbed. 'Right, here we are. Let's go into Madame Raymonde's room first.'

The room was in a silence so deep that she could hear a lorry grinding up Heath Street nearly a mile away. It sounded as though it came from a different world.

'This is where Madame lived. She was what we call an invalid. She spent all her time in bed. See, it hasn't been made. Nothing's been touched. It's just as Mr Ferry said. That's the piano over there. Did she ever play? Did you ever hear the sound of music coming from this room?'

They moved round the TV set and the armchair with the small table in front of it.

'Maybe she watched TV from here, or maybe her daughter sat in this chair and they watched together. And the little boy called David was in another room across the hall.'

Being in the house with David was very moving, an entirely different feeling from the experience of her visit with Ferry.

David was the centre of this tangled web, Wylie's 'wild child', Sophie's autistic child, the tabula rasa that she, Hannah was to write upon, the possible police witness, the 'in care' juvenile of the social services.

What a sad little boy! How much sadder even than Tom, she thought, for Tom did not know what he was or how he differed. Tom was Tom. But David must know somewhere deep inside his psyche who he was and that he had had a terrible experience.

She thought of Genie, tied to the potty-chair month after month, year after year, only to emerge twisted and speechless like a creature from the mind of Hieronymus Bosch. That mustn't happen to David – and she would see that it didn't. But equally she mustn't let it get her down. She must not give way to her feelings, they were unimportant beside David.

'This is Hilda's room,' she said. 'She liked pictures of strong men. Look . . .'

David looked at the weightlifters and surfers on the walls but she could not make out whether he was absorbing anything or not.

245

Didn't matter. This was another layer of lacquer. He might, just might, have been in one or both of these rooms.

'And this is the bathroom they shared,' she said, leading him into the dark room. 'I don't think anyone will mind if I switch on a light. I'll use a tissue on the switch so I won't leave any fingerprints. That's what they do in the movies.'

She switched on the light and looked about the bathroom and abruptly the hairs on her neck rose. She had to control herself from squeezing David's hand and hurting him. It was such a simple but frightening thing: the seat of the lavatory was up.

'They said nothing had been touched! They said everything was exactly as it had been left!'

She wasn't talking to David now, but whispering the thoughts half-aloud.

She thought she heard a slithering, rustling noise, and stood quite still listening. But it didn't come again. She wondered if a rat had got into the house.

'I'm being silly,' she said in a more normal voice. 'Some policeman has been here using the loo. That's all.'

But somehow she didn't believe it.

They went out onto the landing. 'Now we're going into the room where the little boy lived for such a long time. Hold my hand tightly, darling, and don't be afraid. The little boy is never going to be closed into that room again. What we'll do is just look into it for a few moments and then we'll go back to the car.'

She pushed open the door and the smell hit her, a smell of drains, plus the feral smell of a den. A man was standing by the window, the light falling on his cap and coat. She felt David's fingernails drive into her flesh and her breath momentarily left her.

It was Mitchell.

But then he turned and she saw that it wasn't Mitchell.

'Good afternoon, Dr Wilton,' Begg said.

She felt a surge of relief. But David's fingers did not relax.

He came towards them, took off his cap and nodded in greeting.

'Inspector Ferry told me you were bringing David to the house. I thought I would come along and see if anything transpired.'

She was in charge of herself now. 'The idea was that David and I should come here by ourselves. I wanted to try an experiment.'

'I'm sorry, he didn't mention that.'

Begg began to pace slowly up and down the room.

'This is where he lived,' he said. 'I hadn't seen it before.'

He looked odd, she thought. His hair was awry from being under his cap but it wasn't only that. His eyes were flicking one way, then the other, never staying still. His hands played constantly with the cap and he spoke in short jerky sentences.

'You can't imagine anyone doing that. Keeping a child locked up.'

'People do strange things,' she said.

'Yes, don't they? That's very true. Amazing things. Things that on the face of it seem quite out of character. But then I suppose that if they do them they must be in character otherwise they wouldn't.'

She felt David pulling her slightly towards his cot bed and she allowed herself to move in that direction.

'What would friend Freud have said about that?' Begg said.

'Superintendent, David and I are here on an important experiment. I wanted us to be alone so that I could let him refamiliarise himself with the house without interruptions.'

'I had a memo from Ferry this morning. It was on my desk. It said you had made a breakthrough, that David was talking and that you thought it likely he would be able to describe the murder – that's if he saw it.'

'What! That's complete rubbish! He must have got the . . . no, he couldn't have got the wrong idea because I never gave him even a glimmer of hope. He must have been making it up!'

'That occurred to me, but I couldn't be sure. That's why I had to come.'

At that moment she heard a scraping noise outside the door. It was as though someone was rubbing against the wall. Begg heard it too and turned. Ferry was in the doorway. He was holding himself up on the architrave. There was blood all over his face and clothing. He tried to say something but his mouth was filled with blood and he could not articulate.

Hannah said, 'He's been hurt!'

Ferry swayed, gathered himself, and step by step came into the room. Hannah made a move towards him.

Begg had a small pistol in his hand and as she watched he raised it. She could not believe what was happening. It was all stylised and unreal.

'Oh, don't!' she cried.

Begg shot Ferry in the chest and he stumbled and fell into the dark bathroom.

She grabbed David and turned his face against her so he would not see.

'My God, what have you done? I must help him!'

He waved the gun at her.

'Why?' she said. 'Why?'

It was more an exclamation of horror than a question but Begg seemed to take her literally.

'Why?' he said. 'I should have thought that was obvious.'

What was happening in his mind, she thought. Was there something there she could get at? Was it exploding out of control? Would her training come to her aid now that she really needed it? But she was too afraid even to think clearly.

'Was it you? Did you kill the women?'

She knew she had to keep him talking. So long as he talked he would not do anything violent.

'This is your forte, isn't it? The untangling of minds?' His fingers played over the grip of the pistol. 'I'm the kind of person you spend your days listening to.'

'I don't think so.'

He ignored her, his concentration was inward. 'You must have heard stories like mine before.'

'Every story is unique.'

'I suppose so. It's a question of understanding. Know what I mean? Look, let's face it, lots and lots of people have deprived childhoods. A lot of villains use that as an excuse. A lot of weak people, inadequate people too. You can blame any behaviour on it. For some it's a stark choice: you grow up not knowing whether you want to be a criminal or a policeman. They're almost inter-changeable at times.'

She felt David like a fish at the end of a line, every now and then his hand would jerk in hers. She held on tightly to him, trying to blur the scene that was unfolding before their eyes. She desperately wanted him to run, to escape, to flee down the stairs and into the city. But even if it were possible, how could she make him understand?

'You know, doctor, I never had the responsibility for anyone's life before. Not really. I don't mean life and death. So I'm not talking about the two women. Or Ferry. He knew what he was doing – and by the way, he used you and David. You were his bait. So don't feel too badly about him. He's destroyed both of you, if you understand what I'm saying. And it need never have come to this. It's possible David saw nothing, you know. In which case nothing equals nothing. No, I'm talking about someone else entirely . . .'

He began to pace up and down.

'Look, Superintendent I –'

'Don't make things any more difficult than they are. You're a psychiatrist and I want you to understand. I want *someone* to understand. Is that so unreasonable?'

'Let David go. I'll stay and listen.'

'Please, you're an intelligent woman.' He paused and looked around at the dark, empty doorway of the bathroom, then he turned back to her. 'Please sit on the bed.'

She held David as closely as she could, trying to place her body between him and the rest of the room. Her hand felt something hard in the mattress and her fingers touched a tear in the fabric.

'What are you doing?' Begg said.

She held up a pen, a green Pentel. 'It must be one of David's,' she said. 'He must have hidden it. He used it for the drawings.'

He shook his head as though to dismiss the interruption. 'You said psychopaths could not tell right from wrong. I wondered about that. I know what's right and what's wrong. That's the trouble.'

The gun seemed part of his arm now.

'Love's a curious thing. I never realised it before, never thought about sacrifice. I was married. Had kids. I suppose I loved them. Can't remember now, it's all so long ago. There's romantic love and sexual love but I'm not talking about that. I'm talking about

... the responsibility of love ... the caring for someone you love ...'

She could sense the turmoil in his mind, that these were random thoughts he was trying to fit into a pattern if only to explain them to himself.

'I needed the money, you see. Simple as that. And I thought I'd go so far and no further. Just a small operation. I set a limit. But when I reached it I thought: Well, just a little further. I said to Hilda, "What is enough?" Whatever it is, it never is enough, is it?'

Behind Begg there was a movement. A hand appeared at the side of the bathroom door. Ferry was slowly pulling himself upright.

'The old lady had a fractured skull,' Hannah said quickly, talking over any slight noise Ferry was making.

'She fell. But Hilda ... You saw the film *They Shoot Horses, Don't They?*?'

'Yes.'

'That was pretty much the case with Hilda. I mean, who was going to look after her? She was better out of the way.'

Ferry was on his feet now, a dark mass against the dark of the room behind. Hannah tried not to look in his direction in case she communicated her hope and fear to Begg and caused him to turn.

But Begg was still looking inward. 'You can't let people like that loose in society,' he said.

'Do you really think you'll get away with this?' Hannah said, hearing her words come out fast and jerkily.

'That's one of the most famous lines in detective fiction. I first read it in Sherlock Holmes. That's what I've been trying to explain. You don't think. You act. And then before you know it you're involved so deeply you have to go on acting. But what else can you do? From the moment the old woman fell, events took their logical course. I've seen it dozens of times before. You'd think because I was a policeman I could control them. But you can't, you know. You can't control life.'

Like some slow-moving automaton, Ferry was beginning the painful journey from the bathroom. She could hear the slight noise of his feet but Begg was so caught in explanation and memory that he did not seem to register it.

'After the old woman died, Hilda had to go. And once Ferry grew suspicious . . . well . . . he was hidden here waiting for me. What else could I do? Now there's you, and David . . . and there's a policeman called Stacey who will begin to wonder . . . That's the desperate thing about it. It never ends. But so long as there's a chance you go on. I want to go and live in Spain and look after someone. I'm still planning to do that. I still want my place in the sun.'

Ferry was in the room, his face was twisted in pain, the white skin covered in blood. Only his eyes, glittering in the half-light, seemed human.

Hannah felt David squirming and looked down. His mouth was working. He was trying to say something and she thought: God, not now! Don't speak now!

She clapped a hand over his mouth. Begg swiftly brought up the gun.

'I think he's going to be sick,' she said.

Ferry grabbed Begg from behind.

His arm encircled Begg's neck, his other hand felt for the gun. But she could see how weak he was. Begg turned, raised the gun to Ferry's head. She used the only weapon she had, David's pen. She stabbed at Begg's face. He moved as her hand was coming down and the point entered his right eye.

'Oh, God!' he said. 'Oh, Jesus!'

He dropped the gun and held a hand over his eye. Ferry wrestled with him. They swayed and stumbled through the doorway onto the landing. There was a splintering crash as the bannisters gave way and the thud of the bodies hitting the floor below.

'Don't go near!' she shouted at David.

But he was already kneeling at the surviving bannisters, holding one in each hand. He looked down at the bodies below and from his larynx there came a strange and eerie scream. Then he turned to her. His lips began to work, she saw his throat contract as he swallowed, saw his tongue writhing in his open mouth. He began to speak.

But they were words she had never heard before, or thought

she had never heard. They sounded like some primitive language, from the voice box of Palaeolithic man. He repeated them. This time she made out one or two and then, like a pictogram forming in her head she saw rather than heard the words. What he was saying was, 'This is the *Six O'Clock News* from the BBC.'

TWENTY-THREE

It was two days later. Hannah came down the steps of London North police station and into the Finchley Road. Wylie was waiting for her. He watched her come towards him. She was grey-faced and looked ill from her ordeal.

'How did it go?' he said.

'I never knew that taking a statement would go on for so long.' Her voice was strained and shaky. 'They made me repeat everything ten times.'

'You can hardly blame them.' Wylie was emollient.

'And I had to tell them all about Mitchell. A detective called Holder has been investigating him. There really was a legacy from Australia!' They began to walk along the pavement. 'And there's an old man in there. Ferry's father. I was told they had to drag him away from his son's bedside. He spends all his time at the hospital telling the nurses what to do.'

'Did they say how Ferry was?'

'Poorly. He's got holes in him and broken bones, but he'll live. Begg died of a broken neck, by the way.'

'There's a certain poetic justice in that.'

She stopped and looked back. 'That's where I first saw him. On these steps. In your film. He was talking to Ferry. Wearing his cap. God, if only I'd registered the cap.' They began walking again. 'That was what David was drawing all the time. The Brinds thought so too. It was the view he had of it from above

253

the night the two women were killed. He must have squatted at the bannisters and looked directly down on Begg. I must see David.'

He had known this was coming. She had tried the day before but Mrs Brind had said he was unwell.

'What happens now?' Wylie said, still gentle.

'With the police? Paperwork and more paperwork. Listen, I've got to see Sophie today, but first David.'

He knew she was in too febrile a mood for a visit to David just then and said, 'Let's have lunch first.' She looked at her watch. 'I need a drink. And food. I'm frozen.'

'All right, but a quick one, then I must pick up my car.'

'I'll take you round to the Brinds'. I'd like to find out how he is anyway.'

They had lunch at the Berlin. They ate sauerbraten and drank a bottle of riesling. The wine calmed her but even so she talked compulsively about her experience as though talking might dilute its horror.

She described Ferry's movement from the bathroom and Wylie said, 'Did you really think David was trying to say something?'

'I wasn't sure. I wasn't even sure he'd seen Ferry or if he had, whether he was surprised or frightened. But I couldn't let him say anything just at that moment. It would have warned Begg. My God, the irony! Here I've spent weeks and weeks trying to get him to utter a single sound and when he tries I shut him up.'

'And this business of the BBC news. That's what he must have heard over and over again from Madame Raymonde's TV. I suppose it was about the only human speech he did hear.'

'That's why he stuck on the figure six,' she said. 'And why he attacked the set. It was the trigger.' She paused, then said, 'Poor David. I only hope he isn't even more badly scarred.' She looked at her hands. 'I should never have taken him.'

'For God's sake, you weren't to know, A: that Begg was the killer or, B: that Ferry was going to use the two of you. No one knew. That was the whole point of the exercise. By the way, did you ask them about a shotgun or whether Begg was a wildfowler?'

She nodded. 'There was no shotgun in his flat and no one had ever heard him talk about shooting. No, it was as you suggested: you see what you want to see; hear what you want to hear; believe what you want to believe. Finished?'

He drove her round to the Brinds' and used the video camcorder to take her going up the path. He followed, zooming in on the doorway.

Mrs Brind answered her knock and by the time Wylie reached the door the two women were arguing.

'No,' Mrs Brind was saying. 'It wouldn't be right for David. He should be left alone.'

'Mrs Brind, I'm not asking you, I'm –'

But Mrs Brind was dogged. 'He's just recovering and –'

'I'm the psychiatrist in charge of the case! I'm telling you I want to see him!'

The two women stared at each other, then Mrs Brind stepped back into the hall and reappeared a moment later with David.

To Wylie's eyes he seemed much the same as when he had last seen him, a trifle paler perhaps, but to counter that there was more life in his eyes. It was almost as though a button had been pressed somewhere in his head and a light had switched on. Hannah went down on her haunches in front of him and took his hand. He seemed to know who she was for a faint movement of his lips almost became a smile. Mrs Brind hovered; her own lips were a thin white line of disapproval.

Slowly and softly Hannah said, 'Once upon a time, I had a little boy of my own who found it hard to speak or tell people things. And other people thought you were like him. But you're not. His name was Tom and your name is David and you've got your whole life ahead of you.

'It's been a pretty rotten life so far but it'll get better and so will you. One day you'll be talking just like any other person. And one day, I hope, you'll forget all this or at least be able to live with the memory.

'And people will help you to do this, just as they'll help you to talk. I've tried. Now it's someone else's turn; someone who understands more about your problems than I do.'

Wylie realised that Hannah was not only addressing David but Mrs Brind and himself as well. But most of all she was addressing

255

herself. 'You see, David, I was too close to you. And that's not a good thing. So I've come to say goodbye.'

She gathered him in her arms and kissed his cheek and hugged him and gave him back to an astonished Mrs Brind.

'Goodbye,' Hannah said to both of them. 'Goodbye.'

Then she turned and walked back up the path.

Wylie followed her and found that she was crying. He put his arm around her shoulders but she twisted away.

'You'll be able to see him,' he said. 'You'll be able to monitor him. You'll always know where he is and how he's getting on. You'll be a kind of aunt –'

'*Aunt!* For God's sake, shut up!'

'Listen, you're still young enough to have kids of your own!' Again he put his arm around her shoulders. 'Come on.'

'Leave me alone!'

She walked swiftly away, not looking back.

He watched her for a few moments.

'No, I won't leave you alone!' he called after her. 'Not now, not tomorrow, not next week . . . So get used to it!'

He climbed into the camper and followed her slowly down the street.